£1.99

'Frederic Raphael is an ⟨...⟩ author of more than ⟨...⟩ heavyweight literary biographies, and *Eyes Wide Shut*, the late Stanley Kubrick's movie. It is an astonishing career . . . In this collection of short stories and two novellas, Raphael brings to bear his Jewish-American sophistication and upper-crust English education in a way that effortlessly combines brevity, intellect, innovation and wit . . . There is so much to praise in this book. Raphael's audacious blend of script and prose – he is a master of both – bridges the gulf of suspicion that has traditionally divided screenwriting and literature . . . Throughout the book he shows his profound understanding of the virtues of the short story and how to bring them out . . . Raphael deserves serious respect.' Peter Jinks, *The Herald*

'[Raphael] is the nearest thing to Somerset Maugham that we have: a supremely capable professional man of letters . . . Raphael can play with language and concepts of what I think is called "meta-fiction" as brightly as anyone, more brightly, indeed, than most . . . But Raphael can also bring off, and does so again and again here, the kind of story old Maugham himself used to excel at: the kind with a good narrative which also reveals character and leaves you reflecting sadly on people's capacity to deceive themselves and be mean to each other . . . Raphael's world is sweet and sour, and full of brio. He demands much of his readers, who have to keep their wits about them as allusions dart like dragonflies. There is seriousness here without solemnity, and the delight that comes from the act of creation.'

Allan Massie, *The Scotsman*

Frederic Raphael was born in Chicago in 1931. He has written twenty-one novels, biographies of Somerset Maugham and Lord Byron, four volumes of short stories and a number of screenplays, including *Darling,* for which he won an Oscar. For his sequence of television plays *The Glittering Prizes*, he won the Royal Television Society's Writer of the Year Award. His series *After The War* was screened to worldwide acclaim in 1989. His other work includes translations, notably of Aeschylus, Euripides and Catullus (with Kenneth McLeish), essays and radio plays. He is a regular contributor to the *Sunday Times* literary and travel pages. He is a Fellow of the Royal Society of Literature. Married with three children, Frederic Raphael divides his time between France and England.

ALSO BY FREDERIC RAPHAEL

Novels

Obbligato
The Earlsdon Way
The Limits of Love
A Wild Surmise
The Graduate Wife
The Trouble With England
Lindmann
Darling
Orchestra and Beginners
Like Men Betrayed
Who Were You With Last Night?
April, June and November
Richard's Things
California Time
The Glittering Prizes
Heaven and Earth
After The War
The Hidden I
A Double Life
Old Scores
Coast to Coast

Screenplays

Two for the Road
Oxbridge Blues

Short Stories

Sleeps Six
Oxbridge Blues
Think of England
The Latin Lover

Biographies

Somerset Maugham
Byron

Translations

(with Kenneth McLeish)

The Poems of Catullus
The Plays of Aeschylus (2 vols)
Euripides: Medea, Bacchae,
    Hippolytus
Sophocles: Ajax

Essays

Cracks in the Ice
Of Gods and Men
The Necessity of Anti-Semitism
Karl Popper: Historian and its
    Poverty
Eyes Wide Open

All His Sons

FREDERIC RAPHAEL

PHŒNIX

A PHOENIX PAPERBACK

First published in Great Britain by Orion in 1999
This paperback edition published in 2000 by Phoenix,
an imprint of Orion Books Ltd,
Orion House, 5 Upper St Martin's Lane,
London WC2H 9EA

A CIP catalogue record for this book
is available from the British Library.

ISBN: 0 75380 957 5

The characters and events in this book are fictitious.
Any similarity to real persons, living or dead, is
coincidental and not intended by the author.

Printed and bound in Great Britain by
The Guernsey Press Co. Ltd, Guernsey, C.I.

FOR BEETLE

Contents

Shared Credit

I never saw a film on which Noah Benjamin had sole credit, even though he was seldom unemployed. Noah was a rewrite man; he was brought in, at the last moment, by producers who had had enough of off-the-wall originality and decided that what was needed was 'another writer'. When he wanted to spur me to one more effort, Gino Amadei would sometimes mutter, 'I don't know, perhaps what we need now is a Noah Benjamin.'

If Noah was never *the* Noah Benjamin, he did not complain. Writing was a living for him, not a vocation. He left literature to his best friend, Saul Levinson, with whom he had travelled from Hollywood in search of a promising land where Senator McCarthy's *sub poenas* carried no clout. By the time I met them, in the Sixties, Saul was said to be writing the great *un*American novel: the mordant last word on the Black List. Noah regarded his friend's talent without envy; he was a modest star who seemed genuinely to look forward to being eclipsed by a brighter one.

Saul was made of different stuff: if he ever had a kind word to say about anyone, he always thought better of it. Noah was his favourite and willing butt. On the occasion at the bar in the White Elephant, I remember, Noah told us that he had been asked to polish a script of *Mayerling*; Ray wanted it to have a happy ending. 'But I think I've probably got better things to do,' he said.

'Come on!' Saul said. 'You never did a better thing in your whole life.'

Noah flushed, as if at an undeserved compliment, and went to the bar to pay for Saul's round of drinks. He left before we had drunk them: 'Maddy is waiting,' he explained. Maddy was Madeline, his beautiful blonde ex-actress wife, of whom Saul had more than once remarked that she was the well-stacked proof that her husband must have some talent, even if it was not for writing.

The couple had met on the set of *Anna K.*, after Noah had been hired to devise a more sympathetic (and cheaper) way for her to betray her husband in a *nouvelle vague* version of *Anna Karenina*, set in Khruschev's Moscow. To everyone's astonishment, she renounced her career in order, as she put it, to 'be with Noah'.

Meanwhile, Saul had been divorced by Roxanne, his childhood sweetheart and the mother of his four daughters. He was often at the Benjamins' house. He found it a little embarrassing that his friend was so idiotically happy, but a novelist had to be tolerant when he had no place else to go.

Noah's career might not be gaudy with awards, but it was financially very rewarding: by the mid-Sixties, the Benjamins had the house in Wilton Place and a six-cylinder Jensen at the yellow door. Only one thing was missing in their happy lives: Maddy had problems conceiving a baby. Their specialist ran some tests and then he advised them to try going somewhere quiet, by the sea; Noah rented a villa at Le Canadel and planned an undisturbed summer where they could be just the two of them.

However when Saul Levinson turned down a fat script job, because the new novel – working title *Are You Or Have You Ever Been?* – had to come first, Noah asked Maddy if she could bear the thought of inviting him to Le Canadel to stay with them.

'Not really,' she said.

'He can have the staff quarters,' Noah said. 'He wouldn't need to come near us.'

'I love you, Noah,' she said. 'You're such a *schmuck*.'

'We won't ask him then,' Noah said. But he did. What else could he do after hearing that Saul had escaped Gino's prehensile overtures by suggesting that he give Noah a chance to do a *first*-draft screenplay for once?

At first, their guest joined the Benjamins regularly for dinner on the marble terrace overlooking the sea and the railway line (not mentioned in the brochure), but then, one day, he surprised Maddy, naked, at the swimming pool and made an unwise remark. She replied with a selection of unexpectedly acute hypotheses concerning why Roxanne and his daughters now preferred the company of a very handsome, very rich Lebanese. The Benjamins' house guest thereupon became reclusively monastic.

Noah reduced his first first draft of his script to one hundred and seventeen pages – what film producer ever appreciated generosity? – and expressed them to Gino. After ten days, he was abruptly invited to come to London to discuss the scenes that did not work. Taking the summons in dolefully good part, he told Maddy that he would be gone for two weeks and not a day over; if she seriously needed anything, she really should *not* hesitate to call on Saul.

Depressingly, she had once again had the curse. Noah took a cab to Nice to catch the plane. Gino's comments were not pithy, but Noah's professionalism, and his desire to get back to Maddy, made sure that their conferences were less meandering than usual. He worked so hard on the rewrites that he was able to deliver the new scenes within a week. Before Gino could find an unreasonable reason to keep him on hand, Noah flagged a cab and just managed to catch the evening flight to Nice. He could imagine how surprised Maddy would be to see him.

He took a taxi from Nice along the moonlit Corniche road to Le Chanadel. At the wrought-iron gate across the drive up to the villa, he paid off the driver and ambled towards the front door, juggling the key and savouring the zest of the pine trees and the prospect of Maddy. There was no light over the garage, where Saul usually worked late, and he wondered, with a lift of excitement, whether The Novel had at last reached term. Imagine if its creator was sleeping the sleep of that rare being, an author who had been true to his promise!

He crept up the soundless marble stairs and eased open the door of the bedroom. It might have been Gerry Fisher who had artfully lit the scene of the naked couple lying, glisteningly spent, on the uncovered bed. Noah stood in the doorway for a while and then, breathing carefully through his nose, he turned and went out and closed the door on his wife and his friend.

He stood for a while in the hall. Then he took another long breath and walked out of the house and locked the door behind him. He had only a light bag with him and the night was cool. He found a taxi in Le Lavandou which took him back to Nice airport. There was no problem about a seat on the early flight to London.

Once back in Wilton Place, he called Gino – who had no idea that he had ever left London – and was told that the new scenes were much better, except for one, which was, Gino had to say, much worse. It took only a few hours to fix it, so Noah was able to call Maddy and say that he would be on the evening plane.

She was at Nice airport with the Jensen. She kissed him keenly and said that she had some news which she hoped would not upset him: Saul Levinson had finished his novel and had moved out. A senior editor from Simon & Schuster was staying at the Hotel du Cap and had wanted to see him right away. 'So . . . you can imagine: whoosh, right?'

'I can imagine,' Noah said.

They went back to the empty villa and swam together in the pretty pool and then he took her to bed, for a long time. When he had finally finished, she said, 'Wow!'

'Does that beat "whoosh"?' he said.

After they had returned to London, Noah's agent called to say that Gino was going into production with *The Big One*. Noah went out and bought Maddy that red Mini Cooper. A month later, she told him that she was officially pregnant. They could not tell whose tears were whose. When she said that she wanted to talk to him, he kissed her to silence and then asked her what they were going to call the baby. She said that she loved him, but there really was something he ought to know. He said that he knew that she was pregnant and that he knew she loved him and that was enough for anybody to know.

He gave us the news at a poker game that night. Saul Levinson was now both rich and successful; a huge section of *Are You Or Have You Ever Been?* was being serialised in *The New Yorker*. Success had not changed him: he was still drunk and bloody-minded. At two thirty in the morning, Noah outbluffed him with over a hundred pounds on the table; it was not much, but – in those days – it was money, and Saul had lost it. 'Bluff, bluff, bluff,' he said. 'That's all you know, isn't it, Benjamin?'

'Take it easy, Saul,' I said. I felt bad, because Gino had asked me to do a polish on Noah's script.

'So Maddy's pregnant, is she?'

'Three months,' Noah said.

'Good old Riviera nights!' Saul said. 'Bet you that hundred quid it's a girl.'

'I like girls,' Noah said.

When Bathsheba was born, I was working on the script of *Are You or Have You Ever Been?*; Saul said he was tired of the whole overpraised thing (he could not even take his own success graciously), but he consented to point out, over a drink, where I had been incompetent or downright crass. It was then that I asked him why he had bet on the baby being a girl.

'All my kids are girls,' he said. 'Come on, be your age: I was staying with them all summer pretty well.'

I said, 'You're a pretty thorough-going sonofabitch really, aren't you?'

'Am I? She desperately wanted a kid. He couldn't give her one. And you know what they say in the business: if things don't work out, get another writer. He's never going to know, is he?'

God and Mammon

Wirelesses still had valves on the evening when I heard Peter Ashman read an extract from his famous first novel, *Getting Some In*. It was a few weeks before its reprinting-before-publication publication, but who could mistake the breath of fresh air blowing in from the usually dusty Third Programme? *Getting Some In* announced Ashman as the iconic iconoclast of his generation. Being an unsung, and unbroadcast, young novelist myself, I did not, at the time, laugh quite as uncontrollably as the subsequent reviewers. Their sides split when the first khaki-clad, and then unclad, Colin Filth consummated a mould-breaking romance with his sergeant-major's wife, in French-lettered detail, on the noisy boards of a three-ton truck during the late king's funeral. However, I certainly recognised the sound of a page being turned in literary and social history.

Once Peter Ashman had arrived, he stayed. By the mid-Sixties, his ascendancy over his peers had been confirmed: he not only published annual best-sellers, he also wrote thorny poems from which all rosy affectations had been pruned. In addition, he reviewed books he disliked for *The New Yorker*, guest-lectured at Princeton, and outspokenly bucked the

7

trendy tide on late-night chat shows. Canute was his kind of Englishman.

Honesty was Peter's touchstone. Within a few years of fame, he found time to divorce the mother of his four children because it would not be honest to stay with her. He detested cant in all its forms, including romantic love, the so-called fine arts and stupid bloody unselfishness. He put the regular boot into writers who used French words, even if they were French. Literature, for Peter, meant *English* literature, and some of that – he dared to say – was pretty narcotic, beginning with Shakespeare. On *The Brains Trust*, he invited a Regius Professor to try and be honest for once and answer him this: had anyone every stayed awake long enough to read *Cymbeline*? *Winter's Tale* was a frost too.

In his refreshingly four-lettered novels, Peter exposed the fraudulence of shags who kept their word, paid their just debts and admitted that there might be two sides to an argument, even with foreigners. Who can forget the epicentral scene in his fifth novel, *Back in a Minute*, when Fred Crapp grazes a parked Lamborghini as he pulls out in his Consul convertible and is wally enough to leave his name and address, and apology, under some flash bastard's windscreen wiper? Not long afterwards, two Mediterranean types with camel-hair coats and mackerel-coloured chins turn up at Fred's flat, punch him out, do very personal things to his wife and make off with the TV. The visit of Kosta and Tone is only the first lesson in a neo-modernist curriculum from which, as later chapters prove, Fred still has much to learn.

In a page-and-a-bit interview in *The Observer*, Peter refused to agree, or deny, that *Back in a Minute* had a more than transitory significance. He had an endearingly ungrateful way of treating compliments as surplus to requirement. Hence he didn't *entirely* go along with the view that his new novel might prove to be to the Sixties what *Middlemarch* had been to the Victorians. A lot of *Middlemarch* was averagely crappy, if you looked at it closely. What about the view that *Back in a Minute* signalled the end of a suburban *interregnum* in English social history in which courtesy and humbug were synonymous? 'I'm a busy man,' Peter told his aggressively deferential interviewer, 'but if you put a note to that effect under my windscreen wiper, I'll try and give it my divided attention. I only meant it to be a funny book that would tempt people to waste their dibs on it.' As if an intellectual like Peter Ashman could seriously care about money!

I did not wholly endorse the pundits' view that Fred Crapp's milk-and-water *naïveté* thoroughly deserved a jaw broken in two places, the removal of his new sixteen-inch television set and a wife, called Beryl, stripped naked and given one, or two, simply because Fred had done the honourable thing, but I mentioned my pissy reservations only to close friends. And when Victor England telephoned to say that he had bought the film rights to *Back in a Minute*, I was smooth enough to congratulate him on getting in ahead of the rest of the Hollywood crowd who, in the legendary Sixties, had come to London to make movies, talk nicely (at first) to English roses who were on the pill, and go shares in Italian restaurants.

'Freddie,' Victor said, 'here's what's in my head: why don't I produce the movie of Peter's book and you direct it? Did you laugh as much as I did when you read it?'

'There are undoubtedly some very funny things in it,' I said. Like every other screenwriter, I craved the purple authority of being a director. 'Who's going to write the script?'

'Peter wants to. His agent wants him to. I think he's very talented and he loves the movies. He's seen all of yours.'

'*Both* of mine,' I said. '*All* of yours.'

'So that's what I'm going to have him do. He wants a lot of money, but he has a lot of talent. What do you say?'

'Why aren't you going to direct it?'

'I'm too old and I'm too American and I also have a movie you wrote that I promised a couple of people I'd do next.'

Since my first fear had been that Victor was about to dump my script in favour of Ashman's hotter ticket, I was both flattered and relieved. 'I don't know too much about lenses,' I said.

'I know lots of people who do,' Victor said. 'They're called cameramen and what happens is, we hire you a good one. So *now* what do you say?'

'I can't wait.'

'You'll have to. Until Peter has the script written. The contract says he has ten weeks, but he won't take that long. He wouldn't know how, he told me.'

'That's very honest of him,' I said.

In the weeks that followed, I did not *only* wait for Peter to astonish us with what was sure to be his innovatory, and instructive, contribution to the art of screenwriting; I also struggled to finish, or at least to begin, a new novel, before Victor obliged me to turn from what I should be doing to what I really wanted to do.

He called me six weeks later. The way he said, 'Hullo,' suggested to my apprehensive ear that something was wrong. He asked me to come round to his house and read Peter's script before he said anything about it. But his silence had already said something about it; I feared that Peter's sparky iconoclasm had resulted in a screenplay too satirical – and perhaps too unlike the book which Victor had bought – not to alarm an old Hollywood hand, even if he did now have two feet in Chester

Square. Peter was unlikely to have observed the rule which said that there had to be somebody in every story that we could root for.

I sat down between two yard-high alabaster urns in the David Hicks-designed drawing room and Victor handed me the script. He poured me some coffee and it was still hot when I turned the last of the eighty-two pages. I had soon realised that the script was identical with the book, except that it had been broken into so-called scenes and the dialogue was centred instead of beginning at the left-hand margin. There was not a scrap of invention, not a single second thought. Important, seminal even, as his novels might be, when it came to screenwriting, Peter Ashman had given fresh brevity to short measure.

When Victor came back into the room, I said, 'Well, it's very true to the original.'

'He copied it out. He took six weeks to copy it out. If he even did it himself. Is that what you'd call a screenplay?'

'It is a little ... skimpy,' I said. 'But you have to understand ...'

'Do I? *Don't* I?'

'Perhaps Peter likes short films,' I said.

'I got Fox to pay him twenty-five thousand pounds to be a typist. And not a very good one. Plus plenty. If they ever make the picture.'

I could see that my directorial début was not an immediate prospect. I said, 'Perhaps ... if he ...'

'You do agree with me, don't you, that it doesn't work as a movie?'

'I never thought it worked as a book,' I said. The truth will out, unless you watch yourself.

'Will you talk to him, Freddie?'

'You're the producer,' I said.

'You're going to have to be there,' Victor said. 'If you still want to be director. And back me up.'

That was how I met Peter. He arrived for our two-thirty meeting, seventy per cent proof after an A-stream intellectual lunch at Bertorelli's, at two minutes to four. He inquired, with kindly bluntness, why I was never invited to literary occasions, and then he listened with menacing tolerance to Victor's nervous disappointments. He even conceded, without any of the four-lettered explosions I had feared, that he had something to learn about writing for the movies. After all, he reminded us, he had never before done anything that *absolutely wasn't worth doing*. With a slyly obvious wink, Peter offered me free membership in the club of those who, in the normal way of trade, would never think of working for boring Hollywood shags like our transatlantic friend here.

Victor kept his temper, just, by inviting me, 'as the director', to go into detail about what might improve our chances of getting anyone to make – or even be in – the film.

Despite knowing that Peter believed in honesty, I trimmed frankness with discretion. Apart from my desire to keep the project alive, I could guess what the penalty might be, should my new novel come under Ashman's axe after I had been rash enough to teach a modern master how to suck eggs. However, I did point out that dialogue which worked in a book could not always be *directly* transposed to a film. I also mentioned my fear that, despite the new outspokenness, we might not get away with the on-the-nose-as-it-were scene in which Spiro and Tone gave Beryl something to remember them by. In short, I auditioned, at length, for Mr Tactful.

When I was done, Peter put his hands together in front of his bright face in what seemed like a parody of prayer. He looked at me and at Victor England and then again at me. 'Look,' he said.

We looked. Peter sat there with his pursed lips against his vertical fingers. The twitchy Dresden clock on the chimney-piece was the loudest sound in the room. Peter brought his feet closer under him and hunched slightly forward and snapped at the air, as if an unguarded word had escaped from his lips but he had retrieved it before we could hear it.

Victor England said, 'Peter, I loved your book.'

'But what?' Peter said.

'I didn't pay you twenty-five thousand pounds just to type it out again in a different format. I expected a film script.'

Peter said, 'Zip warned me that this would happen.'

'*Zip?* Maybe you should've listened to him. Who's Zip?'

'My fifteen-year-old. He told me you'd want me to make all kinds of silly changes. He even told me what some of them would be. Like making Beryl *attractive*.'

'Who wants to see unattractive women being raped?'

'It's no good, is it?' Peter said. He aimed the question at me, but I avoided taking delivery. I concentrated my attention on a collection of antique paperweights on the Chinese table in front of me. They were very interesting.

'It's no good whatsoever,' Victor said. 'We certainly seem to agree there.'

'You asked me to do this,' Peter said.

'And you didn't do it. And you didn't do it.'

'I happen to have a copy of the book with me,' Peter said. 'Where did I diverge?'

'You didn't,' Victor said. 'That's what I'm complaining about. You said you'd turn your novel into a movie and all you did was take my money and turn it into your novel.'

'Look, sunshine,' Peter said, 'I never pretended to be a

screenwriter. Films are nearly always crap. And "nearly always" is a generous estimate. Zip said I shouldn't have anything to do with people who only care about money. He told me it was simple-minded to imagine that I could be an exception to the rule and serve both God and Mammon. I'm a novelist, I'm a poet, I'm a critic, and I'm also . . .' Peter turned to the blurb of his novel. 'So it says here, and I know it's true because I wrote it myself, "a unique and scathingly satirical voice with a cutting edge which is sharp on one side, serrated on the other".'

Victor England said, 'There's one other thing you are, Peter, that you didn't read out.'

'Someone who suffers fools gladly, but only when they put a glass in my hand?'

'A thief,' Victor England said.

Peter Ashman stood up and I stood up too, interposing my person – as Lytton Strachey once proposed to do should a German show signs of raping his sister – between the novelist and Victor. 'Nobody calls me a thief,' Peter said, through me.

'Then give me back my money,' Victor said, 'and I won't.'

'Talk to my agent.'

'I'm talking to you,' Victor said.

'There's nothing more to say, is there?' Peter said. 'Except the usual four-letter formalities.' He looked around the sumptuous room, like a man returning to consciousness. 'Forty-two shitty films you've made,' he said, 'and this is the best that money can buy. Bloody hell! Cheers then, Freddie old son. I'll mention your name to the Bertorelli boys, if you like. Only don't get your hopes up, will you?'

Victor never got his money back and I never directed a movie, or had lunch at Bertorelli's. Life is not always full of surprises.

L.S.D.

The first Italian I can remember seeing wore blue dungarees with a large white circle painted on the back. I was eleven years old and my school had been evacuated to a remote village in North Devon, near Morte Ho. There was a camp on a nearby nine-hole golf course from which Italian prisoners of war marched, slouchingly out of step, to the farms where they were required to dig for our victory. We watched them with little interest and less emotion. It was a comfort to think that there was one enemy country which seemed easy to beat.

I preferred the Americans. They paraded like conquerors through the high, brambled lanes. Sometimes they chanted songs; more often, they bitched about blisters. After a day's march with rifle and pack, I heard one of them use an adjective I had never heard before in order to describe the state of his back. It caused several of the other GIs to laugh nervously. They were little more than five years older than I was. Despite their sergeants' educational language, some of them still had a certain innocence. On mechanised days, when they had their feet up in Jeeps or swayed in benched trucks, they threw us strips of Wrigley's gum. Their Colgate grins promised that our side was going to win the war, just as the Italians' doleful eyes announced that theirs was going to lose.

When I first met Gino Amadei, it was a long decade after the war, but he reminded me of the hairy, unsmiling eyeties in the farm adjacent to the narrow field where we spent those cricketless wartime summers playing rounders. I had been invited to his flat to discuss rewriting a film script. Legend promised that screen-writing was a contemptible, but well-paid, activity. As a young novelist, I approached Mammon with condescending greed. I allayed my fear of incompetence by reminding myself that a film producer called Amadei was someone on whom I might properly look down, with a victor's magnanimity. After the Rome–Berlin axis, he had something to atone for, didn't he?

The only manuscript copy of my second novel had just been lost by the publisher who had begged me for a prompt sight of it. After having been offered fifty pounds by way of *ex gratia* compensation for months of vanished effort, I was in a mood to give Signor Amadei the benefit of the doubt – whatever his war record – should he offer me gainful employment.

Gino's flat lacked the tasteless ostentation which I had looked forward to despising. It had a quiet view over the wall of the Chelsea Physic Garden and there were a great many books. Gino himself was short and smoothly rounded and well-informed; he even knew that I had already published a novel. Although he was from Trieste, not Venice, there was a lisping, ironic gentleness about his diction. He thought as little of the subject of the film which he was producing as I made it clear that I did. Its working title was 'L.S.D.', which in those days suggested nothing to do with mood-changing substances, but stood for pounds, shillings and pence, or more properly for *Librae, Solidi, Denarii*.

However, if Gino and I discovered that we had both studied the ancient Roman empire, we developed no instant solidarity.

After I had accepted his commission, he was the Consul and I was the foot-soldier. He had the habit of calling me, with nervous regularity, to ask how 'de script' was progressing. After I had delivered my first pages, he was naggingly (and justly) alert to their defects. Once my well-paid, by-the-week servitude was ended, I declined his invitation to go out to Pinewood where at least some of my dialogue was due to be shot. I was happy to pocket Gino's money and concentrate on reconstituting my lost manuscript.

When the novel was rewritten and submitted once again, its trenchant denunciation of the despicable prejudices of the Earlsdon model boat club proved too subversive for my *quondam* publisher's conservative tastes. As he returned my manuscript – which, as I remarked sourly, was itself an achievement – he took leave to warn me that, if I continued to write in this caustic style, I was not going to make any friends.

Although I could not imagine that he would want to buy the film rights of my novel, I sent Gino Amadei a copy of *The Earlsdon Way* when eventually it was published by another house. I simply wanted to demonstrate what I could do when unmoved by crass considerations. However, when Gino telephoned, in what seemed a quite excited voice, and asked me to the flat for tea, hopes of enrichment did slink into my mind.

His wife, Felicity, was blonde and unquestionably English. She sounded to be permanently, and shrilly, on the telephone to Harrod's. At four-fifteen, she took time to roll a trolley into the sitting room. She stayed only to offer me the tips of her fingers. She looked as if she suspected that I had come to repair something. There was bread and butter and strawberry jam and Lyons' Swiss roll. Gino talked briefly about my novel which, to my concealed disappointment, he had not yet finished, in fact not started, to be honest, and then he said, 'Tell me, Fred, what do you know about Byron?'

I quoted his lordship on the Assyrian who had come down like the wolf on the fold and whose cohorts were gleaming with purple and gold. Was I not also right in thinking that he had died fighting for Greek Liberty?

'That is a romantic view. In fact, he was bled to death by incompetent doctors, perhaps while suffering from malaria. I want to ask you one thing, because are you possibly interested in doing a film about him? I tell you why.'

One of Gino's earlier films, directed by someone with whom he had been at university, had won an award at the festival in Venice. As a result, he had been approached by an Italian producer who said that he wanted to do some co-productions with him. Gino had never heard of Luigi Revoltella and asked what kinds of films he made.

'I will tell you quite frankly,' Luigi said, 'I make about four films a year. Two of them, I have to say it, are low-class *merda*. One of them you might say was high-class *merda*, but the fourth one . . .' He apparently did kiss the tips of his fingers. '. . . the fourth one is *merda con zucchero*: shit with sugar!'

Gino now wanted to make a film of Byron's life which was neither shit nor sugar, but he thought Signor Revoltella might be a good partner 'for us'. As a businessman, Gino liked to gamble, if possible, with other people's money.

He presented me with a copy of Byron's *Don Juan* and told me of his lordship's Quixotic part in the Carbonari plot to liberate Italy from the Austrians. It was, he said, on account of Byron that he himself became interested in England, although there was also, to tell the truth, another good reason: thanks to an Englishman he, Gino, ought to have been 'probably, possibly today the richest man in de world'.

As a young man, Gino belonged to a wealthy ship-building family in Trieste. Grandfather Amadei had started the business before the First World War, when the city was a free port, and still part of the Austrian empire. Marcus Samuel, the founder of Shell Oil, had been to every yard in England and asked whether it could build him what he called 'an empty ship'. In those early days, oil was loaded for transport in barrels, but Samuel soon imagined a vessel into whose hold crude oil could be pumped directly. No British yard would think of building such 'an impossible ship', but although Gino's grandfather lacked the resources of Swan, Hunter, he had more nerve than they; he agreed to attempt the impossible.

Samuel now confessed to a further problem: when it came to payment, he could offer only shares in his new company. A deal was struck whereby, in return for building the first oil-tankers in his Triestine yard, Ettore Amadei would receive ten per cent of the share capital of the new company, which Samuel decided to call 'Shell Trading and Transport'.

During the negotiations with Samuel, grandfather Amadei travelled from Trieste to London for the first, and the second, and the third time. He became an unqualified admirer of the British. 'He could not speak de language, of course, like what I can,' Gino said, 'but he recognised one sing which impressed him more than anything else: the people were free! They were not afraid. My grandfather was rich, but he knew all the time that the Austrians could do what they wanted wiz him, wiz everybody. He knew what anti-Semitism was in particular, which was not, I have to tell you, Fred, something that happened a little bit perhaps in the suburbs. He feared the worst, though nothing as bad as what it turned out to happen. So what did he do? He asked Marcus Samuel, who was his friend by now, to keep the shares in a special account in

London, so that one day, if de worst did come to de worst, the family could escape to the land of freedom where they would, with luck, find a fortune waiting for zem. I was his grandson and I would always have a place to go where I would also be rich like hell.'

'And that's why you're here?'

'In 1918, in case you don't know, Trieste became part of Italy and – look, Fred, if you don't mind me saying so, you don't know much about Fascism – because my grandfather was a big supporter of Mussolini. A lot of Italian Jews were. I tell you why: they were more Italian than most Italians; Venetians love Venice, Neapolitans – I have to tell you – love Naples, the Milanese love Milano, the Romans, of course, love demselves. But the Jews, they loved Italy. Imagine what it meant when we escaped the Austrians and joined the motherland! My grand-father, I have to say it, was a Fascist beyond, at least to start with. His son fought in the war; my father, he was at Vittorio Veneto when we beat the Austrians.

'So, you can imagine: as soon as Trieste was joined to Italy, 1918, and things began to look very good, my grandfather wanted us to have a merchant fleet to rival de British. He built new ships, he started a steamship line, he became the biggest man in Trieste. *And* he owned ten per cent of Shell Transport and Trading. You can imagine what we were like in those days, the money, the houses, the servants like hell. But then came the Depression. You heard of it?'

'Why else am I an only child?' I said.

'I don't know. When big things go badly, they go very badly. In the Depression they went worse than that. Finally, all the shares had to be sold, all. Marcus Samuel was now a lord. He advised my father that he would do better to sell the yards and come to England, but my father said that we were Italians, what would we do in England? The shares were sold, and things seemed to get better, a bit. Then came the 1930s, and I have to say it, we had nothing to complain about. My father was a Fascist; I was a Fascist myself.'

'I can't imagine that,' I said.

'Look,' Gino said, 'I'm sorry, but I was at one time the Young Fascist of the Year for the region of Friuli.'

'You were *what*?'

'*Duce! Duce!* Then, one day, we woke up and found that Mussolini had broken his word to us. He had always said that no Italian could be a racist. But then Hitler sneezed and we caught a cold. Nineteen thirty-eight, my father always smoked too much. When they told him that all the yards would have to be "aryanised", which meant that it had to be sold off for whatever price we could get, he right away developed a cancer. They told him that he could have an operation, but with his lungs, there was only a slight chance of success. "In that case," he said, "do it at once."

'He died, of course, in the hospital. I knew that de time had come to leave Italy. But what was I going to do with my mother? All Italians have mothers, all Jews have mothers; it's a fact of life. So: I was about eighteen, nineteenth years old and I called Lord Samuel and explained to his I-don't-know-what, his secretary maybe, who I was. We no longer had a fortune in London; we had no fortune anywhere. But he took the call. And I tell you, Fred, what he did: he fixed for the family business to be bought by one of Shell's companies still operating in Italy. But we were forbidden, of course, to export the money. They still wanted to be able to rob us when they felt like it.

'My uncle told me to take it all, in a suitcase, to Switzerland. I was scared like hell, but . . . thanks to some friends – who were quite experienced crooks I have to tell you – I managed to do it. My mother got away in a ship to Egypt and joined me in London. The money was just about enough to take care of her and I have to tell you that she is still alive.

'I didn't know what to do so I went to the bank to thank Marcus Samuel, who was an old man by now. He came down to see how I was and asked me how I was going to make a living. Well, I must tell you, Fred, I always wanted to be in the films. When I was eleven years old, I had my first camera and made my first film, which was a porno picture. It was very interesting for me, thanks to a friend of mine who had this mistress who was very nice, I must say, in a field near Lake Garda as a matter of fact. So, I said I would like to go into the film business. Samuel asked one of his people, "Do we have any film producers who are clients of the bank?" He owned Shell, he owned a bank, he was an English lord. Not bad. So they said, yes, there were four film producers who had accounts with the bank. "Are any of them overdrawn?" "All of them, my lord." He said to call the one with the biggest overdraft and, in a minute or two, I had a job.'

'And you've never looked back?'

'Almost at once. Because when Mussolini – what a fool, I must say! – declared war on Great Britain, I was immediately interned. Zere was nothing anyone could do, because I – who had always been told what a great country England was, who had come here because my father told me that it was a place that believed in freedom above all – I was "an enemy alien". Alien, all right, but enemy was a bit much, I must say. I wonder what they would have done if we had kept the shares and I had been one of the richest men in England. Probably de same. Possibly.'

'So what did you do during the war?'

'What I did in the war was, until 1943, I worked on a farm in some place, I don't remember what exactly, in de North of de Devon, if you know where that is.'

'Vaguely,' I said.

Who Whom?

Victor England was a very young man when he went to Hollywood to direct his first picture. His memories of the Golden Age were of more gingerbread than gilt. 'The last thing the studios ever wanted to have anyone do in those days was express himself. They wanted product, not *auteurs*, even if they had been able to pronounce them. Oh, Darryl and company liked to make movies all right, and one or two producers, no, *three*, did at least know something about them, but they were all the way out in California to make money and they paid you on the understanding you'd help them do it. Ninety-nine out of a hundred directors shot the scripts they were given, as written, down to and including the close-ups; the other one was on suspension. Directors usually didn't write because they usually didn't know how.'

'Does that stop them now?' I said.

I was sitting with Victor in the new office wing of his house on Stone Canyon, in Bel Air. His air-freshened new space was state-of-the-art with electronic machines and perspex sculpture. There was a big, elliptical desk for Victor and another, hardly smaller, for Sabina. She had been quick to inform me that, in today's Hollywood, she was not a secretary; she 'worked with' people. Sabina had replaced three-day Venetia, who had gotten off on the wrong foot by asking whether her employer wanted her to call him Victor or Vic. 'I want you to call me Mr England,' he said.

Sabina practised the kind of tact that you could not help noticing. She tiptoed to us with silent coffee and then she ducked across the room with written messages so as not to interrupt our conversation. Dialling in the air, she mimed the question of whether she should again call Marc-Antoine Chameau, the expatriate French restaurateur-slash-producer who was keeping us waiting well beyond the promised hour. The three of us were due to discuss the remake of a film whose rights he owned, or part-owned, or *could* part-own, if Victor (and I) agreed to work on it. It just happened to be the favourite European movie of 'one of the overpaid children out at Disney', as Victor put it, though not for publication.

While we sat there pretending not to mind a bit that we were wasting the morning, Sabina was as quiet as the Great Pyramid, and almost as obtrusive. However, Victor entered into no conspiracy of exasperation when our eyes met; his new girl was also slim and dark and pretty and twenty-six years old. It was forty years and three wives ago since Victor England was her age.

Victor said, 'I don't like people who are late. And I didn't like Monsieur Chameau even when he was going to be on time.'

'I guess he's the hoop we have to go through,' I said, 'if we want to make this picture.'

'Nobody will say so,' Victor said, 'but it was better when the big studios decided what they wanted to do, and didn't leave it to the Marc-Antoines to call the shots. Not that we thought so at the time. We all thought we could do better work if they didn't crack the whip so loud. They used to say the writers delivered their best dialogue when they were having lunch in the commissary.'

'Who was the wittiest of them, would you say?'

'Possibly Herman,' Victor said. 'I remember one time, you may have heard this one, there was a whole bunch of us sitting there – I didn't write, but I did eat – and Herman was saying his usual terrible things about Harry, loudly, and someone came by, an executive, and said, "Hi, Herman," and Herman said, "Hullo, Jack," and Jack said, "How's Sarah?" and Herman said, "*Sarah?* Who's Sarah?", and Jack said, "Sarah! Your wife, for Christ's sakes," and Herman said, "Oh, you mean *poor* Sarah." Milton Carver could run Herman close though sometimes. Sabina, I think you should call and cancel Monsieur Chameau.'

'Are you sure you want me to, Mr England?'

'Freddie, do you seriously need this job?'

'They seriously flew me out to talk about it,' I said. 'First-class fares make cowards of us all.'

'It doesn't always take that much. They paid me five hundred bucks a week when I first got out here. I turned yellow right away.'

'Milton Carver,' I said. 'What sort of things did he say?'

'I forget his best. Oh, for instance, he was talking about a producer one day, who was renowned for filling his house with rugs and stuff he'd "bought" from his own movies and Milton said, "Lou is always on the take, but always. Never misses. Like, OK, he ... he even has oilcloth pockets, for stealing *soup*!"'

I said, 'Milton Carver. Why haven't I heard of him? Did he write a lot of pictures?'

'Milt didn't care too much about credits. What he did most was, he rewrote the rewrites. He only worked strictly when he had to, which was when he came back flat broke from the track and a couple of guys in hats and fifteen-dollar suits were out looking for him with an urgent message from the boys, like "Pay up or else". Our crowd liked Milton, but he had this way of waiting till we were all laughing at something he had said and then asking us to lend him fifty dollars. It started out being fifty, but it got to be more as time went by, and the requests also got to be more frequent. We were none of us making a fortune and a lot of us had first wives and families.

'As a matter of fact, Milton and I arrived at Union Station on the same train. He had written a successful play, which Pandro had bought for Cukor to direct, only for some reason he never did. Milt hated California, but he liked the money, and the ponies, so he perched on a branch in the Garden of Allah and that's how come he never wrote another line he cared to put his name to. He was nice to me when I was nobody and I was always glad to see him when he came to the door and at the same time my heart sank, because I knew sooner or later he was going to touch me for money I didn't truly have and could never refuse. It got to be sooner, and sooner. Milt repaid his debts, but only in laughs. Did you ever lend people money?'

'How much do you need?' I said.

'Don't ask! When you even think of working with a guy like Marc-Antoine, it always proves you need a little.'

'I once lent a close friend a few quid,' I said. 'A TV director.'

'Have you spoken to him since?'

'He never forgave me,' I said. 'He became a critic and he always gives his unvarnished opinion of anything I do. Do you want to see the bruises? I have them at home.'

'Milton borrowed and borrowed, but he never blamed you for helping him out. He was genuinely happy when things went well for his friends. In fact, he was instantly on the doorstep, with his hand out. He looked you right in the eye and said, "What did I tell you? Put it there, partner! As much as you can spare." '

I said, 'What happened to him finally?'

Victor looked at me and his look said that he liked me, but that there were things he would as soon not tell me. As it happened, almost luckily, Marc-Antoine's olive-green Range Rover was crunching the imported gravel outside the wide glass windows. We had to go out and be glad to see him. He was wearing Calvin Klein jeans, with a tank-top advertising the Star Spangled Bistro, a jeans waistcoat, a back-to-front cap with A-TEAM on it, and unlaced, cushion-heeled white trainers. He had a purple-and-black designer backpack over one shoulder.

Victor said, 'Hullo, Marco Polo.'

Marc-Antoine put his arms round Victor and kissed him, very near the mouth. I braced myself and he did the same to me. It was no honour; he even kissed agents. 'I was out at Paramount.'

'It happens to us all,' Victor said.

'They love me out there. So, are we going to make *Love*, the three of us?'

'Freddie has some great ideas,' Victor said.

We went into the office. Marc-Antoine did not kiss Sabina, but he did look at her and then at Victor and do something a little unsubtle with his mouth. 'Before we start,' he said, 'I've got something for you both.' He un-velcroed the backpack and pulled out two tank-tops like the one he was wearing. 'Put 'em on,' he said. 'I only have a limited number. Shareholders only.'

'We're shareholders?'

'You will be by the time we close this deal. Or don't you want to make money? You know what Billy suggested as a title for the restaurant when I asked him to invest? "The Moulin de

Muggins"! Instead of the Moulin de Mougins, if you've ever been to it.'

'Many times,' Victor said.

I said, 'Marc-Antoine, *dis-moi* . . .'

'How's France?' he said. 'It's so long since I was there.'

'Hexagonal. About the film. We're going to transfer the whole story to the States, right?'

'I want it to be unrecognisable, even to people who saw *L'Amour*. Even to people who *made* it!'

'They always find out,' Victor said. 'If you don't have the rights.'

'Victor, do I look like a thief? I'm a goddam benefactor. I'm going to make you rich. So you can invest in the Star Spangled B. and get richer still.'

'One thing at a time,' Victor said.

'What for? Like is short, so it better be sweet. Last night I was with two girls and they are both very happy this morning and so am I. I don't know about their husbands. What's your name?'

'Sabina Clip.'

'Well, Sabina Clip, what do I have to do to get a cup of coffee out of you like these gentlemen have? I'm kidding. Do you have a club soda? Give me a club soda. I'm *seco, seco* today. They want it, Frederic; they want it very badly. How soon can they have it?'

'How soon can we close the deal?'

'Writers! It's closed. Why else was I late? But not very, was I?'

Victor said, 'I was talking to Stanley last night . . .'

'That Stanley! I was talking to him this morning. He thinks because his last name has an acute accent on it, he must be able to speak French!'

'. . . and he said that nothing was finally settled.'

'Why else am I here? Dot a tee, cross an eye, and there we are, finally settled. I think Chicago, don't you? Great city, I can make great deals there. Can you write it Chicago, Frederic? I've had some great ideas on casting. I was talking to Dick Dabney about it.'

Victor said, 'I don't care to have my pictures cast for me.'

'When did you last have a picture to cast, Vic, if you don't mind me asking? That looks great on you, Frederic. Doesn't that look great on him? Put yours on, Vic.'

'I like to choose my own cast in my own way. Likewise my own wardrobe.'

'Who do you think you're fooling today? New offices, right?'

'I think you'd better be a little bit careful how you talk to me.'

'Do I need you? I don't have to be careful how I talk to anyone. You need the job, Vic. I know, you know, he knows, they know. All the way down the line. Thank you, Sabina Clip, you have terrific legs. And I bet they go all the way up.'

I looked apologetically at Sabina, but she was looking at Marc-Antoine. I switched and looked at Victor, but his face was thick with angry blood. He seemed to be breathing faster than he wanted.

Marc-Antoine said, 'It was my idea to come to you because of the things you've done in the past I admired. People warned me that you were finished, to be honest, but I didn't listen.'

'Here's something you can listen to, if you want to,' Victor England said, 'because get the hell out of my house.'

'Don't you mean out of your *mortgaged* house? Your mortgaged-to-the-hilt house? I'll tell you something, Frederic, people always make new offices for themselves when they don't have work to do in them. And they hire pretty girls to do nothing. It's OK, I'm out. I should never have goddam well been in.'

After Marc-Antoine had been let go through the electric gates on to Stone Canyon, Victor said, 'He isn't even French. He comes from Abidjan. As if it mattered. Are you upset?'

'Of course not. As long as they still pay my hotel bill.'

'They don't, I will.'

'That's not going to happen,' I said.

'He was right,' Victor said. 'I need the picture. But there are some rug-sellers I still can't deal with. Too old, I guess. Aren't you going to damn well deny it?'

'What happened to Milton Carver?' I felt, rightly or wrongly, that I deserved to get something out of the morning, if only the end of the story.

'He got to be a little too demanding. And not so funny. One day, he came to my door, right after Warren was born, and he said he needed a thousand dollars. Badly. I was supposed to be his friend. Did I want to see him with two broken legs? I said, "A thousand dollars is a lot of money, Milton." "I know, that's why I'm here. I'll never ask you again." I'd had a little bit of a hit, but I was out of patience. I said, "Milton, you're getting to be a pain in the ass. You still owe me like seven hundred and ninety bucks from the last eighteen times you were never going to ask me again. A thousand dollars! I'll lend you five hundred, but that's it. That's *it*." "With only one broken leg," Milton said, "I guess I can always hop to work." I didn't laugh. "Five hundred bucks and it means I never want to see you at this door again. Got it?" "When I have," he said, "you won't." I give him the money and off he goes. An hour later, the bell rings. I go to the door. Milt! I couldn't believe it. I . . . I . . . you saw me just now . . . it was worse than that; I was choking I was so sore. "Listen to me," I said, "because you were never going to come to this door again . . ." He raised a hand. "One thing. One thing I want to get straight, Victor, is all: who owes who five hundred?" '

'Some people,' I said.

'Some people is right,' Victor England said. 'I screwed up just now. What'll you do? Write the picture anyway? He'll call you at the hotel, bet you, and want you to go ahead.'

'If he doesn't have you, why would he want to have me?'

'Who owes who five hundred?' Victor England said. 'You're never entirely sure, are you?'

All His Sons

Stanley Oppenheim is writing a paper to be read to this group of more than averagely bright people which meets in a panelled apartment on the Upper East Side, on the first Tuesday of the month. Why Tuesday? Why not? They have had a sexy seminar – 'Rite and Wrong' – on that exact same topic. The papers are expected to be neither solemn nor facetious. Provocative rather than conclusive is the rule. Topics of choice stimulate Social Thought: 'You want evolution of sensibility?' Max Rifle says. 'Look no further. *Est, est, est!*' That's Max: the resident traveller.

The 92 group consists mostly of Ivy League people. One can no longer say 'men' without embarrassment, though live white males do predominate, unintentionally, which is – as Stanley's brother, Sidney, says – neat. The members are lawyers, clinicians, university teachers (tenured or working like hell at it), critics, a TV anchor (Jay Bamberg, when free), writers (famous or glad still to have their integrity). That about covers it, even if Gerry Lancaster is a geneticist, *and* black, which Stanley's Black Studies colleague, Jesus Armstrong also is, with beard and shaved head.

'92' does not refer to the year of the group's foundation (which *was* '92) but to 92nd Street, where Patsy Lowenstein's

Old New York third-storey apartment is the monthly rallying point. She shares it, but not its ownership, with Mikey Carossa, a top editor at Modern Books. It has a janitor whom you can call in the elevator on the way down and he will have a taxi waiting for you at the kerb when you step out under the canopy, even if it's raining. That's Patsy Lowenstein.

Stanley Oppenheim teaches film studies, twentieth-century literature and the interdisciplinary marches in between with their tough ground cover of cross-referential footnotes and signposted sources here and there, *ici et là* (Lacan, Derrida, Oudart, Baudrillard, Foucault). He is also movie critic for *The Columbia Review*. He gets quoted alongside top critics now and again, though his name is seldom cited. '*The Columbia Review*' evidently sounds more prestigious than 'Stanley Oppenheim'.

Stanley likes to see his words, if not his thumbs, up there on the *NYT* entertainments page (especially in white on black) but he finds something delightful – he *says* – in being the Critic With No Name, a deep voice from the clouds. Is that why he keeps on going to inconvenient mid-Manhattan, mid-morning screenings? Stanley's professorial style would argue against ascription of precise motive or desire for *anything*. He pulls Heisenberg in here as an analogical ally. The middle ground is his preferred terrain; the divided self his favourite character. 'Integrity,' he has written, 'embraces fracture. (*Doesn't* it?)'

Stanley Oppenheim is fifty-one years old. Yes, he has a (second) wife, Melanie Youngman, who reads iffy manuscripts for Mikey Carossa and is two years plus into a Ph.D. on 'Con/version, Di/version, Re/version'. This – to briefly synopsise – will be an account of the ways in which people turn from one faith to another, often 'because an unadmitted similarity in logical, or psychic, form subsists in superficially diverse points of view'. The apparent surprise with which the convert greets a new revelation, Melanie argues, can often hide a con-slash-gruity which is veiled from his own perception. Compare re/veal and re/veil, as Stanley has mentioned a couple of times. Mortality, he has amplified (but only after Melanie has *sworn* she really really wants him to go ahead), is what is *systematically* veiled, not least by claims that go beyond mortality: do we have any conception of immortality except as an infinite continuation of *life*? 'Living-towards-life is user-friendlier than living-towards-death, wouldn't you say so?' Melly never denies it.

Heidegger and his hyphens figure quite regularly in Stanley's dis/courses. The biggest recent laugh he got out of film producer brother, Sidney, was when he *seriously* proposed someone maybe writing a script about the love affair between Hannah Arendt and Martin Heidegger. He also insisted he was serious, which kept Sidney's cackling face covered with a wad of noisy K-K-Kleenex. He was serious because that relationship (in which a *series* of relationships was implicit) encapsulated – it seemed at this point that Sidney might *die* – the whole fascination of Jew for Gentile, and *vice versa*, and for compromised intelligence for what *seemed* uncompromised.

'Don't say "and *vice versa*",' Sidney said. 'Not while I'm still in recovery, OK?'

'You don't think it would be commercial,' Stanley said. 'I actually do.'

'I know you do,' Sidney said. 'Because you are one crazy unworldly fuck. Hannah and Martin. Why not a fucking *musical* already?'

Melanie Youngman's thesis in progress is not *that* frequently shown to her husband. They like each other's brightness, but – because she respects him – she resists intellectual dependency. She also wants *him* to respect *her*. Yes, she has been his student.

And yes, the slogan 'separate but together' might happily apply to them, if it were not politically disreputable (and dated). Stanley and Melanie do not have a child. Stanley's fourteen-year-old son, Francis, is now François. He lives with his mother in Montreal; Elaine Prentice (she has decided to be, again) is a bright, bright therapist and ill-starred screenwriter. She seems to specialise in really good spec adaptations of public domain novels which, unbeknownst to her, are already being adapted by name writers. Unlucky! Isn't it doubly galling that her latest partner, Guy (pronounced *à la française*), is a copyright lawyer? Go figure.

Elaine used to send her scripts to Sidney Oppenheim, who once made the mistake of responding in detail. Now she calls Stanley, occasionally, to tell him how François is doing *great* and what an unfeeling bastard his brother is, not replying to her letters or commenting on her scripts any more. She says to tell him that her sister (remember Regina?) has suspected cervical cancer. Furthermore, if Sidney has anything to do with some people's plans she has heard about for turning *The Golden Bowl* into now a major movie, Stanley ('Yes, I'm still here') can tell Sidney from her that he is going to have major trouble, because Sidney read the version she wrote, and rewrote, at his suggestion. Any ideas that are in the eventual movie, which derive from her version, constitute something which Sidney may not have heard of, but – if they make the movie – he will. 'It's called *evidence*. Are you *listening to me*, Stanley? Then tell your brother.'

Stanley is tall and wiry and naturally tonsured. He keeps what remains of his hair very trim. He favours narrow, rectangular, black-framed spectacles and there is something dark about his pallor; the beard would be black if it could dodge the daily blade. Most of the time, he wears tapering, soft woollen pants and grey-black polo-neck cashmere sweaters. Somewhere along the line – yes, it's a lengthening line now – he can imagine being taken for the younger Arthur Miller, whose work he teaches, without unmitigated enthusiasm but equally without the now standard *lack* of enthusiasm. 'For a polemicist to make, *and become*, a canonical *target* is no small achievement. Attention must, I fear, be paid to this man. So do it.'

Stanley likes to listen to the you-first silence of a class unused to digesting, or even masticating, more than one thought at a time. Then he will say something like, 'Harriet, how do I grab you?' He enjoys the laughter which takes intention for inadvertence. 'Be fair here: I never claimed to be the *first*, but tell me as if I were.'

Stanley Oppenheim is not wanting in opinions or in trenchancy. Incited to provoke, he can deliver provocation like any other trope. He routinely tells a new class that seeing both sides of the question is the most demanding form of partisanship. He leaves a little time for *that* one to sink in, before he asks some guy (lounging with cowboy boots in the aisle) what he thinks he can mean by it. The reduction of male cocksureness is an urgent educational goal. Oh sure, Stanley is *perfectly* willing to go further into this and consider, openly, whether he is not jealous of the young men in front of him, who year by year grow younger than their professor ('A tautology is a tautology,' he concedes, 'and rarely a rose, least of all when you're my age').

Is being cryptic an attempt at sly intellectual castration? Are senior mannerisms Stanley's way of establishing eligibility for the paternal role? He would sooner play the midwife than the sire. He issues his students with an annual invitation to look out the etymology of 'maieutic', if only as a sly way of heading off the embarrassment of correcting ouchy misspellings when the word is served up to him in mimetically servile, but too often last-minute, term papers. He comes out fighting by laying himself open. Systole and diastole? Works for him!

So there's Stanley: tall and slim. This is a man who plays tennis, swims, skis. He eats carefully. Need there be a why? No, but he does indeed want not to be fleshy. His brother, Sidney, is fleshy. Sidney is also short and he does not shave or exercise that regularly. He wears a *yarmulka* a lot. He has been known to make out that he is an Israeli once tank- and now hack-driver: Bund, *Chaim* Bund, licensed to double park. Don't fuck with him, OK? *Ever.* I put you down, I kick you too, both feet. And *Shalom* to you too. P.S.: We're keeping the Golan.

Sidney is four years younger than Stanley, but Stanley sees in him a warning of what he might become. In that sense, Sidney is up ahead of Stanley, like an older brother. He happens also to be richer, although, in Stanley's eyes, his money is the only excuse, and a poor one, for producing the kind of films Sidney does, sometimes for TV. 'So I make phoney shit sometimes,' Sidney says, 'but at least it's *my* shit.' Why does Stanley feel criticised when Sidney makes that statement? Plus, why is he meant to?

Stanley says that he teaches his students *to* think, but not *what* to think. 'That's what *you* think,' Sidney says. When Stanley thinks of Sidney saying those kinds of possibly true things, he has him doing it with his mouth open, and food in it, like James Mason, in close-up, in *The Pumpkin Eater* (Jack Clayton).

The brothers sometimes go to Waxman's deli on the Lower East Side together, Sunday morning. Sidney gets plenty of thumps on the shoulder. 'Hey, Sidney!' from this one, 'Hey, Sidney!' from that one. Stanley stands with legs crossed at the knee, knuckles under his chin. How can Sidney know *that many* overweight people?

Sidney eats a lotta food, and orders more before he's finished. He pulls on a quart of celery and/or carrot juice (two straws for speedy suction). When he sees the flush of *goyisher* disdain on Stanley's face (those compressed lips!), Sidney takes a bite from *lutka* number two. Stanley *never* eats them. 'What's your problem, Stanley? A Jew shouldn't do things like a Jew?'

Trust Stanley to sigh and say, 'How about you don't do this, Sidney, for once? You do this to upset dad and dad's not here.'

'You're dad,' Sidney says.

Stanley shakes his head, as if his partner has led the wrong card, and it was exactly what he expected him to do. Stanley used to play tournament bridge. 1982, he attained Life Master status; then he quit. Elaine encouraged him to play, for love, but not for the love she felt for him. Guy is now; Barry Outwater was then. Elaine, Elaine. What is this with Stanley? He aches for the bitch, although he does *not* miss her; he is happy with Melanie. Yes, he is. What he misses is the Stanley Oppenheim who didn't know certain things, and had hair: the bridge-playing *putz* who thought he and his wife were still what they never were. Elaine, Elaine, cunt and queen (but not aloud).

'You're maybe not a Jew,' Sidney says, 'but you are dad. Look at the hairline. Identical. How *is* Julius?'

'Call him. Ask him,' Stanley says. 'Would it hurt you?' Then he says, 'He seems OK. He grieves. He misses Annette. Fifty-eight years is a long time.'

'Losing a spouse; fifty per cent grief, fifty per cent relief, isn't that what the Talmud says?'

'Tell him that. Tell him that, Sidney, why don't you?'

'He knows it. He's a Jew. Which is why I'm telling you.'

'I'm just not your *kind* of a Jew.'

'The kind that isn't is the kind you are. What do you suppose he's worth? Not that you need it, do you? With tenure already. A man with a pension, *nuch*!'

Stanley has to smile; when bugged he always has to smile. When he's content, he leans forward and frowns and takes a long breath, to fuel the period of time he intends to speak. That intake of breath is a concession to the force of the previous speaker's point. It also heralds a full answer.

Stanley has been writing:

' "This man will die" apparently tells us nothing about a man, except that he is one. But when we say of a *particular* man that he will die, don't we mean that we expect to survive him, that we, the living, will see him dead?

'A man likes to believe of his children that they *bequeath* him a certain immortality. What is truer is that he will not, if he is lucky, live to see them die. The son is more conscious of the father's mortality than the father chooses to be of the son's, and more eager for it. The father would be diminished by the death of his child; the child will be liberated by the death of his father.

'Even if it were to mean something to say that a father and a son love each other, they cannot love each other *in the same way*. Love is a word which proves to us how little we can say about what we insist matters most. Because otherwise . . . *what*?'

INT. 8TH AVENUE APARTMENT. DAY.

Books and records in boxes. Suitcases by the front door.

STANLEY
What your mother and I feel, or don't

feel about each other doesn't affect what
we feel about you.

The boy stands with the baseball bat and the mitt and his
Knicks cap front to back and says nothing.

> STANLEY

You're wrong.

> FRANCIS

I didn't say anything.

> STANLEY

I'll always be here for you.

> FRANCIS

'We' you said. Liar.

> STANLEY

I'm sorry?

> FRANCIS

'What *we* feel about you.' Is the lie.

> STANLEY

She and I . . . your mother and I . . .
we still love you just as much.

> FRANCIS

So why are mom and I leaving here?
You and she don't make a 'we'.

> STANLEY

There are things you don't understand,
son.

> FRANCIS

Yeah. And this is one I do.

'Look at a man about whom we are saying "This man will
die". What information does this give us about him? All men
will die, won't they? But if we say "this man will not die", we
shall be taken for what? Extraterrestrials maybe who imagine
that some humans do and some do not die, like some

extraterrestrials possibly don't. Space visitors might assume – from the virility or the youth of a particular specimen – that this man belongs to an immortal class. *Or* the speaker might not have grasped the meaning of death (taking it from a special kind of curable *illness*, perhaps). Or again, the commentator – when does he become a *critic*? – might be a Christian, magically observing celestial archive footage of the life of Jesus and saying to an ignorant or sceptical person, as the crucifixion takes place, "This man will not die". A (literally) crucial plot-point!'

EXT. 8TH AVENUE. DAY.

STANLEY embraces FRANCIS as ELAINE – an attractive (but that's irrelevant today) woman in her late thirties, muffled against the cold and, maybe, against pain – waits by the car, in impatient tact. She wears a knitted ski-cap, poncho, red pants, boots.

> STANLEY
> You need me, I'm here, Frankie.
> Today, tomorrow, whenever.

FRANCIS endures but does not return the hug STANLEY gives him.

> FRANCIS
> Day after tomorrow?

> STANLEY
> Ask your mother. She'll tell you the
> same thing.

> FRANCIS
> We'll be fine.

> STANLEY
> Good.

> FRANCIS
> Without you.

INT. THE APARTMENT. DAY.

STANLEY comes in and there is wet on his cheeks. His nose is cold.

> NARRATOR
> He has looked forward to and dreaded
> this moment. He is free. And now he
> longs for the chains he no longer has to
> wear.

STANLEY sits at his desk. We watch him closely.

> NARRATOR
> He realises that he need never be
> interrupted again. No one will call for
> help, or lunch, or toilet paper. He puts
> his head in his hands and tries to cry,
> and then to smile.

The telephone rings. He wants to ignore it. He picks up.

'Now consider a scene in a film, in which a man has to go to a meeting. A dull scene, but structurally essential. How to beef it up, give it dramatic urgency? Suppose that the director decides to have a narrator's voice tell us, "This man will die". The subsequent footage need not be altered in the smallest detail, not even re-edited, in order to deliver *a different scene*. Voice moderates vision; ears *are* eyes.

'What was dull before now contains menace; what was slack is tautened. We watch in empowered impotence and excitement. What is tragic inevitability unless it's the categoric promise that tragedy will always be tragic? (Cf. Adler's *Kanal*: we are *promised* that these men will die.)

'The role of the god-like narrator contains all that's left of what used to be morality. "God-like" implying that we may misinterpret the oracle but that it will not, in the logic of our creation, be *false*. We can be promised a scene of fraternal hatred and then witness nothing more unpleasant than two brothers laughing together over lox and cream cheese and celery juice, but sooner or later the narrator's guarantee has to be redeemed. The "erotic" charm of fictions lies in the slow, unexpected, deceitful, sweet redemption of just such cruel promises.'

INT. CLASSROOM. DAY.

The tiered desks of the lecture room are empty. Yet we have the impression that they are *looking down* at STANLEY and the FEMALE STUDENT whose essay is on the flat desk on the podium.

>   STANLEY
> Tell me more about the significance of
> the camera *looking* at a character. How
> does this seem more *moral* – the word
> you use – than a human look . . . ? Can
> machines moralise?

>   STUDENT
> I didn't say 'more'. It's the way the
> camera can *dwell* on a face that *implies*
> an invitation to judgement. The camera
> is *loaded*, we say. Isn't it? It shoots, but
> not to kill. Am I wrong? It *invites*, but
> it doesn't *welcome*, judgement.

>   STANLEY
> (smiles to hear his female voice!)
> How about when a writer describes
> somebody? Isn't that the same kind of
> loaded event? 'Words are loaded pistols,'
> someone once said.

> STUDENT
> Someone once said everything, Professor
> Oppenheim.
>
> STANLEY
> Stanley. Stanley is fine. It's Melanie, isn't
> it?

'Isn't the Holocaust to us what the Lisbon earthquake was to Voltaire? The nature of the human drama changed in the light of a divine narrator with nothing, or nothing coherent, to say. The Supreme (still, small) Voice-Over doesn't carry conviction any more; worse, He can't find anything commanding to say. This dumbness justifies our reluctance or refusal any longer to follow His laws. But, *pace* Zarathustra, don't godless assumptions lead to a general loss of *significance* in daily life?

'Try this: the more we have confidence in the inescapable premiss of an art, the more subtle its practice. (Dare I mention *Seven Against Thebes* aloud?) A determined morality or aesthetic leaves space for *freedom of invention*, the creative exercise of ingenuity. This liberty derives from *already knowing what is inevitable*. Sure, freedom and determinism can ride the same rails, but only when there are rails to ride.'

INT. COLLEGE CAFETERIA. DAY.

STANLEY and his STUDENT (MELANIE) are walking to a table in the almost deserted cafeteria with their coffee. STANLEY also carries a single big cookie in cellophane.
They get to a table by the rainy window and STANLEY breaks the cookie in half before he pulls the cellophane open. He pushes out half the cookie without touching it and offers it to MELANIE.

> NARRATOR
> He has the feeling that he is doing
> something intimate, almost illicit, even

though he knows that he is not. His
smile, which is cousin to a frown, says
that he thinks she must recognise this.

MELANIE

You're married, right?

STANLEY

I'm married wrong. But . . . it's over.
We're separated.

MELANIE

What did she do?

STANLEY

I guess we both did things.

MELANIE

Professionally.

NARRATOR

The question without the question
mark. A feature of the modern style. He
bites his cookie as if it were a significant
act. Because it isn't, it is.

Under this, STANLEY and his STUDENT are talking and what
we do not hear between him and MELANIE seems warmer,
more convincingly intimate, humorous, adult even, than
anything we could.

'Tragedy dies; comedy prevails. We, and our art, are
demoralised. Our lives have lost their dangerous intensity; life is
a *sit com*. We are left in a world in which we can no longer be
relied on to interest ourselves even in who committed *a*
murder. The death of an individual is too limited a problem to
excite the police or a public. We have to be promised that the
killer will strike again, and that *our* lives are conceivably at risk,
before interest is kindled. The notion of murder being the
supreme crime no longer stands up. *Traffic* is murder. There are

worse crimes, and we want to hear about *them*.'

Annette Levinson Oppenheim died two years ago. She and Julius had lived in the apartment at 91 Central Park West, between 70th and 71st streets, ever since he bought it way back in 1943. Before that, they had a house in Brooklyn. Julius was in dress fabrics and imported pieces with his older brother, Rich, and his father, Max, who had done well enough by then to send Julius to Columbia. 'Let the kid go study,' Rich said, 'we can afford a *putz*.'

Julius wanted to major in a liberal arts subject. Possibly he imagined deserving Rich's scorn. But no: he studied management sciences and marketing. Instead of being despised, as he hoped, he learned to despise, as he feared. He came home knowing the business could never make it big the way his father and brother handled things. This was a period that Julius rarely spoke about to Stanley; Brooklyn was the old country.

Rich was a *mensch* much like his father, Max, except he got murdered. Julius found Annette Levinson sobbing and Max with new, vertical lines on his face, either side of his nose, no tears, a man scarred by grief. After his brother was shot down in that alley in Bensonhurst, Julius organised Oppenheim's expansion into wholesaling and then into manufacture. They called him 'the kid', but they didn't kid with him a whole lot. When Max died, in his bed, June 1940, his wife Hannah said, 'Rich killed him. Rich did this to him.' By this time, Julius was all set to get rich. And he did: uniforms, parachutes, the war. He had also married Annette Levinson.

When Stanley came to teach Arthur Miller's *All My Sons*, he hated that play. As soon as he read about the father who made a fortune by knowingly manufacturing aeroplanes with a design fault, in his mind Stanley cast Julius in the Edward G.

Robinson part. Why? His father had not, to Stanley's knowledge, done anything comparable to Miller's bad dad. Until he met Melly, he told no one, not Sidney, not Elaine, that he had dramatised Julius as a villain he had no reason to believe him to be.

INT. COFFEE SHOP. EAST VILLAGE. DAY.

STANLEY and MELANIE in a booth with coffee.

> STANLEY
> I don't know why I told you.

> MELANIE
> He had a good and a bad side, didn't
> he, Edward G., to his face? Camera-
> wise. Is 'Shekel and Hide' overdoing it?
> He seemed like a guy without vanity,
> but he had a lot.

> STANLEY
> He had a career. A man with just a few
> assets likes them well used. My father
> doesn't resemble Edward G. Robinson.
> Except he's not tall.

> MELANIE
> And he's a Jew.

> STANLEY
> Is that a resemblance for you? It's not
> necessarily for me.

> MELANIE
> Did I say the wrong thing?

> STANLEY
> You were right to.

She looks and sees that there are tears shining on STANLEY's cheeks. He is looking out of the window, as if something out there had distressed him. He looks at her and smiles quickly.

STANLEY

I'm sorry. Maybe I'm a Jew too.

MELANIE

Do Jews cry easily?

STANLEY

Some do; some don't. I don't. I guess I
betrayed him. My father. Killed him,
metaphorically, without him ever
guessing. Neat. Not nice, but certainly
neat.

MELANIE

It's very flattering.

STANLEY

Excuse me?

MELANIE

That you told me. Or do you tell
everyone you haven't told anyone else?

STANLEY

It'd be more flattering to say that you're
a very attractive young woman and I
don't know what the hell you're doing
hanging out with a middle-aged
professor who's made a mess of his
marriage.

MELANIE

I guess I want to fuck you.

When Julius got rich-rich, he wanted sons who were
brighter than he had had the chance to be. When he was old
enough to say such things, which wasn't *that* old, Sidney said
that Julius was the kind of businessman who would be
disappointed if at least one of his sons didn't despise him.
Stanley was sponsored to do that by becoming an intellectual.
And Sidney? Oh, Sidney went to college (only not *Harvard*!),

but the way *he* humiliated his father was by being more like him than Julius cared to remember ever being. Sidney wasn't going to watch his mouth and he wasn't going to be afraid of nobody. The member of the family Sidney most hoped to emulate was Max Oppenheim: a word and a blow.

Story had it that, 1937, 1938, there was this march, by the German-American *Bund*, right through the garment district. Nazis! The Jewish dressmakers, most of them, didn't stay around to see the march, but Max Oppenheim had work to do. When the march turned right down the street where he was unloading a truck, Max stood in the middle of the alley and held out his arms and said, 'No punks down here.' This was a man who could lift a bale of material above his head and go on talking price on a take-it-or-leave-it basis for ten minutes, no problem whatsoever.

The leader of the march told him, 'Outta the way, kike.'

Next thing, Max Oppenheim had picked the guy up and was holding him, face to the sky, above his head, high and helpless. Max looked at the Bundists, like he was asking each one of them a simple question: anyone want to fuck with me? No one did. Max took a step back and dumped the leader of the march, bang, on the cobbles, sack of potatoes. No sale: get him out of here.

That was the *mensch* Sidney loved. Sidney played poker like his uncle Rich used to do, two, three days at a time. Rich had been eleven years older than Julius. He had had a frown on him in family photographs that Sidney liked to borrow and take to the office sometimes. Sidney was not free with his fists, but he had a fighter's nose and an ex-fighter's gut. He hung out at the gym and learned to handle himself. One time a network suit threatened to pull the plugs on a production of his and he called him up and threatened to do him 'bodily harm'. The guy said, 'You could find yourself in court, talking to me that way.' Sidney said, 'You could find yourself in the hospital, you stink-fingering asshole fink.' He got to finish his production. It was terrible.

Stanley enjoyed the stories about Max, but he could never remotely imagine *being* Max. As for Rich, that was a dark alley he did not figure on going down. Julius had left Rich in Brooklyn and did not care to tell his children too much about him; yes, he had been a little bit of a demon, but he wouldn't say a gangster; not a *gangster*. How about a low-life? 'He was a low-life, right?'

'If you say so, Sidney.' Julius looked at Annette and, so far as Stanley could see, Annette just went on sitting there with her glasses on, counting stitches. She could make an ordinary armchair seem like a rocker somehow. It was probably the knitting, which – looking back – she totally never needed to do.

Once Julius was rich, he found himself a good tailor, who stocked the best English worsteds. In the 1950s and 60s, he was a regular at the Manufacturers' Club, which was exclusive, but not so exclusive that it would exclude him. He was known to be a charitable man, a soft-spoken, decisive philanthropist. He employed more black people than most of his friends and paid them better. He was not religious, but he joined a Reform temple. All right, Jewish charities were favoured by his benefactions, but the ACLU and the NAACP also benefited, among others.

He had a panelled den in the penthouse at 91 Central Park West, where he kept sets of Will Durant and Mortimer Adler. The *synopticon* introduced him to Plato and Aristotle and

William James. Julius ordered many books; they were ranged on mahogany shelves thick enough never to sag under the weightiest volumes. The minute he had a new book in the house, he removed the dust-jacket and inserted it behind the back cover. Why? That's what he did; absolutely always.

For years, Annette had an Irish maid, called Hilda. She lived in the small-windowed room off the kitchen. One day Annette found her mouth-open dead, as if from astonishment. Another girl was hired. Her name was Fleggy. Annette called her Hilda.

The Oppenheims' first black chaffeur-butler, Harold Beauregard, had started out working at one of Julius's factories during the war. Impressed with the cleanliness of the section for which young Harold was responsible, Julius asked if Harold would care to be employed personally by himself and Mrs Oppenheim. That was how Harold Beauregard came to be a feature of the childhood of Stanley and Sidney. He drove them in the Packard with the spare tyre housed in front of the running-board: Coney Island and Jones' Beach. They went with him to see the Dodgers (Stanley had to be the one that asked, 'Which one is Jackie Robinson?').

When Harold married Juniper Davies, Julius Oppenheim bought the couple a small clapboard house not far from the Van Wyck Parkway (4072 Roosevelt Drive) so that they could raise their family in a good-air neighbourhood. The air got worse as La Guardia and Idlewild took on heavier traffic, but Milton and Amanda Jane went to much better schools than you would find around Lennox Avenue.

Young Sidney asked Harold regularly about Harlem and about what blacks *really* thought. His questions were an innocent accusation that the chauffeur was first cousin to Jack Benny's Rochester. Sidney wanted to know about black pimps and pushers and Holy Rollers and the Reverend Elijah Muhammed. He made a face when Harold Beauregard said that he didn't know too much about most all of those things. Sidney would say, 'What do you know about, Harold?' And Harold would sigh good-naturedly (Stanley winced at the good nature more than the sigh) and then he would say, 'I know what happens under the hood of a Packard and I know your daddy wouldn't want you trailing your shoelaces the way you're doing.' Stanley would be glad that Harold had not said 'I knows' and wonder where the idea came from that he might.

Stanley constructed one Harold Beauregard out of Harold; Sidney, he guessed, constructed another. Today, Harold is a cluster that comes to mind when Stanley wants a class to understand what he means when he says that we can never know a man's motives, or even what a man *really is*, because however we look at why, or who, we only see through a glass, if not darkly, then distortedly; we are part of what we see. With a man ('Yes, or a woman, Harriet'), there is always more to be known, which is the unknown. 'And yet' (like it or no, this is the way Stanley teaches) 'we don't *want* to say that we can never know the truth about him. Or her; especially or her!' Applause.

'What are we so afraid of in black people?' This is something Stanley dares to ask his class, but Sidney is right: he would not necessarily pose the same question out in the street. Stanley guesses he is right, but he cannot accept Sidney's determination to be as loud and crude and nasty about black people as he is about white. Sidney defends himself with authentic shamelessness: 'It's a kind of prejudice to be unprejudiced the way you are, zipper-mouth, and you know it, don't you?'

Stanley *does* know it. He knows that being tactful *and*

articulate entails a gulf between the things thought, and perceived, and the things said. What kind of a *solution* can there be? Don't honesty and civility *di*verge just as candour and abuse *con*verge? Does pluralism *entail* dishonesty? Is this Plato's point about democracy sticking it to us all over again?

Stanley does not have conscious problems with blacks, unless fearing them is a problem. He once asked Jesus Armstrong what black authenticity really was. What would black men *be* if they could be?

INT. FACULTY ROOM. DAY.

> JESUS
>
> How long have you got, Stanley?
>
> STANLEY
>
> As long as it takes.
>
> JESUS
>
> You do? I don't.
>
> STANLEY
>
> How long do you need?
>
> JESUS
>
> No time at all. And that's what I don't
> have.

He smiles with slightly moist eyes (humour or pain?) and touches STANLEY on the shoulder.

> JESUS
>
> You're a good man, Stanley, but I don't
> hate you for it.
>
> STANLEY
>
> Are we always going to win?
>
> JESUS
>
> The white man? I think so. It's about
> all he can do, isn't it?

STANLEY

You don't believe that.

JESUS

No, I don't. Know why we hate Jews?

(STANLEY waits for it, with that stiff smile of his.)

Because they's so *good* to us!

One Sunday in the fall of 1963, Sidney got word that Malcolm X was speaking on Lennox Avenue that afternoon. He wanted Stanley to go down with him and hear what the *Schwarze* had to say. Sidney was driving a big beat-up Chevy station-wagon with loose steering. The city was empty; they had no problem getting down to Harlem. Sidney parked the Chevy on 125th street and they walked round the corner into Lennox Avenue.

'Some crowd,' Stanley said, when he saw the podium with its bracket of folding brown chairs and the wide, deep semicircle of Malcolm's bellying audience in front of it.

'Look at that,' Sidney said. '*Brother* Divine!' Sidney spoke way too loudly. Stanley gave him an unsmiling smile.

They listened to the speech, which was eloquent and not at all stupid. A couple of times they nodded at each other, critics at a show that was turning out better than they expected. In the interval, big-shouldered marshals in reflecting dark glasses and suits came up and offered them literature.

'He can speak,' Sidney said, right in front of the vendors. 'Maybe he can write too.'

Stanley bought a newsletter and ignored the change. 'Are you trying to get us killed?'

'There are cops here,' Sidney said. ''sides, they appreciate us coming down. And besides that, fuck 'em. There's cops here. No one's going to get killed. Fuck 'em, man.'

'Stop this, OK?'

'They want us to be men, to look at them, like men, not like a . . . *problem*. Dad thinks this is something you can scratch your head and find a solution for.' When Stanley sighed his regular sigh at this, Sidney said, 'Don't you, dad? I like these people. I like their nerve. They're aiming to be the kind of Jews Max and Rich were, the kind you don't fuck with.'

'Why am I here, Sidney?'

'Didn't you want to get an education, Stanley? This is the future you have in front of you. Men are men. Men don't *argue*. You argue; men don't.'

'Fuck you, Sidney, finally.'

'Know something? That's nice to hear. From you that's nice to hear. Beats "on the other hand".'

They stayed in the street, a white minority of two, until in mute concert they agreed that speakers were beginning to repeat each other. Without turning their backs, they receded from the meeting and allowed themselves to be borne, as if by an undertow, around the corner. In the empty side-street, its tenement fronts herring-boned with fire escapes, they were symmetrical twins for a moment, holding on to each other and loaded with the same charge of laughter which they did not let out.

They banged the chevy doors and locked them and Sidney hung a wide yewy in the still deserted side-street. They might have been home free, but they were held up by a stop light in Lennox Avenue. While they were lawfully motionless, a bunch of black guys in an open T-bird with a busted silencer came up behind them and, whack!, ran right into their rear end (*Bad Day at Black Rock*, John Sturges).

The brothers did a forward-and-back like a little chorus line and then Sidney said, 'Don't look round. And *don't-get-out-are-you-CRAZY?*'

Stanley smiled, with white lips. He was never going to get out. If he pressed his hand on the door lever, it was precisely because he wanted the reaction from Sidney that he had actually got for once. He enjoyed the fear and then the hate on Sidney's face (hatred for him) and then the light changed and – thank God – the rear bumper wasn't snagged and they were off down Lennox Avenue, heading downtown. The 80's were never so beautiful.

Harold Beauregard raised his son, Milton, with the idea he would go into the military. When Milton's eyes turned out to be a problem, Julius Openheim had Annette's cousin, Leo Levinson, look at the young man. There was nothing ophthalmic that could be done that should not have been tried a dozen years earlier. Harold got old the minute Stanley went away to college and he was left head to head with big little Sidney. The fat boy had a load of questions that asked Harold to step out from his allotted role and he went grey, then white, instead. Truth to tell, he could have killed that kid.

Before he went to the Manufacturers' Club, whose premises would have to be relocated when they came to build 666 Fifth Avenue, Julius would visit Marshall Tringham, his barber, on the first floor of Rockefeller center right under Diego Rivera's edited murals. He took a manicure from Veronica as well as a haircut. 'The less hair a man has,' he told her, 'the more often you see him in a barbershop. Noticed that?'

Veronica wore a white pharmacist-style coat and not too much underwear visible when she leaned forward to buff those almond-shaped fingernails. By the time Sidney first got to see her (sitting on a board across the arms of a regular chair while Marshall cut his damn curls), Veronica was no longer any kind of a babe, but she had a knowing look (like her namesake in *I Married a Witch*). Even when he was ten, eleven years old, Sidney had an idea he knew what it was she knew about, or so he says.

'You're being restrospective here.'

'Mother was old. Annette was old. She chose to be. You know that. Veronica had a great chest. Even I noticed. A lot.'

'So?'

'You were in Cambridge already, engoying yourself. I was an only child. Smart, dirty-minded, ahead of myself. I had boners already at that age.'

'Everybody did.'

'Julius pretended to be a clean-liver, but was he? Was Max? Was Rich? Were you, jerkoff? Because who is finally?'

'You made those things up. How *menschlich* they were.'

'You want him to be your father and not mine. You want to kill him in your own way. With kindness. That's not kind of you, Stanley. Let him be a man. Let him cheat a little. Let him enjoy his money.'

'I don't have the smallest wish to kill Julius.'

'Dad has had a mistress ever since I was eleven years old, at least. You don't believe me? Check with him.'

'I would never do a thing like that.'

'To who? To who would you not do it? And "Whom" me no whoms. You're not Mr Tibbs. Who directed that again?'

'I'm thinking of mother,' Stanley says. 'Norman Jewison.'

'Consider what she maybe once did. *In the Heat of the Night*. Mother. Or more than once. We have time.'

'*Mother?*'

Sidney now has regular manicures himself, Stanley notices, but he does not remark on it. Stanley likes to smile to himself. Sidney smiles at other people. Sidney recruits; Stanley observes. So it goes.

What aged Julius Oppenheim more than wealth, more than hair loss, was the Rosenbergs. He became cautious, as if he feared he was about to miss a step, and correct in his speech. He spent evenings in his study. He had Harold keep everything clean, clean.

'Julius Rosenberg strapped dad right down in that chair,' Sidney said, 'like they were side by side, two of a kind.'

All Stanley could say to that was, Julius Oppenheim had *nothing* but his first name in common with Julius Rosenberg.

Sidney said, 'Know something, Stan? Maybe Julius Rosenberg was also why you got your divorce. From being a Jew.'

Stanley said, 'I never denied I was a Jew in my life.'

'Likewise you never volunteered you were.'

'*Stanley Oppenheim* has to volunteer? Fuck you, Sidney.'

'OK,' Sidney said, 'this one time, OK.'

After the Rosenberg case, Julius signed himself J. Benjamin Oppenheim for a while, but too many people had called him Julius for years for them to imagine he seriously meant them to call him something else. How old was he when the Rosenbergs were executed? Stanley calculated forty-one (*Jesus!*). He considered at one time writing an essay, which might fatten out into a book, about the Rosenberg case and how it affected New York Jewish intellectuals. 'Do it,' Sidney said. 'You could call it "Yes-and-No In Thunder, Maybe". Fiedler on the roof. I just love to hear you heave that sigh of yours, kid.'

When Stanley broached the topic to Julius, his father told

him, 'Why talk to me? Talk to Alfred or Norman. Some of those people. Political people. Talk to Gabe.'

'So how did you feel about the executions? *Gabe?*'

'Gabe King. He put money in some of those liberal magazines. Like a sieve he put it in. And got called all kinds of names. Is there a purpose in this?'

'Did you feel in even the smallest degree that Rosenberg was . . . *justified*? I mean: are you – were you – *entirely* happy with capitalist society?'

'Your hair's going the same way mine did, Stanley, did you notice that?'

'Thank you, I did.'

'I hated him. I thought he was ungrateful and stupid. Also pretentious. He imagined he knew better than the American people. I *feared* them is what I did. They broke the law. People break the law, they have to take the consequence.'

Stanley looked at Julius B. Oppenheim like a work of art, a period piece. 'Given that . . . given that, was Julius Rosenberg in any way whatsoever like . . . a . . . OK, a *brother*? Someone had the nerve to be . . . what he absolutely . . . *decided*. Regardless.'

'What do you know about Rich?'

'Not too much. What is there?'

'He got himself murdered,' Julius said. 'That was the way he lived. Over some money, also over a woman possibly, I don't know exactly.'

'Does Annette?'

'You're into upsetting people suddenly, Stanley, is that it? Why is that? Problems with your wife? You need some trouble that isn't *that* trouble? Rich got himself killed and no one knows exactly on account of what. Maybe Max did, my father;

he never told me. He never told me a lot of things. That was possibly his pleasure.'

'It's almost everybody's pleasure, isn't it?'

'We all go to the bathroom in our own way,' Julius Oppenheim said.

'Do we? Or do we think we do?'

'Sidney . . . your brother . . . he wants Rich to have been what I never was. Well, maybe that's what I want too, but not in the same way. Men, if they're going to be anybody, they have to accept not being somebody else. And that's always who they imagine they might have been happier being. Sidney is no different. Are you?'

'When you're in here in the evenings,' Stanley said, and had to look at his damned watch (Elaine, it was in those days), 'do you only read or do you ever do anything else?'

'Sure. If I have business to do, I do it.'

'You don't keep a diary?'

'If I have charities to attend to, I also do that. Otherwise, yes, I read; and I make notes. Diary, no. Do I disappoint you?'

'I have to go,' Stanley said. 'I was curious is all.'

'We all have to go,' Julius said.

When Annette Levinson Oppenheim died, in her eighty-third year, her sons wondered if Julius would move out of penthouse C, either because it contained memories or because it was now too big. Julius was told that he could sell it for a lot of money, but, listen, he already had a lot of money; he stayed. He let Hilda go though. Milton would take care of him.

Harold Beauregard had died on the day Jimmy Carter was inaugurated (did Julius Oppenheim vote for him? *Somebody* did). Milton Beauregard stepped into his father's place. Milton wore thick eye-glasses, but he was very like his father, without his father's memory. Everybody in the family made the slip – which was hardly Freudian, was it? – of calling him Harold at least a couple of times. Milton disappointed Stanley and Sidney because he was not Harold; he could not remember taking them places when they were small. Sidney showed that he had given up on him by being polite to him.

In due time, Milton had a son called Moss. When his wife, Abigail, was run over, they said by a police car that never *began* to be traced, he took to bringing the kid to the Oppenheims' apartment. This started when Moss was small and continued, during school vacations, as the boy grew bigger. Moss had long skinny legs and a high, narrow head. Milton imagined that he would go into the military, as if he himself had wanted to do that, when in fact it had been Harold who wanted it for him. Milton came in between Harold and Moss and, polite and generous though Julius was with him, he was never much more than the bridge between his father and his son.

When Milton was out, driving Mrs Oppenheim downtown maybe, Julius took Moss into the den and showed him his books. He watched as Moss turned the pages of flags in the big Webster's on the spreadeagle lectern or leaned on both hands – tiptoe feet almost off the floor – and levered himself over Adler's implacably informative pages.

When the kid went to high school, Julius enjoyed to have Moss come and do his homework alongside him, as if what they were doing had equal weight. Sometimes he would stop his own activity and watch for the moment when Moss would look up at him, with the whites of his eyes marble in the spilled lamplight.

Julius Oppenheim did not seem to favour either of his sons. They did not want to go into his business; he never asked them why. Whatever they did, as long as they did something, which both of them did, was fine by him. Maybe Veronica knew something different, but nobody aside from Julius (and Veronica) ever knew what, if anything, she was to him, or what, if anything, he told her.

When Stanley was teaching film, and talked about how the frame might be *composed* but never contained the whole picture, he sometimes thought of Julius walking out of the apartment, with his English suit and his rolled umbrella and his shut, rich man's face, and imagined him walking out of the family frame and into a life where he was no longer anybody's father or Annette's husband and wondered what he did out there, where the imagination's camera could not quite track him down.

'This isn't a criticism,' Stanley said to his brother one time, 'but do you think Julius is hiding something?'

'I hope so,' Sidney said, 'for his sake. Aren't you? *I* am.'

'I'm not talking about me.'

'Is my point. You hope so, right? But your hopes are not my hopes, saith the Lord, and for once He probably has it about right, doesn't He? *I* hope he does because otherwise why has he lived? To give Annette charge accounts and charitable opportunities? To fuck Veronica?'

'We don't know he fucks Veronica. What are you hiding?'

'Stanley, please: I'm hiding it. He fucks Veronica. I hope. You don't. Is what I mean.'

'You hope because then he would be a hypocrite.'

'No, for you he'd then be a hypocrite. For me, he'd then be a *mensch*; part way to Rich. You think he's conceivably gay?'

'*Dad?*'

'Well, come on, out with it, if you do. Alternatively, halfway out with it, as usual. You want me to accuse him of something so you can deny it and scuttle back into your shell.'

'It never *occurred* to me he was gay.'

'Dad and Harold. How did that start? You've never thought about that?'

'You're a reckless bastard sometimes, Sidney.'

'Yeah? What do I do about that? Read something? How about Moss?' Sidney said. 'Is that healthy, would you say?'

'*Moss?*'

'And dad. All that time alone together. How would that look in a movie?'

'Moss is a kid. That dad is glad to help. Sidney, you're way off limits.'

'So it's occurred to you, right?'

'I never remotely thought about Moss,' Stanley said. 'In that sense.'

'Can't loving people also help them sometimes?'

'There's love and what you're talking about.'

'You think it's a good thing what he does for Moss? How good a man does Julius have to be finally?'

'He's someone likes to be generous.'

'Which differs how from *being* generous? He was an operator. Must've been. He made the big bucks, not Max. Not Rich. What happened yesterday that makes him have to be this good today? Ever think about that?'

'He does those things, one way and another.'

'He doesn't do with anyone else what he does with Moss. That I know of. So how do you read it, professor?'

'I truly have to go,' Stanley said.

'He loves the kid. You can say it; I can't. Why is that?'

Julius fixed for Moss to go to a good college. He came and visited with Julius in the vacations and showed him some of his written work. Julius passed it on to Stanley and it was good enough for him to wonder, secretly, if it was all really Moss's. At one point Julius suggested Moss might do post-graduate work instead of going into the military. Did Moss really *want* to go into the military or was he wanting what he thought Milton, and Julius, wanted him to want? Moss was six foot three inches tall now. He was slim and elegant and, when he came to visit, conservative in his dress. Julius appreciated the whiteness of his shirts. He gave him some cuff-links he never used.

When Milton brought coffee and cookies into the den, Julius and Moss would stop talking about whatever they were talking about and they watched Milton as he put down the tray. Moss looked at Julius and sometimes Julius looked at Moss, and they waited for Milton to say, 'Anything else?' There never was. 'Thank you, Milton.'

Sidney said, 'I've been known to feel jealous.'

'By whom?' Stanley said.

'OK, I observed myself to feel jealous, and inadequate.'

'Inadequate I can understand,' Stanley said.

'Tongue like a lizard,' Sidney said. 'You have sometimes. Mother said that to me once.'

'Annette said that?'

'With a smile to her knitting she said it. Who did she knit *for*? Did she knit for you ever? She never knitted for me.'

'For Francis she did,' Stanley said, 'coupla times. Jealous?'

'Does Julius like us?' Sidney said. 'Not like he likes Moss. Or fears him.'

'Moss needs him, he thinks. What's to fear?'

'Blackness. Colour of death. And we don't need him?'

'Sidney, do you know how old you are?'

'Every minute. I will never again come twice without

65

pulling out, even when she's blonde, built on top, and a *shikse*. Life is as good as over, but otherwise terrific. He thinks we *didn't* need him. He thinks Annette took care of taking care of us, when in truth it was Harold. Wasn't it?'

'Suddenly we're we, you and I,' Stanley said. 'Why is that?'

'He would've liked us better if we'd seriously wanted his money. I don't say if we'd gone into the business before he sold out, but if we'd been greedy, *after* something. Fastidious is another thing she called you. Annette. Meaning she never saw you picking your nose like she saw me.'

'Like she saw you plenty. Why do you do that?'

'Because you don't wanna see, don't look. Moss is *so* good he's a little too good to be black, don't you think that?'

'He's dad's house-plant, is that what you think he is?'

'With dem white flowers on dere! Dad's making an example of him, but of what? To whom? And also why?'

'It could be, *could* be, that he feels bad about Milton.'

'*Milton?*'

'He took him on. He treated him politely. He helped him like he helps a lot of people, but he never liked him, not like like. If he hadn't been black, and Harold's son, he would've let him go before he ever took him on.'

'You're making sense here,' Sidney said. 'What happened?'

'Don't spoil me, Sidney, now.'

'Why aren't we close, Stan? Close–close?'

'Because it would embarrass – embarrass you.'

'Embarrass *me*? Isn't that misaddressed possibly?'

'We need the distance; that way we don't clash.'

'Something happened to you didn't happen to me. What?'

'You,' Stanley said. 'But don't think I haven't appreciated the company. Now and again.'

'Moss is going to be Julius's white man. White *goy* even.

When Abigail was killed, that was when it really began. He turned into the kid's mother. Annette never wanted Moss in the house.'

'No? How can you tell?'

'Because I can't. You know Annette. Bravery and coward-ice, what's the difference in her case? Why didn't dad push to find out which cop in a hurry for dinner it was killed Abigail? Milton didn't have the clout; dad did. He knew the mayor.'

'It's not the kind of thing he ever did, ever. He can't do everything. Why didn't *you* push? You know people in the mayor's office. And the Police Department.'

'Yes, I do, and I need those guys. And I don't care who killed Abigail. Neither did Julius. One bit. Me, I don't care to make people guilty, and *hunted*, just for the righteous hell of it. You're the critic; me, I'm not. So some cop got away with accidentally killing a *Schwarze*. Shame! But life goes on. Answer me this: who *said* that it was a cop car killed her?'

'That's what the word was. I don't know *who* exactly.'

'Is Moss a little too good to be true? Can he *really* be that *much* of a credit to his race? Not to mention ours, which is what he is being bribed to be, isn't it? Is that really what *he* wants? A man who never ever has to look behind him because when he wipes his ass that paper is clean enough to blow his nose on? Guaranteed. Is it healthy for him to be *that* civilised?'

'What would you prefer he was?'

'I saw him once,' Sidney said, 'downtown. Strutting down 42nd street. With some white chick. In wraparound Ray-Bans and a black velour outfit. Looking like a guy might ask you if you wanted to buy a watch, or pay twenty bucks to get blown by his bitch. Six inches taller than he ever is over at 91. Moss is a closet stud, is my point.'

'Except it wasn't Moss you saw, was it?'

'Maybe it was, probably it wasn't. But what happens when the brakes come off, or he finds they're jammed?'

Stanley goes to see his father, but not regularly. Regularity would soon mean that he did it only out of duty. He likes to surprise Julius, although his father never *sounds* surprised when Stanley calls to say that he happens to be a couple of blocks away and how about if he drops by?

Since Annette died, Julius no longer uses the den too much. Mostly, he sits in a wing-chair in the living room. The two four-place brocaded couches on either side of the cold fireplace rarely have their tasselled cushions dented unless an insensitive stranger comes by. When he visits, Stanley sits close to his father in an upright *fauteuil*, as if one day he might take his hand. He refuses refreshment so as to make it clear that he has come only to talk. One afternoon though, when his father had a telephone call (Gabe King), gimme-a-second eyes urged Stanley into the kitchen for a glass of water. The marble work surface under the closets was active with tiny, translucent insects like grains of busy sand. Stanley did not care to deal with them, still less follow their trail into the corner closet. He left the kitchen, with his thirst, as though he had never been there.

Soon after Annette's death, Julius had to have a hernia operation. Stanley said that it was as if he had swallowed his pain and it had erupted below the belt. Brian Rohde had once told the 92 group that the body can transfer pain to an area which is not of prime importance to the subject: for instance, a right-handed art director patient of his fell, skiing, on his right shoulder. After an interval, he experienced agonising symptoms in the left scapula.

When Stanley applied this theory to Julius, Sidney said, 'The guy has a hernia, not a secret grief. He had it *before* Annette died. You're saying that dad *prepared* to grieve before Annette died and then ...? Or are you saying that he's *punishing* himself because he feels responsible? Because there, maybe, you're on to something. Maybe he created the pain because he didn't feel pain. Is that what you're saying?'

'I'm not saying anything,' Stanley said.

'Talk, talk, talk,' Sidney said. 'What is it with you?'

Stanley went to see his father on the eighteenth floor in the hospital. Julius was eighty-six years old or he could have been in and out in a day. But with insurance why be in a hurry?

Stanley reached the door of Julius's room and heard voices; in particular, *a* voice, which seemed familiar *and* strange. Its volubility, but not what it said, came through the wide blond door muffled, somehow high and low at the same time, as impossible to understand – except as a kind of *number* – as those black radio stations Stanley sometimes picked up on the way to work, where rapid speech was a kind of dance.

When there was a small silence in the room, it left space for a murmur which Stanley took to be Julius's voice, and there was a note in *that* which was also familiar and strange. Stanley stood outside. He thought – because he was a professor and it seems more mature to think than to feel – of two scenes, one from reality (if Papa Hemingway and reality ever met) and one from Marcel Proust. He remembered Hemingway telling (*A Moveable Feast*) of the time he went to Gertrude Stein's Paris house and heard that dominant, opinionated woman speaking, upstairs, in a wheedling tone which he, Ernest, had never heard from her before. He realised all of a sudden that it was not she but the meek Miss Toklas who wielded the power in their relationship. He was accordingly and for ever dispensed from awe and emancipated from apprenticeship. Horror and relief were indistinguishable: a rose was no longer a rose. Did this ever happen? How can we tell whether Papa once told the truth?

The passage from Proust was equally perverse: the moment when the narrator looks through the window of the country house near Combray and sees the beloved daughter – what was her name again, Harriet? – defiling the photograph of her (once) beloved dead father, in order to gratify her lesbian lover. Before Stanley dropped his shoulders to look through the judas window (the jailer surveying a condemned man), he was already seeing the narrow head and shaved neck and the roof of hair that said Moss Beauregard. Something was happening – no, had happened – between Moss and Stanley's father.

INT. 76TH STREET APARTMENT HOUSE. DAY.

STANLEY is pulling out his keys as he climbs the steps to his third-storey front door. He passes another TENANT on her doorstep, a grey-haired LADY talking back into her apartment to an unseen person, and when she turns and sees STANLEY, she frowns and pulls her head slightly back: who are you?

>STANLEY
>
>Hullo, Mrs Weintraub.

>MRS WEINTRAUB
>
>Professor! I'm so sorry. You startled me.

>STANLEY
>
>Then I'm sorry too.

He goes on upstairs, amused at what he might have said but didn't. He puts the key into the lock of his apartment and eases the door open.

He hears: *what?* The quiet sound of *haste.*

NARRATOR

He cannot say what is being done in a
hurry. He cannot tell where, exactly, it
is being done. The sound is a quiet
version of what would be done more
loudly, if it were. Can people whisper
voicelessly? *That* is what he hears.

ELAINE comes into the hall.

ELAINE

Stanley! What are you doing here?

STANLEY

Don't I live here?

ELAINE comes and puts her arms around him, sort of.

ELAINE

You were supposed to be going to a
screening, I thought.

STANLEY

Somebody here?

ELAINE

What happened?

STANLEY

Electrical problems.

ELAINE

Guess who dropped by.

STANLEY

I don't think so. Who?

ELAINE

(Calls back)
It's OK. It's Stanley.
(To STANLEY)
Barry. Outwater.

BARRY

(Comes into the hall from the living room)

71

Stanley! This is lucky.

STANLEY

I'm glad to hear that.

They shake hands. BARRY pats STANLEY on the back.

BARRY

I came round with something I wanted
you to have.

ELAINE

It's on the side.

When BARRY turns to go back into the living room, STANLEY
can see that the back of his shirt is over his pants.

INT. THE LIVING ROOM. DAY.

BARRY

You won't believe this.

STANLEY is quite radiant. He is blooming with anguish. He
notices that ELAINE is not wearing stockings.
BARRY takes a book off the television and holds it behind his
back.

BARRY

Guess what I've got for you.

STANLEY

It's truly my big day for making guesses.
What?

BARRY produces a book without a dust-cover. STANLEY looks
at the spine: *A Garland of Ibids for Van Wyck Brooks.*

BARRY

Gotham Book Mart. How many times
have we talked about that book? Rare
as rare. Soon as I found it, I made
tracks over here. It's yours.

STANLEY

How much do I owe you?

BARRY

Stanley, come on, don't be silly!

STANLEY

This is something I've truly always
wanted.

BARRY

My pleasure.

STANLEY hits him right in the mouth. God, that hurts!

Stanley said, 'How goes it, Moss?'

Moss looked at Julius and then he said, 'Fine. Great.'

'When do you go back to school?'

'When I'm ready. Right now, I'm taking some time out to think about things. Time for reflection!'

Money was what had happened between Julius and Moss Beauregard, wasn't it? When Moss stood up, *very* tall, he did not shake hands with Julius; but that was a conspiracy: they understood each other. Then it was as if, in the small room, Stanley was too far away from Moss to reach him. After the young man left, Stanley and his father traded smiles before they got to it.

'He's dropping out of school,' Stanley said, 'is that how it is?'

'He has problems,' Julius said, 'but he didn't say exactly what.'

'And you didn't ask.'

'I don't want him to feel that he owes me anything.'

'Doesn't he?'

'Maybe I was too ambitious for him. Kindness can be . . . authoritarian. Judgemental even.'

'So you aim to be kinder. How are you feeling, dad?'

'Like I'm joined together with metal clips, which I am, I

guess, and I have to be careful.'

'Then be careful,' Stanley said. 'When are they letting you out?'

'Tomorrow, the day after. Whenever.'

'Are you getting some help, around the house?'

'From you?' Julius said.

'I was thinking of nursing,' Stanley said.

'Moss wants to take care of me for a while,' Julius said.

'And you then said what?' Sidney says.

'I said, "Why Moss?"'

'And Julius said, "Why not?"'

'Is exactly what Julius said.'

'And then he tightened his lips and there was the ghost of a smile pinched between them, and he looked right at you, only sideways, so you couldn't look right at him.'

'You were evidently there,' Stanley says.

'Is the little bastard dropping out of college? He shouldn't do that. Why can't Milton move in with dad?'

'Milton is getting old. He has a hip. You resented the kid going to college is the truth. And now you resent his not going. You're a tough one, Sidney.'

'I have a question. Do you *like* Moss?'

'I don't know. He's young.'

'You have young people in your classes all the time. You know if you like them.'

'I feel like I ought to. Like him. He's clean, he's tall, he's polite . . .'

'Dad bought him, is the simple truth, isn't it?'

'Is that simple? Bought him for what?'

'To whitewash. Or hadn't you noticed he was black at one point? He took him across the line. Like Catholics did with

Jewish kids during the war. They took them into their convents and stuff and protected them and there was a price to pay, and they paid it. Hail Mary.'

'Julius only wants to be a good man and help Moss be one.'

'Is this about us partly also?'

'Us. Remind me.'

'He's the good kid, Moss. The stepson who cares for the old guy his own kids don't.'

'Don't we care? Where'd you get that one from? Julius ever say he felt that way?'

'Do you care enough to wipe his ass for him? I don't. I don't want to see his rumpled butt and help him with his buttons. I was never in with Julius the way Moss was. Were you? Working right there in the den with him. With dad over my shoulder. Moss was his personal four-leaf clover, his lucky charm. His thing.'

'The way he shut the door, when we were kids, it said "Stay out". That's the way I always saw it.'

'Is he going to leave Moss money?'

'I don't know that he's made a will even.'

'Ask him.'

'How can I ask him a thing like that?'

'There isn't a damn thing we can ask him, is there? Not one damn thing. And yet he seems totally straightforward, totally . . . accessible. Is he? Are you happy, Stanley?'

'Today? Yes, I am. I haven't always been, but I am now.'

'Am I?'

'Why doesn't he want a female nurse? He could hire somebody really competent . . .'

'Does he need one? Julius had a hernia. Today, what's a hernia? What's *yesterday's* hernia? A small scar. Am I happy, I asked you? It's not medical attention he primarily needs. Well?'

'You're a sonofabitch,' Stanley said, 'so I guess yes. Yes, you are. You're trouble; you're happy.'

'Janice is leaving me.'

'She is? What do I say?'

'Are you sorry?'

'For her or for you?'

'Either. Guess why.'

'You treated her like shit.'

'She liked that. My sperm count is approaching zero. Is why. Thirty-seven years old. She wants a kid. *Adios* time.'

'Can't they give you something?'

'She's not waiting to find out. Know what finally triggered her walking out? I said maybe you could help out, sperm-wise.'

'*Sidney.*'

'So you're a busy man, so how long would it take you?'

'Janice doesn't like me that well.'

'So? I'm only asking you to fuck her. You kissed her one time. We had to pull you off.'

'New Year's Eve. Jesus.'

'Right after Elaine took off.'

'I was drunk.'

'And Janny had that come-and-get-it red dress on.'

'She didn't walk out because of your sperm count, Sidney, and I'll tell you something.'

'Do it. It's time.'

'You suggested that so I'd be responsible somehow. You fixed it so it was the thought of *me*'d be the last straw for her. I said you were a sonofabitch. You are a sonofabitch.'

'So: we're going to let it happen, are we? Moss. We're just going to watch the parade go by.'

'Julius is a free man. Moss too.'

'You think dad's going to leave him all his money?'

'You want me to talk to Moss about what he ought to do and what really bothers you is dad's money. He *can't* leave it all to Moss.'

'Are we entitled to see the will?'

'I don't think so. We can contest it, I guess, eventually, but the right to see it as of now? I can talk to Herbie Hornik, but . . . You think Moss is seriously positioning himself . . . ?'

'Fuck Moss. I'm thinking about what Julius is seriously doing, possibly.'

'You figure he doesn't like us?'

'Why? Hoping he still might like you, professor? Why else are you in an elegant job that pays pennies?'

'Can we ever stop doing this, do you suppose?'

'Am I hurting you, darling?'

Before going to read his paper to the 92 group, Stanley calls in to see Julius. Nineteen months after the hernia operation, Julius claims to be as mobile as he ever was, but he rarely leaves the house. Stanley no longer considers it necessary to telephone to make sure that the old man is at home.

Moss undoes the locks and opens the door of the penthouse. He is neatly dressed, in black slacks and a woollen top, flat slippers. Truth to tell, he looks not unlike a stretched version of Stanley.

'Hi, Moss.'

'He's not here,' Moss says.

'Not here?'

'He want to the Manufacturers' Club.'

'He did? *Alone?*'

'He had a car come. They have their annual meeting. They're making him an honorary life vice-president.'

'That's good. That's great.' The apartment smells polished; no, the *air* smells polished. 'So . . . what are you doing?'

'This minute? I was checking out your father's shoes, making sure they were clean.'

'Moss, are you ever going back to college?'

'I don't truly know.'

'I hope you are. For your sake. There's a big world out there. And you could do pretty well in it. You don't need to be cleaning shoes.'

'I don't do it because I need to. Your dad likes to have me around.'

'Listen, it's none of my business . . .'

'That's right,' Moss says.

'. . . but I know my father would not like to be thought to have stood between you and what you could be. He always believed that . . . that black people deserved to have the chance to be full citizens, in every way.'

'He wants me here. I want to be here.'

'But are you *right* to want to be here? Is the question.'

'I can always go to college.'

'Always doesn't necessarily last as long as people think. How's *your* father these days?'

'They look after him fine where he is,' Moss says.

'Because say hullo to him from me.'

'And how about your father?' Moss says. 'Do you say that to him too?'

Sonofabitch! What would Sidney say now? Something involving 'bodily harm' maybe. Stanley is merely damned if he will leave. He is due at Patsy Lowenstein's, but he sidles past Moss into the apartment. Not saying 'Excuse me' is as nasty as he gets. He walks into the living room. Moss follows. Does he think Stanley is going to *steal* something? Stanley acts as if he is looking for something, or checking something, or *something*. He goes through into the den and opens the thick Webster's on the spreadeagle lectern. His heart beating-towards-rage, he makes himself a scholar checking an etymology; and winds up thinking about Dotty Lamour and *The Road to Morocco* (Paramount). Moss stays in the doorway. Is he fooled for one moment?

Now he can go, Stanley says, 'What I wanted to indicate was this: if there's anything *I* can do, checking out courses or scholarships, anything like that, because I'd be glad to help.'

'He'll be home around ten, ten thirty,' Moss says. 'In all probability.'

Mikey Carossa is in his early thirties. He went to school in Europe. Mikey is not short; he is rounded, which makes him seem short. He has no angles. He wears a maroon cashmere cardigan and a pink shirt and a black silk tie with hoofy, high-kneed yellow centaurs on it. His hair is thick and dark and neat. It looks too expensive to be only hair. Mikey has the layered ends singed when he goes to the barber's.

'Stanley!' he says. Mikey's voice is both melodious and exclamatory.

'Am I late?'

'*Nous avons failli d'attendre.*' Mikey quotes Louis *quatorze* with a smile that insists that Stanley be flattered when he doesn't translate.

'Stanley.' There is nothing exclamatory about Patsy: she states. She is a small, groomed woman, in a grey, herring-boned Armani trouser suit, little button boots. She is in her early sixties and was married for many years to rich-*rich* Arthur Lowenstein. They had had five children before Patsy concluded that she had made a mistake. She has kept her husband's name, but she did not stay Jewish; only rich. She now identifies herself as a transactional therapist; confidences are lodged in her as in a vault. When the discussion requires ginger, she will unlock a box in her mind and unseal an anonymised detail. For instance, she tells of one client who made a lot of money dealing drugs. Now he can neither spend it nor give it away. He has a paralysed right hand and can shake hands only with the left. This, he says, puts people on their guard against him. Needlessly. Unfairly?

Stanley is settled in *the* chair. He frowns over his notes as though they had been thrust into his hands by a stranger and contain ideas and opinions which do not squarely address the agenda which he meant to raise. Somewhere in the back of his mind, a voice very like Sidney's would like to know the sense in the same people meeting once a month to exchange ideas which can only be inoffensively bold, so that everybody will want to come again. Stimulus without satisfaction: America, 'tis of thee.

Great horrors haunt the room, but only as issues. Mute phantoms of Massacre, and Bigotry, and Unreason mind their manners. The humidifier, with its timely gasps of steam, is a domestic dragon standing in for scalier, snappier monsters.

INT. PATSY LOWENSTEIN'S APARTMENT. NIGHT.

We can see STANLEY as he raises an issue, asks questions, scratches his head, licks his lips, looks round, continues, pauses, thinks, doubts himself, confronts himself, qualifiedly satisfies himself. He continues to speak, and pause, but all we hear, for the moment, is:

NARRATOR
He has the illusion, the possibly true
illusion, that he is conducting a

dialogue, although no one else is
speaking, yet. He points out the flaws in
his argument. The audience seem to be
watching a contest in which the speaker
is on both sides of the net at the same
time and returns his own service with
interest. When he finishes, it is as if they
appreciate his attentive evaluation of
what, in fact, they have not yet had the
opportunity to say.

                  STANLEY
              (Now speaking audibly)
Tolerance *without* repression is barbarism;
there *is* no gate any more for the
barbarians to be at. Dante got it wrong:
'Abandon Hope' is the sign that hangs
over *paradise*.

An impressed pause is gently breached by the thin, considered,
applause of people who have been given something to think
about here tonight.

' "Dante Got It Wrong",' Mikey Carossa says, 'haven't we
practically got a book there almost already?'

'On an earlier point,' Jay Bamberg says, 'if we had your
celestial narrator working overtime here, imagine if he was
saying, listen to these rarefied people . . .'

' "Rarefied" he calls us,' Max Rifle says, 'after all I've done
for the kid.'

' ". . . because it's the last time they're ever going to meet
like this." '

'Jay's getting that long-awaited shot at the evening news, do
we gather?' Chloe Globe says.

'I hadn't heard that yet,' Jay says.

'Not meeting like this any more, you said, didn't you?'

Stanley said, 'Here's my point, Jay. If the selfsame words were said (a) audibly to all of us and (b) quietly to one of us, they wouldn't have the same impact, wouldn't mean the same thing. Which is why today we have no common public philosophy.'

'*Why?*' Jesus Armstrong says.

'Jesus is right,' Stanley says. '*Not* why.'

'Ten second knockout,' Max Rifle says. 'Champion of the world, Jesus. How does it feel? What are your plans? How many girls do you want?'

'I'm up again,' Stanley says, 'because –'

'I'll take Melanie's word for that,' Max says. '*When I get it.* My italics.'

'The loss of common meaning is a *symptom* of social *and personal* disintegration.'

'And so what?' Max says.

'Tell you what, Maximilian,' Stanley says. 'Go write some pieces for the paper about, oh, *Carpathia*. Be away for quite a while.'

'Don't lose it, Stanley. Don't lose it. It's probably only slipped behind a cushion.'

'It took me some time to write that paper, Max. You write one and then I'll do the one-liners.'

'Cake and coffee-time, don't you think so?' Patsy says.

' "Last time we're going to meet like this." What does Jay Bamberg know that I don't?'

'Aside from how to behave himself? Why do you do this, Max, every time?'

'My theory is, even people who make trouble contribute to keeping the peace. Long as we keep the numbers down. Like the man said, few are chosen: T. S. Eliot's point, which I do not intend to sharpen for him, but which, totally between ourselves, under the dome of silence, never totally lacked acuteness. Now we have that footnote in place, tell me: is Jay's the moving finger writing on Patsy Lowenstein's hand-printed wall or what's he doing?'

'How about contributing to the discussion? Constructively. Did you ever hear of that?'

Max pushes himself up from his chair and comes towards Stanley with his hand out. 'Max Rifle,' he says. His bushy grin looms in at Stanley and his exercised hand squeezes pain into Stanley's arm. 'We've known each other for twenty years, Stanley. What's the matter all of a sudden? That Melly of yours working so hard she won't come to bed?'

Patsy — the rich lady who likes to be seen doing it all herself, very occasionally — wheels in coffee and cookies and cake, head-to-one-side careful where the Bedou rugs join.

'You don't want a civilised discussion, why do you come?' Stanley says.

'Maybe I like to get to rub thighs with Chloe Globe.'

'Can't you arrange to do that without all this?'

'Sure, but I like the pretence that that isn't what I come here to do. Pretending is what I come here to do, just like you, don't I? Who needs the real thing? *Ever.*'

Mikey Carossa is listening closely and also watching Patsy pouring and passing. He is solicitously unhelpful; his eyes follow Patsy's movements.

'You know what Mikey is?' Max says. 'A tennis mother.'

Stanley says, 'You know what I think sometimes. Maximilian? I think you want somebody to ask you what the hell is really the matter with you.'

'Remember Groucho in the elevator at the hospital: "I can't get it up, what floor is that?" No, no, no. Me, I can't get it *down*. One sight of Chloe's intelligent little ass, quivering for further information, and . . .'

Chloe turns round and says, 'OK, Max, you're turning into a parody of yourself. I have to admit I like "little" though. Makes all the pedalling worthwhile.'

'She likes "little" because it isn't too true; right, baby? What do they actually *do*, Stanley, have you ever asked yourself, those two?' Max indicates Patsy and Mikey. 'Chloe, any ideas?'

'Max,' Chloe Globe says, 'are you going to be*have* ever possibly?'

'And lose your attention?'

Patsy is holding out coffee and Black Forest *gâteau*. 'You were as good as I've heard you, Stanley, tonight. But you made me wonder something: is it a mistake possibly we always meet in this apartment?'

'We *are* the people who meet in this apartment. 92 is 92.'

'I was only asking Mikey earlier: are we getting stale possibly here?'

'And my dry paper answered your question?'

'Your paper,' Patsy says, 'was *significant*. Apropos, Mikey has something he wants to ask you, I think.'

'When you think, Patsy, you *know*. About what?'

'Doing this book.' Mikey Carossa was right there.

'About?'

'What you were analysing tonight. The end of nuance. The publication of the previously secret world; the closure of the cave as place of reverence and lame retreat. The desecration of privacy.'

'Sex with the lights on,' Max says. 'And the critics in.'

As Stanley walks down Fifth Avenue past the snappy flags for 'QUATTROCENTO SIENA' which the Met is flying, he looks through the brown leaves in the park and sees the irregular firmament of lights scaling the apartment building where Julius lives. Isn't it time he called Francis and checked on his grades? François. What if, as is a likely shot, Elaine picks up? Stanley screws himself round, scanning for empty cabs. Soon he sees one waiting to come out of 65th Street, but he crosses right in front of it. He walks along Central Park South and turns north.

'Did he get home yet?'
  'It's after midnight.'
  'Is that "yes, he did" or what is it?'
  'Are you OK?'
  'I'm here. I'm fine. And I'm asking you a question.'
  'He's home. He's in bed. So was I.'
  'He's my father. I have a right to know how he is.'
  'Yes, you do.'
  'And he's all right?'
  'And he's all right.'
  'Please tell him I called by.'
  'I already told him.'
  'Again.'
  'I certainly will.'
  'Please be sure to.'
  'Is something wrong?'
  'I hope not.'
  'Do you want to come in?'
  'If he's asleep, no.'
  'He's asleep.'
  'I'll call in the morning.'
  'He'd like that, I'm sure.'

'How was his evening?'

'Just fine. He made a short speech and it was . . . well received. They gave him a plaque, which pleased him.'

'If not in the morning, then certainly in the afternoon.'

'You want to come in, you can come in.'

'I did, I would,' Stanley said.

EXT. BROADWAY. NIGHT.

STANLEY walks up from Columbus Circle towards 66th Street, which is his preferred way home. How can we see that he suspects that he has made some kind of a fool of himself? Is he angry with MOSS or with MAX? And about what? It is, he feels, but cannot express, as if in the time between leaving MOSS before the 92 group meeting and returning to 91 C.P.W. after it, he and MOSS have had an unpleasant exchange, almost a fight. Nothing happening has somehow amounted to *something* having happened.

EXT. 66TH STREET TOWARDS SEVENTH AVENUE. NIGHT.

STANLEY sees a GIRL standing in the doorway of an Open-24-hours drugstore. How does he know she's a hooker? At first she is just a GIRL lighting a cigarette.

GIRL

Hey, mister . . .

STANLEY's answer is not answering, but he is not walking *quite* as fast as he was. The GIRL steps out of the doorway and is walking along with him. Free country.

GIRL

I'll blow you for fifty. Is that fair?

'Is this all right?'

'This is fine,' Stanley said. 'I'm a professor. What's wrong with it?'

'Italian, I meant. It's convenient, for me, anyway.'

'For people like me there will always be such a thing as a free lunch.'

'I talked to some people, Charlie Worth not least, and there's a gathering consensus in favour of your book. Will it be sexy? Is their only question.'

'And I half want to agree with whoever asked it,' Stanley said. 'But yes, I think finally it will be, because it's *particularly* in the area of, let's say, morals that the narrator has fallen silent, not to say dumb. Take the novel . . .'

'Menus?' the waiter said.

'Menus,' Mikey Carossa said. 'You were taking the novel.'

'Adultery was its key trope, its emblematic transgression was sexual. And now? Now we have to construct new outrages, new scandals to make sex any kind of a crime. Look at half the movies . . .'

'Half is all I do ever stay to look at.'

'Enough to see that adultery can license fatal attractions, but it's not fatal *itself*. Today we have a society that refuses to regard sexual activity as a moral field. Who gives a fuck when they can sell one? Can I start with the stuffed eggplant?'

'For me too,' Mike Carossa said to the aproned man who was delivering puddles of olive oil to their side plates. 'Then the *spaghetti alle vongole*. For Professor Oppenheim also. And a bottle of '43. The *Classico*. How soon can you get to this? I'd appreciate a specimen chapter or two. That I can show people unofficially. Let's make 'em whistle a little. As in "Wow! Tell me more."'

'Not before the summer, *possibly*.'

'Understand something: I want this to be the birth of a new Stanley Oppenheim.'

'Fine. One stipulation: no forceps.'

'Who lets himself go. No forceps! And of whom we had glimpses at Patsy's Tuesday night. I don't want you to be humble. Or qualified. By which I mean . . .'

'Less than totally convinced of my own genius.'

'Is this a time to be alone?' Mikey sniffed and nodded at the wine. Then he looked out of the window as if the traffic hadn't been there before, and then he said: '*Stanley*.'

'Mikey.'

'Patsy.'

'Wants us to meet some other place.'

'Excuse me?'

'I had the impression. The group.'

'I was her patient, right? Is how we met.'

'I assumed.'

'Do you know anything about me? Why should you?'

'Outside of your reputation?'

'You imagined I was gay, right?'

'Not particularly.'

'Why not? I did too. But here's the funny part. You were looking forward to it, right? Then this'll cheer you up.'

'Be warned: I can get depressed being cheered up.'

'I tried. I found I didn't like it. I didn't like *anything*. I was happy! And that worried me. Because I couldn't *really* be, could I? Which is when I went to Patsy. Who was fabulous. She was fabulous. She *is* fabulous.'

'I hear she is.'

'She is. The last thing in the world I want to do is hurt her. She's sixty-three years old. I'm thirty-two.'

'So who's the problem?' Stanley said.

★

'What did you advise him? Not plain speaking, did you?'

'Did he want me to tell him that he was wrong, or did he not want me to tell him that?'

'Did this occur to you as a possibility: he told you not because he wanted out, but because he wanted to be tempted to kill her?'

'Are you crazy?'

'Am I? Think about it. He appointed you a witness. She dies, you're the evidence he was afraid to leave her, but wanted to. So now he can still want to, openly, at least to himself, but he can't kill her.'

'Sidney, you're the Movie of the Week. Why kill her? When he can just walk?'

'Answer's right there in the terrible script we call life: he doesn't want to hurt her. He loves her. He makes her happy; she makes him. These are two people in paradise, Stanley. You have to feel sorry for them.'

'You know who the snake is? Max Rifle.'

'On the nose,' Sidney says. 'And what a nose! What did Max do? Is parental guidance required before you tell me?'

'The guy's in love with him.'

'That's some shirt to lift. Mikey should see a shrink. Like now. Race.'

'He lives with one.'

'And . . . OK, OK. I see the rewritten plot-line. I don't buy it, but I see it: the poor schnook knows he's a schnook, and he can live with that, possibly, but he can't stand for her to know he is. He could endure humiliation and rejection, which he is surely going to get, if Max has anything to do with it, but he can't stand to have her as a witness to it. So what happens next? Tell me. I'm a producer. Since when does one of those go all the way to the bottom of the page?'

'Does Max Rifle have any kind of a history with guys? Does Mikey have a *hope*?'

'Of broken bones. *Sure*. A full Nelson is his idea of fun? He couldn't've chosen a better bastard. Max is a bully. He knows that. He's not going to get anywhere. Why else did he tell you about it? That's what he got off on, for Christ's sake. Your face. The damned can come to that.'

'He wants me to do a book.'

'All the marks of desperate measures. He's told you he wants to leave her because he wants to stay with her. Likewise, he's invested his feelings about Max in you because you're the nearest thing there is to giving lunch to a Swiss bank.'

'He's afraid of what it would do to Patsy.'

'Who probably wouldn't give a *shit*. Who'd possibly *welcome* it. Who'd likely grab a pencil and want to take notes.'

'You're saying life is a farce.'

'And it isn't? History repeats itself: first as tragedy, then as Mikey Carossa. Only it's not over yet. Man is a killer *first*, then a joker. Then *both*. Take Moss.'

'Excuse me.'

'What are we secretly both of us wanting to have happen there? We want that guy *out*, and the outest form of out is under a subway train – or a prowl car (remember Abigail?) – with neither of us around to be suspected of having done the pushing.'

'I don't want anything like that to happen to Moss.'

'No, because I suggested it and now you can be the voice of *humanitas*. Always your big favourite. Boldness is dissent; hesitancy is leadership. The mark of the alienated Jewish intellectual down the ages. With the wraparound frown of the righteous man as far up his own ass as he can go.'

'Sidney, what are you afraid of?'

'I'm not. You are. Why did you go back to 91 the other night? To confirm something, didn't you? What?'

'Julius was OK. You want Moss to be a bastard, don't you?'

'It would make him human. It would give him some respect. He's that or he's a white-faced black guy with a brown nose.'

'Why can't he just be someone deeply appreciates what Julius has done for him?'

'He can. There's nothing wrong with fortune-hunters. Us included. Why else do we want Moss under a train?'

'Julius leaves Moss a bunch of money. Won't he deserve it?'

'You are what you eat. But who's eating who, and for what? And who's turning into what? Ask Abbott and Costello. They're the experts. Our attitude is a measure of what Moss is doing for Julius and we're not. He's the death-watch beetle, and all we're getting to do is to watch him.'

'Keeping Julius alive,' Stanley says. 'Is *that* it? We really want *Julius* dead, not Moss. Moss is a side issue.'

'*But* if he doesn't keep Julius alive . . . we have problems with ourselves. So . . .'

'There's still something I want to hear from Julius,' Stanley says, 'and I don't know what it is. Which is why I want to hear it.'

'I know what. You want him to accuse you of something. That you can deny, and still take the fall. You don't dream of the crime half as much as you dream of being punished for it. Or – how about this? – that you *can't* deny, but also didn't do. That'd be the perfect murder for you, Stan. Only what can it be?'

Stanley walks home across town from the St Regis. The refurbished bar is his and Sidney's uptown safe house.

On the corner of Seventh Avenue, he gives an old
BLIND AND HOMELESS black guy some 'change'. Handing
over a dollar fifty launches him into thinking about his motive
for doing it, and Julius's. This segues into a resumé of the Jews,
the Blacks, and the United States. The ghosts of the Scottsboro
Boys can still walk a man across town. There is no one in the
doorway of the drugstore.

When Stanley walks into the apartment, Melanie looks up
from the table Elaine used to sit at. She has four flagged books
in front of her. She unlatches her glasses and there are shiny
dents either side of her nose: work, work, work. Stanley kisses
her scratched head and rests his jaw over her skull while he
scans her notes. He realises that Melanie and Elaine are damn
nearly anagrams of each other. So what?

Melanie's chin comes up for her to try to look over the top
of her own head at him. 'You didn't find a bridge game, right?'

'I never tried.'

'Why was that?'

'I wanted to see you. Can we go someplace and eat, and talk?'

'I ate,' she says. 'Are you OK?'

'If you are. Guess who I had lunch with. Mikey Carossa.'

'And?'

'He wants me to do a book.'

'He wanted you to do a book the other night.'

'But he *still* wants me to do a book. This is a man who runs
with the ball.'

Melanie says, 'How did he seem?'

'Seem.'

'Mikey. Was he OK?'

'He seemed Mikey.'

'You should eat,' she says. Her glasses are back on.

★

'Stan?'

'What's the problem, Sidney? I know that unfamiliar voice.'

'OK, when did you last speak to Julius?'

'Julius. I spoke to *Moss*; Friday last week. He said dad was
. . . resting. He seemed . . . concerned, but he said I shouldn't
be.'

'I didn't get an answer from the apartment day before
yesterday, yesterday, or this morning again. Here's my
question. Do you have a key?'

'To the apartment? No. Do you?'

'I had one, why would I ask you? We should get over there.'

'I have a shit load of work in front of me here.'

'Stanley, you're the good son. *I*'m the bad son. Don't trade
roles on me here. I don't know what's happening over there. I
think we should. I can hear you sighing. You disappoint me.
Sigh no more. This is no time for woeful shepherds.'

'I'll see you in the lobby, at 91 C.P.W. in . . . Jesus . . . at
this hour? Forty-five, fifty minutes. Minimum.'

'Take the subway. Quicker than a cab.'

'And I bet you I'm the one has to wait. But tell me
something: what is it you're afraid of exactly?'

'Same thing you are.'

When Sidney comes into the lobby where Stanley is waiting
for him, he is wearing a long, wide green raglan coat and a fur
hat.

Stanley says, 'Look at you! I didn't know it was that cold.'

'I like the coat,' Sidney says. 'Fuck the weather. *And* the hat.
Harry Levitt bought it for me.'

'You're fucking Harry Levitt?'

'For all I'm worth; all *he's* worth. Which is now plenty. I
gave him three points on "Downtown Hooker". For the *title*.

How could I know they'd be worth a dime? Coat says I was a *schmuck*. Shall we go up? You think I'm wasting your time.'

'Hoping.'

'I share that with you.' They stand together in the elevator. At the penthouse floor, Sidney says, 'Harold Beauregard didn't like me, did he, one bit?'

'I wouldn't say that.'

'As you've so often said, Stanley, there isn't a damn thing you would say. He didn't. One bit. And who will say he was wrong? I'm waiting.'

'What are you *really* hoping at this moment?'

'I'm worried like any son would be.'

'I hope you're wasting our time. But, yes, not only that, if that's what you're assuming.'

'I don't assume too much about you, brother. Same hen, different eggs. Settle for that.'

They walk along the new rug to the front door of penthouse C. When they get there, each appraises himself by looking at the other. Harold Beauregard used to take them to the big hall of distorting mirrors at Coney Island. That was the last time Sidney was tall and thin and Stanley squat and plump. Stanley remembers the scene from *Lady From Shanghai* (Orson Welles); Sidney just remembers being taller than Stanley. Worth every penny.

Sidney pushes the button with a big thumb. The bells rings with an antique note that belongs to black-and-white movies. It rings as if the apartment had no furniture in it.

'Now what?'

'We get the super. What else can we do?'

Harvey Novak is not new but he was not there when Sidney and Stanley lived in the building. He understands their problem but they have to see it this way: his duty is to Mr

Oppenheim. All right, they're his sons, but what way does he have of knowing whether there's any kind of a problem between the old gentleman and his kids or anyone else? Isn't a gentleman like Mr Oppenheim allowed to take a vacation or even be out for the day? How can they expect him to open the door in the absence of permission from the tenant?

Stanley says, 'Mr Novak, we haven't gotten through to him personally on the telephone for . . . eight days it is now.'

'How about the black guy looks after him?'

'He said Mr Oppenheim was not . . . so well. That was four, five days ago. Since when . . . I'm sorry, but somebody has to get in there and see what's going on. If anything.'

'He and the old gentleman seem to get along fine.'

'No one is denying that. Maybe *Moss* has been taken sick. No one's exempt. Maybe they shared a take-away. We need to have this door open. Do we call the cops? Would you be happier with that?'

'They won't thank you.'

'I'm not looking for thanks. We need to make sure there hasn't been an accident. We give you fifty bucks, which I don't believe I have any obligation to do, will *you* thank me?'

'This isn't about money.'

'Good, because our father could be lying there, needing help, two feet from the phone and not be able to get it. Moss may be . . . anywhere in the world. Open this door for us, will you, Mr Novak, please?'

'He doesn't let you have a key?'

'We don't live here. Does your father give you a key to his house?'

'He lives in my house,' Harvey Novak says. Then the money is in his pocket. 'This one time, OK?'

There is still the smell of polish in the air, but it is very faint.

The apartment seems bigger. The brothers look in the living room, the kitchen, the spare room. 'Moss?'

The bedroom door is shut. Stanley knocks. They wait. It gives them time to check that each of them is ready for this.

Julius is lying flat, full length, which is not very long, in the big bed. Sunshine falls in bent rectangles across the hardly rumpled covers. One luminous panel droops off the end of the bed and brightens the fawn carpet. The silence in the room has a certain smell to it. The air is unbreathed. The brothers inhale with hesitation.

JBO's monogrammed slippers are neat at the bedside. The blue silk dressing gown is over a chair. An open *New York Times* makes a flat tent to Julius Oppenheim's right, where Annette used to sleep. The three-day-old newspaper seems already to have yellowed. Julius does not have his glasses on. He has his head pressed into a shallow pillow; little linen wings cuff his ears. Another pillow, bigger, less resilient, lies next to Julius. At an acute angle to his regular pillow, it throws a soft shadow over the low head.

Sidney says, 'Where is that cowardly black sonofabitch?'

'Let's not . . .'

'No? So fabricate something, Stan. Run something up. He ran away is where he is, and who knows what he took with him?'

'Do you see anything missing?'

'Is that a damnfool question or what?'

'Sidney . . .'

'Yeahyeah. OK. Fuck you. Because look what we did. We talked and we talked and look what happened. Poor little bastard.'

'You can't cry, don't cry.'

'Pretend you're not here, Stan. Try that. I'll do what I want to do. You know what this could be, don't you?'

'Which doesn't mean it has to be.'

'Nothing does. Ever. Not with you. Know what? I'm still waiting for him to say something. This is quite a performance from Julius, being dead like this, but I'm still not sure we're through with him. Did he die or was he pushed?'

'We have no right . . .'

'Right? Right? What right *do* we have? Spell it out to me, fuck. Where is the bastard was supposed to be caring for him?'

'Eighty-seven years old, Sidney. Don't start flailing around before we have the facts. He maybe panicked and took off.'

'They never do shit, do they? They never do shit. They commit three-quarters of all the crimes in this city and none of them has ever done a thing they're accused of.'

'This won't do.'

'We're alone. We're alone. Who are you afraid of?'

'We should call the cops. Or Dr Beck.'

'The truth is what you're afraid of. To do what?'

'Whatever's usually done.'

'Let's always do that. Put the phone down. Give it a few minutes, can we at least do that? Let's not *instantly* run away from everything.'

'What is this routine with you, Sidney, all the time?'

'When did you last talk to Julius?'

'I stopped by before the 92 group meeting, which I always do, but dad wasn't here, Moss said. Which proves . . .'

'*What?*'

'Sidney . . . Moss said he went to the annual general meeting of the Manufacturers' Club, so he probably did. We can check.'

'Lousy sons, is what it comes to, doesn't it? He shoulda had a daughter.'

'We will have to be defective in your eyes always, why is that? Fathers have to be left to grow up on their own sometimes. We have lives of our own. You always said he did. Veronica and all. So so do we. Now can I make the call?'

'We get the cops in here, what are they going to see, what are they going to find out? I'm not ready to talk to cops about this whole thing yet.'

'What whole thing is that in your estimation?'

'They could just as well say *we* did it. You watch *Columbo*.'

'I never watched *Columbo* since Francis went to live with his mother; and Ghee. Did what?'

They stand together by the bed looking down at the body. Julius has his eyes closed but they still seem to be watching from behind the chalky lids. The unpuckered innocence of that small face, naked without its glasses, makes it seem newly born; ready, at least, for some further activity. It does not look to be the end of Julius. He still might be dangerous, this old man who was never – to his sons' knowledge – a danger to anyone.

'How much pressure does it need to suffocate an old man while he's sleeping?'

'What's making you say this, Sidney?'

'He wasn't sick.'

'He was old. Old people die. He's dead. What makes you hate Moss Beauregard so much?'

'I don't.' The tears shine on Sidney's cheeks but they do not fall; they burn. They accuse. 'I don't hate him.'

Stanley draws more breath than he needs. 'We should call someone if only because that sonofabitch Polack knows what time we came in here and – you know what? – *we* could wind up accused of something.'

'Believe the date on the *Times* and he's been dead since Monday.'

'Felix Beck can tell us easy. Also whether Julius was in more discomfort than we possibly know about.'

'Know what? I'm waiting for the old bastard to spring a surprise.'

'I remember . . .'

'I remember that,' Sidney says. 'The way he'd be sitting, eyes shut, on the big chair of Max's they threw out finally with the radio on next to him and Annette would come and turn it off, thinking he needed to sleep, and the minute she did that . . .'

' "Annette, I'm *listening*." '

'Catch that Brooklyn intonation you put in there? He was tougher in those days, he wore more . . . like he was in the old country. He should nevera left it. None of us should.'

'Bullshit, Sidney, and you know it.'

'That's your *father*.'

'Fathers are strangers we try to be close to. But when are we? Before we're born. I'm extrapolating, but –'

'At a time like this, the good brother *extrapolates*?'

'There's no one else here, *alive*, Sidney, in this room and you're playing to an *audience*. Do you notice that in yourself? Trying to feel something, right? What? What do you feel?'

'Suppose Moss killed Julius. What's your reaction? Your reaction is, "Suppose he *didn't*!" Leaving an apartment with a dead man in it, not calling anybody. Even if all he did was come in and find Julius dead in his bed, what kind of a bastard leaves the house and doesn't contact a soul?'

'Why do you want a fight at a time like this?'

'I want a fight with *God*,' Sidney says. 'Is who I want a fight with. I want to fight Him because that way I would have some grounds for thinking He exists.'

'Or for thinking *you* do. I have this urge to take him and shake him awake.'

'Because you want *him* to be God. Me, I never gave him due respect. Why? I guess he was my Milton. He came between Max and me and he was never as real to me as somebody I never saw and who never saw me. So Julius built up the business, made the fortune; for me he was always a little bit shadowy. And who cast the shadow? Max.'

'Rich. There's another shadow that weighs heavy.'

'Who – I once heard more than once – was not the man with the cleanest hands in the garment district, when it came to muscling union organisers and stuff like that. Funny thing is, I don't care what Rich and Max did, which was quite a lot between them, as I understand. But I *do* care what *he* did, which was, we keep telling ourselves, a lot of good. By "care", I mean . . .'

'Judge. Want to crap on. Why?'

'I don't like good Jews. I don't trust them. This guy built up a semi-major business and I never knew a good man did that. Some do that and *then* they're good, but . . . He wouldn't let us know him, Stanley. You think all he did in that den of his was read Mortimer Adler? Do we know for sure he ever got beyond volume eighty-five? Why didn't he want either of us to work in the business? When he sold it, he did it *against* us. It's like there were things we'da had to know he didn't want us to know; it *pleased* him we didn't know. He needed to have the last laugh on us, Stanley, is how I see it. He never wanted to share the joke any more than he did the business. That's what he enjoyed, keeping us out. Keeping the fun to himself. And the dirt. Look at him. He's still enjoying it. Taking it all with him. The secrets. Because what happened to Rich, *exactly*?'

'He won too much at cards. From the wrong people.'

'And what did Max die of, come to that, exactly? Do we know?'

'"Rich killed him," is what grandma Hannah said when he died.'

'Meaning?'

'Rich's death, I assume.'

'How about if Julius killed him and she was lying? His mother. How about if they did it together? I love to make you shake your head, Stanley, you prick.'

'We should call someone before it's too late.'

'For what? Imagine if Julius has left his money to Moss Beauregard. What're we going to do about it? Alternatively, he stole it; what are we?'

'All we know, he could be under a train.'

'Right where you pushed him. Your secret's safe with me.'

'Not guilty. I never go in the subway.'

'Scared of muggers? Julius too. So he bought himself his own *personal* mugger. He brought back slavery is what he did.'

'This is not a nice way to talk, even about your father.'

'Nice! You're a man can never close the door, Stanley, and be truly alone with himself. You don't trust yourself enough. That's where you lost it; *we* lost it. Because I only pretend to have it. Rich and Max, they had it. Lucky bastards.'

'Self-assessment makes liars of us all. The IRS relies on it. Look at those penalty clauses.'

'Moss has to be aware sooner or later they're going to catch up with him. He has an *identity*, for Chrissake; he has a social security number. He can't just go black on black, hit the ghetto, and that's it. Painted bird. *Hand*-painted. He isn't

brothers with the brothers any more . . . So why did he leave
the apartment?'

'How about if Julius asked him to?'

'Before doing what?' Sidney says. 'Alternatively, *after* doing
what?'

'Can't a man want to die by himself?'

'Maybe he was tired of Moss being so damn good to him.
Maybe he wanted to lie here for a while without anyone asking
him if there was anything he wanted. Maybe *that* was what he
wanted.'

'Suppose Moss took nothing,' Stanley says, '*and* had nothing
to wait for. What kind of a bastard does that make him?
Shouldn't we cover his face? Don't they do that?'

'Leave him as he is,' Sidney says. 'He's enjoying it.'

'Is that smell something's happened since we came in here or
was it here all the time?'

'Or is it us?' Sidney sits on the end of the bed. He seems to
be a long way from Julius's upright feet, but his weight tightens
the covers over the toes as if the old man had straightened
them. Sidney's unshaved cheeks make it seem that he had
advance warning to look like a mourner. Stanley feels lonely in
his height above his brother and the body in the bed.

'Rich fucked Annette. Did that ever go through your
mind?'

'You're sick, Sidney.'

'It did. She was Rich's, wasn't she, before she was Julius's?
And all their marriage, she was doing the same thing, in her
way, as he was: covering up. It was a sweet lifetime's work, the
pair of them. I bet he was lonely without her because of that.
Nothing to do with love. They kept each other happy with the
knowledge that they'd pulled something off. When she died,

where was the fun any more? No fun in hiding what no one knows or cares was there.'

'I'm going to go look in the den,' Stanley says, 'and then when I've done that, I'm calling Felix Beck.'

'His eyes are shut. Did somebody have to shut people's eyes or do they shut naturally sometimes?'

'If he died in his sleep, I guess. Which is the likeliest thing. And then Moss panicked, or was . . . maybe they have a thing about dead . . .'

'. . . white males? Maybe *they* do.'

'It must be strange, someone dying on you and you're all alone with him. I'm going to go look in the den. For nothing I can think of.'

'For trouble.'

'Not really.'

'Really. Believe me, Stanley, trouble is what you're looking for.'

The den has a heavier door, it feels, than any other room in the apartment. It is a large room, two-thirds the way to a library. There is the walnut desk and two deeply buttoned cigar-coloured leather chairs. The books are mostly sombre in their unjacketed binding. There is a long yellow section, however, where Julius kept back numbers of the *National Geographic Magazine*. He subscribed for seven years. It was cheaper than travelling, was what he said when Annette asked him why. A year later, he didn't renew.

What do people look for, Stanley would ask his film class, when they search places? And why do they always finally find something? Or if they don't, why do we always know that there *is* something they haven't? Even third-rate movies have moments that make you think. Stanley regularly instances that one where the gay villain, and his friend, leave a house where they have been camping aggressively. The owner finds that they have picked the place clean before they drove away, so as not to be traced: furniture, carpets, pictures, nothing remains. And then – wouldn't you know it? – in a crack in the uncarpeted boards he finds just one thing: a photograph with an address on the back. It is all the clue he needs to take up the chase, and allow the movie to continue. At no time is it suggested that this clue was left *deliberately*. Which is why the movie, the professor teaches, lacks prehensile quality. But suppose that someone had seen how much better it would have been if that one little clue had indeed been *meant* to be found. Then the runaways would *want* the hero to come after them; the prey and the hunter are also the hunter and the prey. As long as fictional accidents have a purpose, art is alive, because eminently distinct from life.

The desk drawers are not locked. Top right, there are three black leather folders. Julius's wish to be learned is written all over the enclosed pages. Look at those numbered paragraphs! Some of the numbers have circles around them: issues to be pursued another time? A few of the circles are thick, as if Julius had gone round and round them in pensive perplexity.

When Stanley opens the next drawer down, its contents rise slightly to meet him. It seems that the stifled stack is taking a furtive breath. The old diaries are skimpily inscribed: they contain appointments and birthdays to remember; yes, Stanley's included. And Elaine's. Yes, and Francis. Some of the named appointments in those dead years have a few words written by them: 'How is his dog?', for instance. Stanley now knows that Jack D. had a dog, but not who Jack D. was. *Deisenhofer*?

Is there going to be a gun someplace? In the bottom drawer,

Stanley finds a leather-bound photo album, black pages interleaved with tissue, a cellophane sleeve over the whole thing; inanimate virginity. There are no photographs inside. Maybe Julius bought it for somebody and never gave it; maybe it was a stand-by for when he needs to give somebody a present and never did. Veronica? A question for Felix: does the hymen have *nerves*?

Stanley lifts the album out and there is a sheet of legal paper underneath. Is he hoping for answers? He finds questions. At the head of the lined yellow page Julius has written, and underlined, 'Twenty Questions'. The ball-point has been pressed into the page, weighted with deliberation:

1. Why lie? Why tell the truth? Truth being?
2. Hiding what, *when* I hide, from whom? Without God, who is God?
3. Only the man who hides them cares about things?
4. What kind of gold is silence?
5. Do I *have* to cheat? If yes (yes), a *vice* or a duty?
6. What a man does alone: is there *anything*?
7. Have they a need to hate us? And?
8. Why want power; why be Rich? *Hiding what?*
9. In families begin lies. No? Yes: fami*lies*. [Encircled in the text] A. [Encircled darkly.]

Sidney says, 'Anything?'

'Eleven missing questions.' Stanley holds out the sheet of paper. 'Did he know what they were?'

'Maybe he just ran out.'

Stanley looks at where the ghosts of words pressed through from the previous page dent the striped paper below the list of questions.

'Nothing left in Moss's room,' Sidney says. 'Might just as well never have been there. Gone for keeps.'

Stanley chooses a 3B pencil from the blue Venini glass tub on the desk and rubs the side of the lead across the indentations. They fill out into:

'Finally, *he and S.* are hers. *M.* is mine.'

Stanley turns the shiny revelation to Sidney. 'Meaning?'

Sidney reads and then he hits Stanley on the shoulder, a solid blow. Sidney sits on the desk, feet in that open bottom drawer, and looks at the sheet of paper and then at Stanley.

'Is S. you or me?'

'Probably.'

'We're both hers. Meaning Annette's?'

'Why does he write that down, Stanley? If it's true, why trouble to write it?'

'Suppose it's not true,' Stanley says. '*What* isn't?'

'What's missing? He's not saying, is he? Even to himself. He's your father all right, Stanley.'

'M. is Moss, is that your conclusion?'

'Will that wrap it up? Not for me.'

'Can it be anyone else? And how is M. *his*?'

'You know the answer to that one, professor. He bought him: he's his.'

'Yeah? I don't know. This is said in the same breath as the stuff about S., it's against Annette, isn't it, the train of thought here? This is angry. Vindictive even. About what?'

'You're the hermeneutics man. Sing a song for me.'

' "He and S.". Why not "they"? Why not "S. and S." or "the Esses"? What does "and" mean in there?'

'How would he write that — "the esses"?'

' "He" is one of us, presumably, you or me, and "S." is the other. There's a *distinction* in there, Sidney. "He" is one of us and "S." is – on the other hand, by contrast, someone else, someone in a different category.'

'The force is with you, Stan. Keep flying. So we're in different categories in Julius's mind. Why?'

'I'm not convinced Julius's *mind* is the field of operations here. This is more like . . . an inventory. It's not about feelings. It's a resumé. Of facts. But what?'

'Look at number eight. Rich. With a big R.'

'Telling us what?'

'You know what happened in the old country, don't you, when an older brother died and he left a widow?'

'Rich wasn't married to Annette.'

'Was Rich a man to wait for a *huppah* over his head before he went to action stations?' Sidney holds out his hand. 'You'll have to check out the dates, but meanwhile call me "cousin Sid".'

'Well, I'll be a sonofabitch.'

'Looks that way. "Why stay what we are?" What does that mean? He wanted to divorce Annette?'

Sidney and Stanley Oppenheim sit together on the desk and examine the paper which examines them.

'Did I tell you Janny finally left me?'

'You said she was going to.'

'She did.'

'That circle around A. seems to signify some kind of an obsession. Like Annette had a circle around *him* and he was matching it maybe.'

'Did you find that just before Elaine walked out you had all the sex you ever wanted to have and never did before?'

'I don't think so. Even assuming I know what you're saying.'

'I'm saying I finally fucked her good. I fucked her good.'

'Oh. OK.'

'I did what she wanted only I never did it before. I didn't give a damn about her is what I'm saying. I didn't save a damn thing for another time. I did what men are supposed to do to those bitches.'

'You hurt her, is that what you're saying?'

'I gave her what she wanted and it didn't matter if, later on, she pretended that wasn't what she wanted because there wasn't going to be a later on. I wanted her to be sorry. I didn't hurt her like to *hurt* her. I just . . . didn't stop, not until there was nothing left to go on with. You're not even my brother and I'm telling you this.'

' "Why be Rich?" How do you read that, Sidney? You're my brother. That Julius was being Rich? To whom? To her? "Hiding fear". Of what? Of her ever saying that she still thought about him.'

'Maybe he did too kill Rich.'

'He was at school practically when Rich was killed.'

'Rich was what Julius knew he was never going to be. Not once they sent him off to study. Imagine that. I can; you can. Imagine what Julius musta felt when he realised that he'd been set up to be castrated. Sure. Privileged castration maybe, but . . . no balls is no balls. Which left Rich and Julius two of a kind he was never going to be, thanks to them.'

'This is your idea of what they were.'

'Rich was this street kid, Max's own; he was muscle, he was *bad*. And Julius goes away to school and he learns about laws and contracts; he learns about respect for other people's rights on paper. He gets castrated. He can never be the kind of Jew his brother is, his father is. But he also gets clever. He learns that business doesn't have to just be arm-wrestling; it isn't breaking the garment workers' balls *only*. You can break them with pieces of paper, the kind he's learning how to write. And then, when he graduates, he sees Rich sitting there, the big bastard. Little Julie, he's right behind the eight ball, and it's a big one. Maybe A. is just what comes before B., except it didn't because he ran out of time, or inclination. Or started a new sheet of paper we have yet to find, or never will. That cover it? I'll tell you something, Stan, I get horny remembering what I did to her. I gave her something to take away with her and she only deprived me of one pleasure, telling her to go to hell after she changed her mind, because she didn't. Yet. Julius was right, about fammy-*lies*. Being nice is not natural. Showing respect, that's where lies begin.'

' "A vice or a duty?" ' Stanley says. 'Where does that come from?'

'The Tree of Knowledge. First bite.'

'This is a text for the ages Julius left in the drawer. Just add boiling water, you know? You don't have to be right, Sidney, about Rich being my father. Someone woulda told us.'

'Annette? Would she? He never made her that mad maybe. She kept her mouth shut, which was her pleasure, and she had a lot of charge accounts. Is what he means by "duty" perhaps. As in paying it. No hint of Veronica, which is kind of a pity.'

'What was her last name?'

'Who asks a manicurist her last name? We can probably find out. I don't even know if she's still alive.'

'We should call Felix. We should call somebody. That Kovak character knows when we got in here. He could make things unpleasant.'

'He could also make them pleasant. Which button do we press? Julius has been dead more than half an hour. So we can't have done it, whoever did.'

'There's no evidence Julius wasn't my father.'

'You look like him. Rich. You look just like him. You even

have his frown suddenly. Like you found his shoes, and you stepped right into them. Did I ever tell you my theory about the Kennedys?'

'We have to phone Felix.'

'Probably not, because it just came to me. I've played around with it for a while and now, all of a sudden, I have it pat. Are you ready for this?'

'I don't think so, Sidney. Not now.'

'Yes, you are too. Because here it comes. Too late to stop now, baby. Do you suppose Bobby knew, had any idea, that old Joe and brother Jack had made their deal with the devil? i.e. the Mafia. Do you think Bobby didn't know that they had bought Cook County as well as West Virginia and that they only did it with help from the Mob? Was Bobby *stupid* as well as young?'

The telephone is a phoney antique from the 1940s. Stanley looks at Sidney each time the dial rolls back to encircle the denuded zero.

'So. Jack is elected. Right after we went down to Harlem that time, remember that?'

'You were Spencer Tracy. With two hands.'

'You were never going to get out the car, were you?'

'Wasn't I?'

'OK, so what does Bobby do as soon as he gets into the Justice Department? He goes after Hoffa; he goes after the Mob. The very people that Joe and Jack owe something to; owe plenty; owe *everything*. He goes after them with all the muscle he can muster. Maybe with J. Edgar Hoover's help. No, no; *enemies* help each other, a lot sometimes. He goes after them like it was a *crusade*. Bobby's a street-fighter; he can't feel like he's a man without he has a rumble planned . . .'

'Dr Beck, please. Professor Stanley Oppenheim. We're up here with my father who . . . I fear is dead. I'd appreciate it if Dr Beck could get over here. Julius Oppenheim. Please do that. We're at . . . Yes, we are. Thank you.'

'Bobby knows, and he has to know, that those guys are not going to accept being fucked over. But he goes right ahead.'

'What choice did he have?'

'Jesus Christ, since when was the Kennedys' favourite car a Fiat *Justitia*? Not long afterwards – it *wasn't* long, check the dates – Jack gets killed in a hit. And who's all ready to be measured for his mantle? No, this is not paranoia. I don't have to be saying that Bobby did anything *consciously*. These people are icons, which is why even what we know about them we can't admit. Marilyn and stuff. They are icons who aren't above or below *anything*. That's *why* they're icons. We've been clinging to illusions about them for decades; when we lose one, we just hold tighter to another, like we still believe the brothers loved each other. Did they? Both of them loved Marilyn and they didn't have a moment of jealousy, we like to think, because for Kennedys no woman is anything but three holes to fill. And who gives a damn about last names? Is that what you think?'

'Sidney . . .'

'It's exactly what you think. Because everybody does. But wait! Because Bobby'd seen Jack take Joe junior's place and why wouldn't he imagine taking Jack's? Because it's *immoral*? Fammy-*lies*, that was the Kennedy idea of fun; sell the *goyim* happy photographs, make out Jackie and Jack were sweethearts, fuck the American people right up the ass. Come in their faces. That was the big bang for those people. *They* were the Mafia, if you don't know that, is two and two too difficult

for you? Bobby killed Jack by taking off after the Mob and he
knew damn well what would happen. Now think about Julius
and Rich. And Max is old Joe.'

'You have no evidence.'

'Of *course* I don't. But imagine Julius coming home from
business school, whatever they called it then, and persuading
his father Rich was out of control, muscling competitors,
paying the Bensonhurst mob to strong-arm union organisers,
helping himself to cash to pay for his poker losses. Imagine he
also knew where certain bodies were buried that Max was
involved in . . .'

'You're fantasising.'

'Somebody has to. If we're going to get to the truth. "Rich
killed him", remember?'

'I remember. I don't see . . .'

'Shut your eyes and look. Rich was trouble. Max wasn't
about to stand in Julie's way, but Rich was. Max was old. He
was tired. He wanted to be comfortable. What did Julius have
to do? He didn't have to do *anything*. All he had to do, *they* had
to do, was let Rich get poor. Wither on the vine. Was he
going to stop gambling? He was way down in the hole already.
Cut off his credit and what could he get but deeper? He didn't
win too much, Stan; he lost too much. And once he was weak,
he was dead. And Rich had to live with that, and died with it.
Julius too, but it didn't kill Julius, it kept him alive. Until
maybe Moss came along.'

'Imagine if this was an emergency,' Stanley says. 'And the
guy was dying and it took this long.'

'We'da called the paramedics. You want lightning, you have
to pay for it. You know what I think? I think we'll find there's
an empty safe somewhere in the apartment. And whether it's

empty because it's empty or because it's emptied, we'll never know. And you know something else? Good luck to the bastard finally. Let's hope he took off back to the old country.'

INT. THE BEDROOM. PENTHOUSE C. DAY.

FELIX BECK stands up from examining JULIUS's body.

> FELIX
> I can't say.

> SIDNEY
> He coulda been suffocated though,
> right?

> FELIX
> 'Could've' covers all kinds of stuff. He
> could've, but I don't see any clear
> evidence.

> SIDNEY
> Bruises?

> FELIX
> Maybe a pathologist would say
> differently.

> SIDNEY
> He killed him, he got away with it,
> right?

> FELIX
> If is a big word.

> SIDNEY
> Which I did not use.

> STANLEY
> Felix, thank you for . . .

> FELIX
> He didn't suffer. That I think I can
> promise.

STANLEY

Or struggle.

FELIX

There again.

SIDNEY

There again, Stanley!

FELIX

He was a member of a Temple, wasn't
he? I'll make the calls I have to make,
and you call them.

STANLEY

Should we stay here? We should.

FELIX

It's usual, I guess. I can't, because . . . I
have the living to think about.

SIDNEY looks at STANLEY and STANLEY's look asks SIDNEY
not to say what has occurred to both of them: 'Whose living?'

INT. THE ELEVATOR. 91 C.P.W. DAY.

STANLEY and SIDNEY going down.
STANLEY draws breath and looks at SIDNEY and lets it out
again.

INT. THE LOBBY. 91 C.P.W. DAY.

The doors open and STANLEY and SIDNEY come out.

SIDNEY

I don't know for sure, cousin, but
maybe we're both going to be rich men
suddenly.

STANLEY

Assuming he's finished joking. Could
you possibly not do the cousin thing
again?

SIDNEY
And what are you going to not do?

EXT. 66TH STREET. NEW YORK CITY.
DAY.

STANLEY walking towards Eighth Avenue. He is looking
around him with a searching energy we have not noticed
before. Perhaps he imagines that he will see MOSS
BEAUREGARD dressed as he was when SIDNEY saw, or *maybe*
saw him. How can we tell from looking at STANLEY that
something like this is in his mind? He *scans*, perhaps, and does
not flinch from looking at tall black men.

His father is dead, either just now or long ago. *Both* his fathers
are dead and he feels the weight lifted from him. Is he a
different man? He would not want to say that. Perhaps his
unexcited expectation of money makes him look the world in
the eye. He can have what he wants as soon as he can think
what that is.

INT. STANLEY'S APARTMENT. EIGHTH AVENUE.
DAY.

He unlocks the front door, eases it open, and comes in. He is
like a thief in his own place. He listens and hears no unusual
sound. He walks into the living room on careful feet.

MELANIE is not at the table.

STANLEY hears his breath coming out of just one nostril: the
smallest possible indication of surprise. He goes along to the
bedroom.

STANLEY
Melly.

It is more a statement than a question. No one answers. He looks at his watch. Mid-afternoon. The apartment is empty. Why should it not be?

STANLEY opens his hand and slaps five straight fingers against the dressing table. Why?

INT. THE LIVING ROOM. THE SAME. DAY.

STANLEY picks up the telephone and dials SIDNEY's number. SIDNEY's voice mail answers.

> STANLEY
> It's me. Suppose 'A.' is Abigail. And she
> was another Veronica. What does that
> make Moss? I'm not going to mention
> this again, OK, brother? And you don't
> call me cousin. Agreed?

He is glad that SIDNEY was not there. Would he have said what he just said if he had been? He thinks probably not.

He stands there for a while looking down at the street. He neither wants MELANIE to come home nor does he not want her to.

He smiles. Is he happy or is he not happy?

> STANLEY
> All his sons.

The autopsy on Julius Oppenheim was inconclusive. It seemed likely that he had died from suffocation, but it was not clear whether he had been forcibly denied air. When his will was published, it was found that Julius had left Moss Beauregard half-a-million dollars conditional on his completing his Master's degree. Moss Beauregard did not come forward and the money was never claimed. Sidney and Stanley were their father's main heirs and both were made richer than they expected.

Sidney Oppenheim was dating a spectacular (to look at) actress called Honey Pegler when his undivorced wife, Janice, called to say that she had some news he might like to hear. This meant, to Sidney, that he might equally not like to. Janice was pregnant and he was the father. 'So?'

One afternoon, when Stanley was working on his book, provisionally entitled 'Changing Tracks', in which (according to the outline submitted to Modern Books) he aimed to show how, in the second half of the century, post-literate (wo)man sees her/himself increasingly as a character in a visual, not a moral/literary context. Versatility wins over integrity; if we are lucky, we appear in many roles, with different actors; we care less about morality than opportunity, *much*.

Stanley is discovering an exhilarating fluency as he writes what does not, now, greatly matter to him, except as an exercise. He winces when the telephone rings and answers it. 'Yeah?'

'Dad, this is Francis.'

'Francis? *Francis!* I'm sorry. Are you OK? I think of you as François. Well, that is, I don't actually; but I expect you to. What's happening?'

'I want to come and live in New York.'

'You do? What does Elaine, what does your mother say about that?'

'I haven't told her. But I want to come. Like now. Can I, please? Dad?'

When Stanley puts the telephone down, he makes a note: 'Instead of closure, sequel.' Then Melanie is coming in the door. And before he can mention Francis, she is going to say, 'Stanley: Mikey Carossa . . .'

Bread, Money and Liberty

The Ramplings had flown in from Mexico City on the early plane. Raymond bet Rosalie anything she liked, within reason, against the promised minibus from the hotel being at Oaxaca airport, but there it was. The driver, in khaki shorts, floral shirt, black baseball cap, asked if Sharon *Th*ompson was on the plane with them.

'*Th*ompson,' Raymond said. 'Not that I know of. Why?'

'We wait for her, please.'

'Remember what I said about *paciencia*?' Raymond said. 'I really want to hear that brass band, *and* see it. It's quite a sight apparently. Bob Manning told me it only played till two o'clock. He covered Mexico for us before Johnny gave him the Arts.'

'There's always tomorrow, isn't there?'

'It only plays in full fig on Sundays.'

'Ah,' Rosalie said. 'What *did* you say about *paciencia*?'

'Ha!' Raymond said.

The Ramplings sat for twenty minutes in the hot tub of the minibus until the displeased woman who had to be Ms Thompson came into view. 'My luggage is now apparently – can you believe it? – in Acapulco. Forget the Alamo, don't you wish they would?' Despite her loss, Ms Thompson was lopsided with a bolster-sized duffel-bag. It seemed unlikely that she was going to be marooned without a change of clothes.

After climbing aboard, she cold-eyed Rosalie and Raymond as if they had connived at her vexation. She wore a white shirt, a dark blue linen trouser suit and a major canvas hat. Following her sharp, no-nonsense nose, she went to the back of the minibus. Her shoulders were braced in expectations of an imminent last straw.

Raymond leant towards Rosalie's ear. 'If you want to know what Dorothy looked like . . .'

Ms Thompson scowled at the potholed suburbs of Oaxaca and made aggrieved alterations of her position on the wide bench which she had to herself. The driver's horn croaked at scampering children and sidling dogs as the minibus lurched through the prolonged outskirts of what had been promised to be an unspoilt relic of Spanish colonialism. Had Manning possibly taken his latest budget cuts less well than previously assumed?

Raymond watched his wife's face for signs that she shared his disappointment. It would be unforgivable if she did. Rosalie remained impassive. She had been Raymond's secretary, then – when he became managing editor – his personal assistant. It had taken her four years to displace Dorothy, though she had been in Raymond's bed rather more quickly than that. It remained her policy to insist that he was the boss.

The minibus reached the old quarter and began to roll over regular, and promisingly antique, streets. The driver stopped where a chain across the wide, empty Avenida Benito Juárez denied wheeled access to the Hotel Tamayo. A squat porter in an embroidered blouse and cotton trousers trotted to the rear of the minibus, lowered the flap and began to pull out the bags.

Sharon Thompson slipped past the Ramplings and stepped out, unencumbered, for the hotel.

When everything was unloaded, the driver gave Raymond a look tantamount to an upturned palm. 'You go on in, Rosie, why don't you?' Raymond said. 'See if our bloody voucher rings any happy bells. I'll . . .'

The driver told him that it was five pesos per bag. Raymond, whose position at editorial conferences was constructively left of centre, took the noble view and coughed up for Ms Thompson's duffel-bag as well as for their own two rigid suitcases.

Meanwhile, Rosalie had discovered why Sharon Thompson had hurried ahead of them. Since Oaxaca's famous Day of the Dead was imminent, the coconut-matted hotel lobby was garrulous with guests. Checkout time was noon and the Ramplings had arrived at the high tide of activity. Ms Thompson spoke Spanish in a low voice which procured impressive, and infuriating, priority.

When Raymond – who had, after all, done her tipping – cleared his throat to solicit her good offices, the sharp nose was keyed to more urgent scents: Ms Thompson followed the bellboy into the palmy interior of the hotel. The Ramplings had to wait until their room had been vacated and serviced. The old clerk advised them to go to the travel office and book places for the hotel tour to the colourful festivities. After some serious accusatory dawdling had had no effect on the clerk, Raymond decided that they might as well do as the chap had suggested.

They found that Ms Thompson was already making her reservation. When the jet-haired *chica* behind the desk said, '*Diez y seis dólares, señora,*' and the American woman nodded,

Raymond was relieved to think that at least he need not bargain.

'You get driven everywhere, you get free flowers to throw on the graves, and plenty of *mescal* apparently. *And* a guide.'

'Whose grave do we want to throw flowers on? We don't know anyone who's dead, do we, locally?'

'There's always D. H. Lawrence,' Raymond said. 'He lived here at one point. He might be around. The dead don't need to book, do they?'

'Do I like *mescal*?' Rosalie said. 'I bet I don't.'

'I bet you don't.' Raymond saw that Ms Thompson was looking at him with a certain complicity. 'In which case, darling,' he said, 'you absolutely don't have to drink any of it. Promise.'

Ms Thompson gathered her tickets, muttered something fluent to the girl behind the desk and, with a little swish, as if she were wearing a skirt and not trousers, went along the arcaded patio to her enviably available room.

'After all, the Day of the Dead is why we're here.'

'I thought we were having a belated honeymoon.'

'It's why we're having a belated honeymoon *here*,' Raymond said. He refrained from saying that he and Rosalie had been together for three years and that, although it was technically their honeymoon, since it did indeed follow their wedding, it was not even their first time abroad together (their thing had basically started at a management seminar in Barcelona) and hence he did not find it incumbent to act as though she were his sole object of attention. Raymond reckoned that he was a man who refrained from saying quite a lot of things. What he did not reckon was that Rosalie was a woman who guessed most of them.

'We could go up to the main square,' Raymond said, 'and

come back when the room's ready. That way, we just might still be in time for the band.'

'Why not?' Rosalie said. 'Incidentally, they call it the *zócalo*, the main square.'

'Good for them,' Raymond said. 'You know, I don't mind that woman knowing her way around, but she might have done her own bloody tipping, I must say. "Forget the Alamo." What was that supposed to mean?'

'Didn't Dorothy say things like that?' Rosalie said.

'Dorothy? Of course not.'

As they turned the corner by the cathedral, the band was still gleaming and blaring in the *zócalo*. Fountains splashed silently under the surge of sound as grey-uniformed bandsmen swelled to their shiny work. Clouds of silver balloons were tethered above the barefooted salesmen who ambled along the arcades. Tall trees with greeny-black foliage threw shade over the cushioned high chairs of the shoeshine men. Their owners looked with resignation at the trainers on the feet of most of the *gringos*, but some of them snapped their fingers and pointed at Raymond's dustless toecaps.

'I seriously wish they wouldn't do that,' Raymond said.

'Raymond, can you think of any reason why those men are wheeling all that sand from all the way over there and dumping it in heaps in front of the cathedral?'

'I was going to ask you exactly the same question. Except that I was going to call you Rosalie, not Raymond.'

'*Paciencia*! They're going to make quite remarkable things out of it.' They turned and saw Ms Thompson, bent gymnastically at the waist, scanning the silver earrings and local artefacts displayed on two *serapes*. The Indian woman in charge gave a show of creased indifference as she turned over the bright zippered purses and appraised the heaps of toys skulls and black-ribbed skeletons that danced on strings.

'Now's your chance to ask her for the money for the tipping,' Rosalie said.

'Rosie, come on!' Raymond turned and smiled and said, 'What sort of things exactly?'

'If you don't know, I wouldn't want to spoil the surprise.'

Ms Thompson was gone before Raymond could ask for advice about where to have a spot of lunch. There was something disconcerting about the unhurried briskness which enabled her to be here and over there at pretty well the same time. The more he disliked her, the more Raymond felt inclined to believe in her competence.

The band finished with a prolonged diapason as the Ramplings were inspecting a café menu. They decided that they could not go seriously wrong with what was translated as 'chicken spit'. They were waiting for it in ravenous apprehension when the first marchers came into the square, carrying banners and waving flags with what Rosalie presumed to be provocative initials on them. As they shuffled past, the demonstrators chanted slogans in a good-natured version of righteous indignation.

Raymond said, 'Any idea what it's all about?'

'Bread, money and liberty, roughly, I think.'

'There's nothing too much wrong with this chicken, you know,' Raymond said. 'I don't think we'll risk pudding though, do you? There might well be fruit in the room.'

The marchers began to spread on to the pavement under the arcade and were soon handing out pamphlets to people in the café. Raymond advised Rosalie to hang on to her bag while he spoke diplomatically loud English in order to reassure the cops as they passed between the police cars which blocked the exits from the *zócalo*. They strolled along the wide, untroubled avenue to the Hotel Tamayo, where their room was said to be ready. The tiled floor was blood-red from puddles of unmopped water.

'*Now* I know what I fancy for pudding,' Raymond said, when Rosalie stepped out of the shower feeling much, much better. 'Peaches.'

On the day of the dead, they had a siesta and ate an overpriced, unincluded supper in the hotel before being summoned to the bus for the tour of the cemeteries. Thunder rumbled in the Sierra Madre, so Rosalie went back for her folding umbrella. When she came out, she saw Raymond in the aisle of the bus, talking to Sharon Thompson, who already had her window seat. Rosalie watched without jealousy. She realised, without it being very important really, that she did not love the man she had married and that that was why she had married him.

They drove back through the suburbs as the storm became more aggressive. By the time they were walking the gauntlet of an alley lined with stalls offering the usual souvenirs and *serapes*, Rosalie was congratulating herself on the umbrella. Most of the tourists, whom the guide had issued with unsubtle bunches of long, slightly smelly marigolds, seemed to imagine that the storm, like the political demonstration in the *zócalo*, could not possibly apply to them.

The white-gated cemetery did not seem old. Whatever ancestors were buried there had to be of quite recent vintage. There were many wavery candles, wind-shielded in plastic cups. Indian families stood by the graves or sat on stone benches. There was no sign of either grief or enthusiasm. The Indians murmured and leaned together to select food from unfolkloric boxes. Having collected paper cups of *mescal*, the tourists went in search of something to be impressed or, if possible, slightly frightened by. They held their marigolds more like weapons than tributes.

'Where do we throw them exactly?' Raymond said.

'Anywhere you like,' Ms Thompson said. 'Nobody's going to be offended. How about someone who doesn't seem to have too many friends?'

'Why are you here, if I may ask? You've obviously done all this before.'

'My grandmother was Mexican,' she said. 'She's buried right over there.'

'Let's give our flowers to your grandmother then.'

'I'd as soon you didn't.' She left them with unhurried suddenness and went on her high-stepped way across the humped ground.

'Some people always put you in the wrong,' Raymond said.

'And it's starting to rain,' Rosalie said.

'Let's get rid of these damned flowers and get back to the bus. Do you think it's true, the Mexican grandmother?'

'Why would she lie?'

'She likes to play games,' Raymond said. 'She's the kind of woman who always has to leave you with egg on your face.'

'And what does that make you want to do to her?' Rosalie said.

Rain began to fall. It was warmer than the hotel shower. Rosalie offered Raymond some of the umbrella but he left her to it and seemed to enjoy the downpour. He waited outside the bus and watched for Sharon Thompson and then came, in his now transparent shirt, and sat beside Rosalie in a bad mood. She was not worried; he never made love to her as she liked unless he was angry.

The next morning, the storm had cleared. After an ample

buffet breakfast, which – as Raymond pointed out – basically took care of lunch, they walked to the market, where Raymond bought a 1930s-style straw hat with a snap brim and a dent in the middle. Then they ambled into the *zócalo* to think about a drink.

The sun, after the rain, had crisped the demonstrators' abandoned pamphlets into brittle wafers. There were rumours about shootings. However, the main thing was that, over by the cathedral, beyond the bookstalls, what had been heaps of sand had been transformed into a gaudy bestiary of sprawling, skeletal monsters with sooty ribs. Green-spotted dragons coiled round lamp-posts. Christian crosses adorned mildly revolution-ary slogans picked out in red. Stilted skeletons, in paper dresses and hats, stood among the recumbent sculptures. 'She was quite right,' Raymond said. 'Well worth the price of admis-sion, this is. What's that?'

'I just found it,' Rosalie said. 'Lying on the ground.'

'Anything in it?'

She unzipped the purse. There was a thick roll of notes inside. 'About fifteen hundreds pesos. Plus some small change.'

'That's over a hundred quid.' Raymond was scanning the *zócalo* for anyone who might be slapping his pockets with increasing desperation. 'Any name or anything?'

'Only the money. It's very like the one she bought, isn't it? Your friend.'

'It's like the one everyone bought. What the hell are we going to do with it?'

'How about taking it to the police?'

'In which case, it'll never be seen or heard of again. We could stick around and see whether anyone comes looking for it. Better walk on a bit, meanwhile. The shoeshine chap seems a bit unduly interested.'

'Maybe it's his,' Rosalie said.

'Don't be bloody silly, Rosie.'

'Oh I wouldn't want to be that,' she said.

'Ms Thompson!' Raymond said. 'You're always around when you're needed!'

Sharon Thompson was coming towards them in a dress with a long skirt. She had jettisoned her major hat for a new one which was very much like Raymond's. He would have been interested to know what she paid for it, but it probably wasn't the time to ask.

'Rosalie's found something. Could it possibly be yours?'

Ms Thompson looked at the wallet and said, 'Nothing to do with me.'

'My wife spotted it lying on the ground. What do you think we should do with it?'

'Buy yourselves a good lunch. No sense giving it to the police.'

Rosalie saw Raymond's little smirk and she did not mind a bit that he was pleased that the American woman thought as he did. She did not mind that he was asking Ms Thompson if she wanted to come and have some lunch with them, if she knew somewhere good. While Sharon and Raymond began to walk across the square, Rosalie went over to the shoeshine man and gave the purse to him to keep in case someone came looking for it right by where he had his pitch. She wasn't totally against walking back to the hotel and collecting her things and never seeing Raymond again in her whole life. But then he turned back and indicated that there was a worthwhile restaurant on the first-floor terrace overlooking the *zócalo*. And then he was frowning at the smiling shoeshine man and refraining from saying anything and Rosalie was abruptly happy about almost everything.

An Older Woman

When Simon Erskine told me that Ricky Tarrant's mother was Lithuanian, his remark was not based on serene genealogical interest. The Erskine Gallery had just lost one of its best artists to Ricky's candid poaching. However, since one of my grandmothers happened to have been born in Vilnius, before having the wisdom to leave it for St Jo, Missouri, Simon's revelation had the odd – almost irritating – effect of giving me a tenuous affinity with a man whom I had regarded with both suspicion and envy.

My suspicion had been excited by Ricky's too evident determination to take London's art, and social, world by unsubtle storm; the envy was the consequence of his handsome facility for befriending those who were talented, famous or rich enough to merit his calculated attention. He also had access to a large number of very pretty girls, one of whom – Jilly Langridge – told me, without a hint of reproach, that he always behaved towards her like a perfect gentleman, even after she was married.

All the same, Ricky never denied that he was an adventurer. 'I don't see what else life can be,' he once said to me, '*except* an adventure, do you?'

'I certainly do,' I said. 'But don't let me blunt your thrust by telling you what.'

'*Blunt my thrust?* Did you really say that? You'd better be careful, Freddie, you're turning into a parody of yourself.'

'Takes one to spot one,' I said.

'Oh? And what am I a parody of exactly then?'

'Julien Sorel in *Le Rouge et le Noir*, aren't you? Or the Larry Harvey character in *Room at the Top*. Joe Lampton. Like all the best parodies, you have both style and premeditation and, of course, no sincerity whatever.'

'I'm going to have a haircut,' Ricky said. 'Do you feel like one? You're beginning to lose your hair, aren't you? Does that bother you?'

In those early 1970s, Ricky's own hair was expensively layered and gleaming black, almost blue. If anyone but he had made personal remarks about my incipient middle age, I might have been insulted, or indignant, but I told myself that Ricky was only reminding himself of how brief a span of hirsute handsomeness might be available to him. He was, after all, already twenty-seven and – despite the urgency of his ambition – he did not yet have a Bond Street gallery with Ricardo Tarrant incised in the window.

As Ricky and I lounged, side by sheeted side, in our Jermyn Street barbers' chairs, he confessed that Harvard (as he chose to call Harvey Hilyard) was getting restless at not being more visible to the critics and the smart money. He wanted his next show to be closer to w.1 than Ladbroke Grove, where the Ricardo Tarrant Gallery had hung his work on the bare brick walls of a bankrupt fruiterer's shop. Harvey was aggrieved because the show had only been a sell-out; the reviews had been unflatteringly skimpy. Since the artist had sworn nothing more durable than undying gratitude, Ricky was afraid that his poached prize would soon do to him what Ricky had persuaded him to do to Simon Erskine.

Ricardo Tarrant had been in London only five years. He had jetted to Paris, from New York, in May 1968, in order to clench a comradely fist at the student revolution before acquiring a truck-load of its ephemeral fly-posters and manifestos, which he had stored against the day when they would be collectors' items. Soon after hitting unrevolutionary London, he bought a derelict house in Camden Town, with capital borrowed from an undisclosed source, and renovated it into four flats, three of which he sold, each of them for more than he had paid for the whole property. The one at the top was, as Joe Lampton would advise, kept for himself. Having proved that he could make money from a standing start, Ricky paraded his credentials in the world of art, where a new Midas seldom lacks a welcome.

He was convinced that he could steer Harvey Hilyard into being the major painter of our time. But that could happen only if he could raise prompt cash for a West End gallery, which was why, as we had our shoulders brushed by our well-tipped barbers, Ricky wondered if I could lend him two hundred grand. I told him that I had left my wallet in my other coat.

Sylvia and I, and our small children, were living in a terrace house in Seymour Walk in those last fat years when the Sixties swung terminally into the early Seventies. Since the street was a *cul-de-sac*, it was full of aggressively new cars either coming in or backing snarlingly out towards the Fulham Road. We gave occasional dinner parties in our windowless, mirrored basement dining room. I was trying to believe that a busy social life was a sign of contentment, although I had not written in several years and feared that I was wasting my overpaid time in the movies.

Juliet Rotman was one of the American producers, then
resident in London, who sponsored my cushioned malaise.
Juliet had been married to – and had four children by – Baruch
Rotman, the quiet son of one of the founders of Republic
Pictures. Their amicable divorce had left her a very rich
woman. That was why it had been amicable. Juliet often asked
us to her house in Chester Square and, to avoid seeming to be
spongers, Sylvia and I invited her, from time to time, to
Seymour Walk.

Juliet was a small, elegant, only slightly wrinkled woman in,
I suppose, her mid-fifties. If she wanted another husband, she
gave no anxious sign of it. She dressed in not too girlish fashion
– Jean Muir, not Mary Quant – and she spoke in the husky
tones of someone who never had to raise her voice in order to
get what she wanted. Juliet had both taste and money; I liked
to believe that it was her taste which I found so likeable.
However, she had also promised to get me a very good deal to
write a movie about Benjamin Disraeli.

When I arrived home from Jermyn Street, Sylvia told me
that Jacob Seligman had called to say that he could not, after all,
make it to our dinner party the following evening. We had
hoped that his titled fortune would provide Juliet with a
partner to reckon with.

'We need a bit of glamour,' Sylvia said.

'Why don't we ask Ricky Tarrant?' I said.

Sylvia said, 'Apart from the eight immediately obvious good
reasons, you mean?'

'I had a haircut with him today,' I said. 'He was all right.
And Juliet loves art. Ricky is at least lively.'

'At *most* lively,' Sylvia said.

When I called him, Ricky said, 'Want me to bring

someone? Do you need a pretty girl? Or two? Do you know the Danieli twins? You should.'

'Sylvia and I are asking you to dinner,' I said. 'You really don't have to bring the pudding.'

'I don't want to sit next to one of your old biddies who says she's given up sex, by which she means it's given her up.'

'There goes the seating plan,' I said.

Ricky was late. We were seriously thinking of going downstairs to the pear salad when he finally knocked at the door. He was wearing a raspberry-coloured corduroy suit, with flared trousers, a black shirt, a Cordoba hat and a knitted white tie. His usual suntan seemed, however, to have faded since the previous day. His voice was paler too.

'I'm sorry,' he said, 'but I've just escaped being run over in the Fulham Road. By a whisker. Chap in a bloody great Roller came straight at me.'

Sebastian Leek surveyed Ricky's raspberry-coloured outfit. 'Probably didn't notice you,' he said.

Juliet had an attack of the giggles. She stopped, as we went into the dining room, but then a renewed spasm almost choked her over the *filet en croûte*. Ricky regarded her, for a moment, with less than his usual scheming charm. 'Very rare to find money with a sense of humour,' he said.

I feared that the evening would not recover. There was a streak of mischief in Ricky which now led him to pay aggressive court to Angela Leek, presumably in order to pay Sebastian back for a remark which none of us was likely to forget. Soon after eleven o'clock, Juliet's chauffeur returned for her. The *café-au-lait* Corniche filled the street. Ricky said, 'My God, it's the same man who tried to kill me: he's come back to have another try.'

Juliet said, 'Do you need a lift?'

'Preferable to an ambulance,' Ricky said, and in no time he was in the Rolls with her.

I had a meeting with Juliet in Chester Square a couple of days later. Her solemn expression disposed me to expect bad news about Disraeli. *Dizzy*, however, was not the problem; she wanted to talk about Ricky Tarrant. Did I know about his Venezuelan mother and his Venetian father? How could I explain the extraordinary precociousness of his taste? What kind of a country was an England in which such energy and sensibility were not recognised? She had decided to become Ricky's partner in his new Bond Street Gallery. It did not require a great deal of wit to guess that Ricky's eye for antiques had spotted, and landed, a bargain in Juliet Rotman.

When I next saw Ricky, he put an arm round me and hugged me. 'I don't know how to thank you,' he said, 'for introducing me to Juliet. Come and see the gallery.'

I was, I confess, surprised both by its size (huge) and its prime location (opposite Agnew's); I was still more surprised to see the names Tarrant *and* Rotman incised on the wide window facing Bond Street. 'I could hardly do less,' Ricky said. 'Because, as far as I am concerned, Juliet isn't just a source of money, you know.'

'That's very touching,' I said.

'Christ, you happily married men, you can't believe that anyone has motives that aren't mercenary or disgusting, can you? Juliet's changed my life. And my attitude *to* life. She's a wonderful woman. She shouldn't be wasting her time producing movies. I've told her to give it up.'

'Thanks very much,' I said.

When I went to Chester Square to finalise the plans for *Dizzy*, Juliet took the opportunity to mention, rather shyly, that she was going to the Cannes Festival with Ricky, who was really interested in film. If she was allowing herself to be measured for a painful drop, I had to admit that she looked, for the moment, amazingly well on it.

'You're afraid that he only wants me for my money, aren't you?' she said. 'Well, I have got it, haven't I? And what does it matter? After all, what do *you* want to know me for?'

'The cases aren't exactly alike,' I said.

'He's wonderful in bed,' she said.

'There you are,' I said.

'Do you know what worries him most?'

'Probably not,' I said.

'He's afraid of losing his hair. His father –'

'The Venetian.'

'Yes, was bald when he was forty. I made the mistake of telling him that I could never fancy bald men. I know it's a very . . . improbable love,' Juliet said. 'I know that one day he may very well walk out on me for a younger woman. Meanwhile, I intend to be happy with him for just as long as I can.'

'Why not?' I said.

The Tarrant and Rotman Gallery soon became the only place where the new generation of artists cared to show their work. When Emmy Figgis, whose self-portraits – as enticing as they were accurate – had lent a new aesthetic dimension to pubic hair, moved from across the road to become Ricky's latest client, the rumours of an amorous motive were quickly into print. Knowing what kind of an operator Ricky was, I feared that Juliet's lease of happiness was, like Jim Callaghan's doleful government, in its last weeks.

Some time later, I found myself adjacent to Ricky at our favourite barber's. His face was juddering under the supposedly benign agitations of a friction machine. He rolled his eyes and looked at me balefully. His anxious air was no great advertisement for being on top of the world.

'What's the matter with you?' I said.

His fingers went to his brow. Was it my imagination, or his, that his hairline had receded slightly?

'What've you heard, you grinning bastard?'

'On what topic?' I said.

'Come on, Freddie, don't do this. Juliet.'

'I don't think *Dizzy*'s going to happen,' I said. 'She says she loves the script but my guess is, she's gone cold on it.'

'Doesn't surprise me,' he said. 'I offered to marry her.'

'Then you have nothing to be ashamed of,' I said, 'do you?'

'Do you always have to be cynical?'

'It's often the quickest way to the truth,' I said.

'I thought she really cared about me,' he said.

'How's Emmy?' I said.

'That little tart. I never realised how much it hurt.'

'What did, Ricky, exactly?'

'Juliet dumping me. She's even giving me the gallery. She wants her name off the window.'

I said, 'You don't seriously expect me to believe that everything working out, exactly as you planned it, has broken your innocent little heart, do you?'

He looked at me with what appeared very sincere loathing. Tears distressed his recently renovated face. 'She's walked out on me, you bastard. She's dumped me. She never gave a damn about me, did she? She just wanted what she wanted.'

There was, I supposed, something at least *slightly* decent, if also laughable, about Ricky's very lifelike parody of a wounded party. What I found less amusing was the prospect of seeing the state to which Juliet had been reduced.

I saw her back view at Glyndebourne a few days later at a

new production of Giacomo Ferrara's *Phaedra*, for which Harvey Hilyard had done the *fortissimo* décor. May I be forgiven, I hesitated about going up to her. I dreaded the grievous ravages which abandoned love might have deepened in her face. What amazing courage it must have needed to put on a new Jean Muir and ride all that way, painfully alone, in the *café-au-lait* Roller! As I pushed towards her, a tall man, with a shock of fair hair, anticipated me. He was carrying two glasses of champagne and, as he held one out to Juliet, I could see that he was hardly out of his teens. It was then that I realised that receding Ricky had been telling the truth: Juliet had left him for a younger man. Why not? She could afford it.

Emile

The first thing I heard about the man who lived in the Manoir des Trois Chemins was that he was a Belgian. When a Frenchman remarks of someone '*C'est un Belge*', it is as if he were already telling you a joke. If you smile, because he has, and because you do not wish to seem to have missed the point, you may also feel slightly uneasy: you have already accepted that there is something innately comic about belonging to a minority. Although Belgium is not a part of France, many Belgians speak French, with a distinct accent which the French are pleased to find laughable; they provide a butt which, rather conveniently, does not have to live within France's borders in order to incur the derision of the French. Since Belgium is famous for fried potatoes, waffles and chocolates, its standard citizen is also assumed to be a rounded buffoon of whom it is said, for notorious example, that he can be recognised in a submarine because he is the man carrying an umbrella. Despite his laughable role, the Belgian is also taken to be a man of shrewdness, with more brains and almost certainly more money than he cares to display.

The Manoir des Trois Chemins is in the valley of the Dordogne. It overlooks a road which comes along the valley of the river Céou to where it gushes into the Dordogne at

Castelnaud, and another road – on the right bank of the great river – which drives along the valley towards Beynac, and also a third road, which cuts inland towards Sarlat. Those are the 'trois chemins' on whose unhurrying traffic Emile Bouguereau, and his wife Eugénie-Béatrice, could look down from the long stone terrace at which, I confess, I have often looked up, with a measure of covetousness.

Although I am very happy with the modest farmhouse where we have lived for many summers, the Manoir des Trois Chemins – something between a manor house and a château – stands so proud on its high ledge, above sloping fields, with the silvery Dordogne flowing below its left shoulder and then sliding leftwards towards Beynac, whose great château commands the limestone bluffs high above the deep cut of the river, that it would be pusillanimous not to be tempted, very slightly, to be its master. On the other side of the river from Beynac, the château of Castelnaud, which was built by the English during the Hundred Years War, is on an equally steep cliff. There is a combative confidence in the style of the two castles whose commanders laid claim to the same fief and tried, in the turreted arrogance of their fortresses, to give the impression that their authority was unquestionable.

The Manoir, by contrast, is long and flat-faced and unassertive. Two rows of wide, unsuspicious windows, with their slatted shutters thrown wide, overlook the enviable terrace and the widening valley below it. There are round towers at each end, witchily hatted with pointed slate roofs. The shade of green-black fir trees fans the face of the house as the sun melts the morning mist and takes charge of the landscape. The grey, lichened mass and deferential outhouses of the Manoir announce the standing of the Récollet family, whose valour was established in the famous siege of Sarlat, in

1649, when the town resisted a savage assault by the supporters of the Prince de Condé, who was seeking to overthrow the young king Louis XIV before his sun could reach its zenith. Madame Récollet-Bouguereau, as she always called herself when answering the telephone, was a voluble expert in the history of her family and of its loyalty which, she gave one to understand, deserved more liberal rewards than it had received down the years.

It may well be that, in her perhaps passionate, certainly beautiful youth, Eugénie-Béatrice entertained a pure and ardent love for Emile. However, she had left it to her younger sister, Sophie, to continue the Récollet line, which she had done, *la pauvre*, with repeated (and fattening) piety. By the time I met the Récollet-Bouguereaux, Emile was a thinly moustached, rather tall and certainly not rotund man in his early seventies. He had made a fortune in the Belgian frozen food business. Only on retirement had he comes to live in his wife's ancestral property. Who, she would ask, loudly, would choose to stay in Belgium if he could have a historic home in the Périgord? Eugénie-Béatrice often reminded you that she was the true, and sole, proprietor of the Manoir; it had been in her family since before the siege of Sarlat at which, as she might well have told you before, her ancestor had distinguished himself.

Since she brought Emile to retirement in it, the Manoir had had a completely new roof – the earlier one had been riddled with termites – and new wiring and new plumbing. The formal garden had been beautifully, and very expensively, restored to the plans which an enterprising Récollet originally brought back from Renaissance Italy. However, her husband's money did not entitle him to anything but the privilege of sharing the house with its *châtelaine*.

Eugénie-Béatrice was a few years younger than her husband and, as time went by, she seemed to grow younger still. Her evidently Parisian clothes were mostly black, but they were somehow *bright* black and advertised their unprovincial provenance; her jewellery flashed with inherited good taste; when she smiled and put one small, gloved hand on your sleeve and whispered a privileged invitation to one of her little gatherings, you were supposed to know that all further resistance was futile. Madame wore her silvering hair in a bun whose tightness seemed to pull the skin smooth across her cheek-bones. She was a remarkably good-looking woman, but I confess to the impolite fantasy that, should her hair come loose, her entire skin might fall in a wrinkled heap around her ankles.

The Dordogne is a department notoriously congenial to retired persons. Since writers never retire, and fade away only with the greatest reluctance, I have no notion that I truly belong in the community of British, Dutch, and Scandinavian expatriates to whom, over the years, we happen to have been introduced. I have perfected a wave – almost a salute – which is at once immensely friendly (and unaffected) and which says that I should love to spend the next hour comparing the price of meals in Sarlat and Bergerac, or of a round of golf at Lolivarie as against Rochebois, but that I am at the mercy of my pensionless way of life and must rush home, immediately, to write an important novel.

However, every Achilles has his heel. I can resist our neighbour's seductive invitation to join in culturally rewarding rambles to the eighteen Norman churches between Domme and Beaumont; I have foregone the pleasure of seeing a Dutch ex-ambasssador's slides of his tour of the Kalahari Desert; I have not even been able to find time for a canoeing and camping weekend under the aegis of a retired public school chaplain.

But when Eugénie-Béatrice came up to me, in the interval of a performance of Molière's *Le Malade Imaginaire*, during the summer festival in Sarlat, and accused me of being a bridge player, I could not – as a distinguished novelist once put it – deny the soft impeachment.

It was as a result of my too easily secured guilty plea that I became an irregular visitor to the Manoir des Trois Chemins. Sylvia neither disapproved of my boldly furtive visits to the Récollet-Bouguereaux nor did she feel any duty, let alone temptation, to share them; my wife was not amused by Eugénie-Béatrice's rumoured admiration for the National Front, whose leader, she had said, was the only French politician who told the truth. Sylvia preferred her garden to the smoke-filled *salon* in which all the best old bones of the Périgord sighed at their bad cards and drank Eugénie-Béatrice's thin tea and pliable biscuits. Even I affected reluctance; I told Emile that I would come only if they had genuine need of a fourth, or an eighth; the Récollet-Bouguereaux often had two tables, in order to vary the ordeal of partnering Casimir Malachowski, a Franco-Polish ex-colonel, of princely origins, who wore a monocle and thought himself the best player in the room.

I had played at the house five or six times, with a certain lightheartedness, since the stakes were negligible, when Casimir asked me – after I had done something rather bold and considerably to our mutual advantage – whether I minded if, as my partner, he spoke very frankly to me. Something in his manner suggested that his frankness might not be as complimentary as I deserved, so I said, 'Not a bit, *pas du tout* even, as long as I am allowed to speak equally frankly to you afterwards.'

As he considered what retort would best deal with my

insolence, the ex-colonel's clenched mouth began to – how shall I say? – *rotate*. His left brow bore down on his monocle so heavily that I feared he might spring a dangerous wound. Then he said, 'You, Monsieur, are a *guest* here.'

I said, 'Are you now resident in this house, Colonel?'

'In France,' he said. '*I* am French.'

'And have been for some time, I gather.'

'You are a guest in this country. You are, if I may say so, someone who should watch himself. You are, if I may also say so, as good as . . . as *apatride*.'

I was not deeply wounded to be accused of being a stateless person, even though I was able to guess on exactly what racial grounds I was being put in my place, or my placelessness. Fortunately, the Colonel was too old to hit, so I simply said, 'I think I shall go home.' It was not witty, but it was, I thought, in the circumstances, diplomatic.

'Casimir dear,' Eugénie-Béatrice said, 'we're not all as expert as you are. I am sure Frédéric is sorry if he did the wrong thing.'

It was at that point that Emile said, 'Frédéric is a friend of mine. He is our guest, Casimir, as you are, and I cannot understand by what right you criticise a better player than yourself, but cannot accept his right to criticise you in turn.'

'I did not bid one spade with only three spades in my hand,' Casimir Malachowski said.

'Frédéric plays with us although he has better things to do, and has had better partners than any of us.'

I said, 'Emile, Emile, don't worry. If the Colonel wants to advertise his Frenchness, I am sure that we are all willing to ignore the accent in which he does it.'

The Colonel did not reciprocate my magnanimity. He stood up with careful clumsiness, so that every eye was fastened on him. Then he said, 'I regard the way he chooses to play as little better than cheating.'

Fearing that my diplomacy had had too broad a yellow streak in it, I now said, 'If I ever see you in this house again, Colonel, I shall know that it is time to leave it, as it is now.'

Emile said, 'Casimir, kindly leave my house. At once.'

Casimir said, 'His house! *Ecoutez le Belge!*'

I do not know how these things happen, but the way that he said 'Listen to the Belgian' told me what perhaps everyone knew already, that the Colonel was, or certainly had been, Eugénie-Béatrice's lover. If Emile had always known it, he had borne his cuckoldry with dignity. And now that Casimir had as good as publicly horned him, Emile simply winked at me. While the rest of the guests blinked with embarrassment or pretended that it was all a joke, I felt a sudden, happy fraternity with a man whom I had previously regarded with distant indifference.

I also felt that I could not simply stalk out of the house without first holding out my hand to him. '*Mon cher Emile,*' I said, 'if I can ever be of any service to you, you may call upon me without hesitation.'

Having thanked the unsmiling Eugénie-Béatrice for the usual skimpy refreshments, I left the seven of them to enjoy the rest of their afternoon as best they might. It was a pleasure to return to the pursuit of the *mot juste*.

I did not receive an apology from Eugénie-Béatrice. I was told by a Norwegian art dealer that she expected one from me. I continued to admire the Manoir des Trois Chemins, but I did not again park my car under the green-black fir trees until, one day almost a full year later, Emile telephoned me. His voice seemed nervous and a little thin. He wondered whether I played chess. I said, 'I know the moves, Emile, but I'm not a chess player. You can't bid three-card suits at chess, can you?'

I am not sure whether I went back to the Manoir des Trois Chemins out of generosity or insolence. Eugénie-Béatrice passed me in the doorway as if I were a tradesman or a *notaire*. I gathered the impression that Emile himself shared the shadow which fell across me. He was older and frailer than he had been a year before. It was no surprise when he told me that he was ill. He told me with a smile which said that, by 'ill', he meant dying. The strange thing about the dying is how often they surprise you by their vitality. Emile played chess well enough certainly to make me pleased if I could prolong our games beyond twenty moves or so. His illness even turned me into quite a good loser; I was able to turn incompetence into tact.

I began to go up to the big house pretty well every week. I had the silly feeling that my regularity was keeping him alive. He told me, with a strange smile, that he had never missed Belgium, but that he had recently decided that he would be buried in the same churchyard as his parents and the young brother who was executed during the war. It was the first hint of tragedy in a life which, so far as I knew, had been devoted entirely to frozen food and to Eugénie-Béatrice.

One Wednesday afternoon, I drove up to the house as usual, knowing that my coming would be the signal for Eugénie-Béatrice to leave, almost certainly in order to go and see her lover, and I was admitted by the unsmiling Hilaire, the Bouguereaux' factotum. Hilaire indicated that Monsieur was upstairs. I thought that Emile had finally taken to his bed and I hesitated to intrude, but then I heard him call 'Frédéric' and I climbed the oak steps which I had not climbed before.

Although he was clearly in more pain than his usual

morphine could prevent, he was not in bed. He was packing a suitcase, one shirt at a time.

I said, 'Emile, what are you doing?'

'I want you to drive me to Périgueux,' he said. 'If you would.'

'Of course, but what's going to happen in Périgueux?'

'I'm going to catch a train.' To speak seemed to require so much effort that he could not even fold a shirt until he had fallen silent again. 'To Antwerp.'

I said, 'You're not going anywhere. Except to bed. You're much too ill to travel.'

'That's why I must,' he said. 'I'm going to join my mother and father.'

I said, 'I was looking forward to a game of chess.'

'It's now or never,' he said. 'So it must be now. She says so.'

'Does she really? A journey like that'll kill you.'

'I shall be lucky,' he said, 'if I last that long, but I must try.'

I said, 'What does she mean by "it must be now"? Why must it?'

'Because,' Emile said, 'it's cheaper to buy a ticket when you're alive than be transported in a coffin when you're dead. She says it's up to me. If I don't go now, I can't go at all.'

I said, 'What kind of a woman is she, for God's sake?'

'Practical,' he said. 'Very practical, and very French.'

I drove him to Périgueux. He bought a second-class ticket and I carried his light case on to the train. I suppose I should have gone with him, but what kind of a joke would it have been to be alone with a dying, or dead, man in Belgium?

Lo and Behold!

*Annotated edition specially compiled
by Dr Appels N. Pears, jr.*

Re: *The Life of Dolores Hayes*

The Penthouse Apartment,
30 W. 69th St. N.Y., N.Y.

To Augustus Merkin,[1] *President/C.E.O. Alpha/Betta*[2]*/Delta*[3]
Books Inc.

Extra-Dear Gusset,[4]

I gather from the panic in your voice that you asked
Floyd to find out how the Dolores Hayes[5] opus was
coming along. Before you withdraw your advance or rattle
your writ, herewith preface and specimen chapter, plus the
early blurb to catch the catalogue. This is going to be a
humdinger, if you want my totally biased opinion. My bet
is you'll be making it your stack-'em-hi Big One for the
Fall. It has everything, and that's not all.

Kiss, kiss,

(signed) K-K-Katie

Draft Blurbette:

LO AND BEHOLD!

by Dolores Hayes (with Katie Kite)

The long-awaited autobiography of one of the most enigmatic, probably best-loved, certainly *most* loved stars of the modern screen: 'Marlene Dietrich[1] without ze knotty vowels and with legs longer and shapelier than any poppola Coppola[2] crapola,' once gushed K.T.[3], the witty English critic who seldom gushed twice. Up to now, Dolores Hayes has always been extremely reticent, but award-winning authoress and syndicated columnist Katie Kite has succeeded in turning the key in Lady Lo's lock. And how!

For the first time, we learn what really happened between Lo and 'Uncle Louis'[4] in those tumultuous Hollywoo days when she was under con trick at Metro. We hear how come she plummeted to stardom in *Hummingbird*, The Musical That Never Was.[5] She comes clean on that mysterious first marriage to Dick Schiller, Alaska's pet poet who dove in and joined the whales at the false news of Dolores' death in childbirth. She is refreshingly explicit on her hurricane-farce relationship with Worn Baity[6] which blew itself out (*or did it*?!) only when she married Nubar 'Boom-Boom' Gemujian, the Texan steal magnate and Olympic deckathlete.[7] B.B.'s broken neck, after a trampoline tussle, at the hands – four or six, shall we ever really know? – of the Tarlo[8] triplets left Dolores a widow with a king's ransom in heirloom throw-rugs alone.

Later, we travel first-class behind the scenes (and into the flies) in swinging *and* roundabouting London, where Dolores inspired Barry Quint's[1] quantum leap into designer legend with the See-Through Dress That Never Was! We discover how she co-created *Cunnin'*, the best-smelling perfume, and where *exactly* Dolores was when slalom legend Matto Massimo[2] went through one gate too many, too fast at Kloucesters.[3] Oh and mush, mush more!

Lo and Behold is not for the blushful hypocrite. It is a story of success and failure, of ups and downs, of loves (and truly adorable puppy dogs) lost and found. Above all, we find out that, even if Dolores Hayes still looks like a woman a third her age, her one regret is that too many people called her sweetheart and no one ever yet called her Mom and meant it.

Katie Kite's In Person Preface

The traditional, see-through kind of ghosts clank chains as they re-enact the deaths of kings. I am a modern ghost who collects sexy stories of the lives of kinks. Other ghosts walk the bloody tower, their heads underneath their arms; Katie is happy to walk off with her subject's full-face profile, first taped, then typed.

I am not a ghost who hangs around in ruined choirs. I *much* prefer what Dolores Hayes offered, and abundantly: superb French Riviera hospitality topped with the *crème fraîche*[4] of total honesty! From the moment when her ornamental gates parted inwards, at the shy whisper of my name, to disclose heavenly bushes, plush gushes of bougainvillea ('Give me purple *and* red, I told them, and to hell with taste') and a curvaceous vista mounting, oh so sensuously, to a front door guarded with antique Grecian pillars – from the Temple of Venus, *s'il vous plaît*[5] – I knew that Miss Dolores Hayes was going to be one of this author's very special people. A villa like *Les Roches Roses*,[1] if its like there be with a God-knows-what-it-cost graded Carrara marble terrace overlooking a Mediterranean view which only the *most* blasé could overlook, provided the idyllic setting for memorable *al fresco* sessions that combined fascinating work with pure, pure one-on-one pleasure.

The public can always rely on my book to come richly truffled with a fat sliver of photographs. Thanks to its subject's unrivalled albums, *Lo and Behold!* will in no way disappoint them. They will not only enjoy the full-colour contrast of seeing today's baldies and biddies when they were yesteryear's baddies and buddies, but they can also revel in the unpublished – blue-noses will say unpublishable! – stills from the early, earthy, never publicly projected *Gee-Gee*.[2] Straight-laced equestrians may balk, but I am with Dolores: we both believe that we owe it to history to leave frolicking sweethearts unexpurgated. 'Let the chippies fall where they lay,' as Lo put it. 'After all, check out Botticello.'[3]

Yes, Dolores has lived an art-loving and sophisticated life, but never fear, all you who lose heart at the sight of a third syllable. If you – like me! – tend to reach for the remote at the hint of a foreign language, *calmez-vous!*[4] My breakfast serials are always edited to go down digestibly. Gals who live by syndication can be relied on for an unfancy prose style.

Before I slip into the more comfortable third person, I must go public on undying gratitude to my agent, Floyd ('Can I get back to you?') Austin. Plus, where would I have been without the literal fountain of information anent the superstar's Ramsdale schooldays supplied by Marguerite Byron (no relation of the poet,[5] she confesses, nor – alas! – of the quarterback![6])?

From her Palm Beach wheelchair, Louise Windmuller[7]

(finalist at Flashing Meadow, 1960 – oh that cruel, cruel net-cord at match point, Louise!) found time, and neck-braced courage, to remember Dolores the demon of the courts. She gave me her two-fisted, back-handed view of Dolly Hayes-Robillo's[1] disqualification at Sydney in 1961, which ended her tennis career in taboo-breaking and tearful controversy. What *really* happened later in the Gwen Fairplay Memorial Locker-room Complex? Like the trouper she is, Dolores swears that her racket flew out of her hand because of perspiration on the handle. Would she ever have deliberately fractured Louise's skull in as many as two places? The overly-publicised occasion, in Major Key, Fla. 81171, when she pushed over an umpire's chair was – Dolores swears again – completely inadvertent. The way she tells it, she tripped over her opponent's outstretched ankle as the gals changed ends. It was a pure, pure coincidence that both incidents involved 'that prize bitch Louise Windmuller'. There are two sides to every net, remember.

Thanks are due to the Humming Bird Animal Orphanage, in Little Zembla, Colo. 71635,[2] whose simply outstanding benefactress Dolores has been (up to 5% of the royalties from her best-loved hits with the group *Suck*[3] go directly to the Foundation). Irving Flashman,[4] the film critic who has been Philippines-based ever since he skipped bail on that controversial statutory rape charge (C-cupped Belle Ann[5] looked eighteen going on thirty-five and *promised* she was twice married), took me through every single out-take in the whole of Dolores' movie career, and assessed her very unique achievement in pithy detail. (Irv reiterated that Circuit Judge G. Rodias's[6] own personal life had a question mark or two to contend with, stretching back to 1956.) Oleg Sherva,[7] John Shade[8] Distinguished Professor Emeritus of Local Journalism in the University of Red Rock,[9] unzipped his unique collection

of press releases and also helped me, with rope and piton, to
surmount the pinnacle of the eponymous rock from which, by
a macabre coincidence, Dolores' third husband, two-time
studio head Harry 'Beat it' Carry, plunged to his tragic death,
when – by yet another coincidental twist of fate, of which
more anon – he was literally flattened into the macadam by the
(eight) wheels of a Get Lucky icecream truck. The usually slow
driver – Jehu Johnson, 32 – was rushing the Flavor of the
Week (Macadamia Raspberry Sensation, didn't it have to be?)
to a Get Lucky outlet right on campus. My investigation of
company records establishes that they were short of sugar cones
too, but that need not concern us directly here.

What can I say that he does not deserve to hear about Dr B.
Boyd,[1] who has devoted much of his life to clocking Dolores'
life, second by second, with awesome, adulatory accuracy? The
man is evidently nuts. I have likewise benefited from reminis-
cences, short and not so short, of working (and playing!) with
Dolores Hayes from fellow-stars Tony Quim, Greg 'Quick'
Puck, Worn Baity, Diane Kitten, Megan Rye, Sophie Mor-
ceau, Mob Bitchum, Jilly 'Hank' Collins and Dawn Patrol;[2] I
talked, often in spectacular homes where telephones never
stopped ringing, to directors Willy 'Ernst' Bilder, Manley
Dunnin, Ellen Peculiar, Jo-Ann Scheissinger and Clove 'Turkey' Dinner. To one and all, I send a big, big thank you; their
mistakes are, of course, all mine.

(Start checking on releases, clearances etc., Gusset, OK? –
K.K.)

LO AND BEHOLD!

Being the Life and Times of Dolores Hayes,
as told to Katie Kite

Beginning at the beginning is not that easy, because since when does anything start there? At what point did I truly begin to be – or think of myself as – Dolores Hayes? Mom always called me 'Lo', unless she called me other things. I was a pretty ordinary little girl, sometimes pretty, more often ornery. Either way, I was being something I wasn't *really*: I was always like *experimenting*, from as far back as I can remember. My life has been a search, lonelier than people can sometimes imagine, for an identity that is truly my size (my favourite cooturiers will tell you that I still bridle at a tight sleeve). Does that help explain why my closets are full of dresses and things I seldom wear more than once (no, *carissimo* Tonino, I am not being snitty about you)? Isn't an actress someone who feels happier and more comfortable being someone else? My semi-permanent, live-in self is only Dolores Hayes until some writer dreams me up a better part. Pencils out, scribes!

Small-town life in Ramsdale, Mass., during WW2, was safe and sweet and, to be honest, painfully painless! The only excitement was when some kid's dad got wounded or killed in the Pacific or someplace. You had to be nice to them then, even to Phyllis 'Crabs' Chatfield,[1] which stretched my patriotism gossamer thin. Then all of a sudden, I got lucky: *my* dad was killed. I cried and cried and everybody had to console me, so I acted crying some more.

Dad died on the selfsame beach in Italy where Miss Conti and I later made *Quattro Stagioni* (released Stateside as *Pizza*

Pie),[1] with Nessie Bedrave and Shag Daley.[2] The place had changed a lot since dad was pancaked by the falling flap of a landing-craft but it was sincerely an experience to be working in a dump where pop had been a hero. To go back to my childhood, mom was devastated all one evening by dad's passing. Dr Noah Backoff,[3] the incredible shrink to whom I owe so much, has a theory that I've been looking for a father ever since – someone to live up to and punish for my original dad leaving me without anyone to rebel against. As part of one analytic hour, Dr Backoff once read me this poem with the line 'I hate you, daddy' in it.[4] When he wanted my free associational reaction, I hoed and hummed.

Right in after mom became a widow she had to rent rooms. That was how come this French professor came to live with us. He called himself Humbert Humbert: ''um-*bare* 'um-*bare*,' he instructed me to say if I ever went to Paris and felt like it, which I subsequently have many times, staying in five-star hotels. Almost right away, *Le Professeur*[5] H. was crazy about my mom; and she was crazy about him. Was I maybe a little bit jealous? Hum was old in places, but he had major looks and he had travelled all over France, Italy and parts of Belgium. I also do rate chest hair, in moderation, on men.

I realise now that Humbert was certainly using me a little bit to make a good impression on mom, but he sure did take a lot of trouble. Candy bars, bedtime tales, expeditions to isolated beauty spots? All I had to do was sit in his lap and off we went. Thanks to Hum, mom – who seriously might have been a movie star herself, if she had had the brakes[6] – rediscovered herself as a beloved and a loving woman. Hum, as he asked me to call him (instead of, as I tended to, 'daddles'!), was very courtly. Ooh *là là*, did I get some French from him! *En effet*[7] and on reflection, I probably owe it to him I homed in on *Les Roches Roses*. His dad once owned a hotel right along the *côte* from here, which is where Hum had (or *very* nearly had) this first love, Annabel,[1] that he could never, never get out of his mind. My mom reminded him of her.

At first, Mom was reluctant to undertake a second marriage, but H.H. said it with flowers. Truth to tell, he said it with just about *tout le bazar*,[2] and finally she yielded. I used to lean over the banisters (one cutey-pie, bobby-soxed leg in the air!) to spy on them as he did his Sharle Bo-yeah. What was I? Eleven or twelve years old, but little Miss Flat-Top always imagined that it was her at the receiving end of his Parisian parleyvoo! Was my weaving fantasies that Hum loved *me* maybe the start of my learning curve as an actress? 200-an-hour Dr Backoff hints as much.

H.H. was decidedly patient – positively *heroic*, in retrospect! – in pandering to my girlish dreams that it was really little Lo he fancied. Dr Backoff, who I still visit sometimes (his professional insurance fortunately covered him for retirement to a sanatorium for terminally deluded witch-doctors in St Paul de Vence), vunce sug-*ch*ested that, in my particular case, 'hunger preceded appetite'. Could that be why I am permanently unsatisfied, even when, as I do, I have everything I could possibly want? That's my dear friend Sarah 'Gabby' Volumnia's[3] take on things. I can't deny that I have had my fair share of pleasure from unhappiness, but there could still be *someone* out there that I haven't had yet and who would possibly give me what I really yearn for. It could always be God. On the other hand, I go along with St Augustine[4] and I won't pretend I don't: chastity is great, but don't rush me.

I heard about saints, and sinners, from one of my sadly deceased friends here on the *côte*, the fabulous atheistic religious author, Grimm Gryn.[5] In spite of his success, bangers remained his favourite dish right to the end. I am only sorry he never

ALL HIS SONS

wrote one of his frightening movies for me. You could always rely on him to produce a big part for a woman. Why oh why did he never get that Nobel?

Am I digressing? Gallon Gallon,[1] the pro-life philosopher and rated poker player, once told me that life *is* a digression. Time flies but, apparently, it flies back and forth. I wasn't going to the mat with him even if we did happen to be in the gymnasium at Ramsdale U. We had both received *honoris causa* degrees. (Yes, I *am* entitled to be called *Doctor* Hayes, but forget house calls!) For reasons only loosely connected with time, I eventually told G.G.[2] to take a running jump, which he did, with incredible agility for an eighty-two-year-old Limey.[3] He vaulted right over the horse and succeeded in remaining rigid on landing. He told me he still felt eighteen years old. Then he died: his pacemaker couldn't keep up. He fell on top of me and knocked me out, which is how we were discovered, dead and alive respectively (luckily for me), by Dean Redkneck.[4] It looked as though we had been lovers, but – believe you me – *rigor mortis* is no fun to live with. My life has been undeniably glamorous, yet persistently dogged by tragedy.

My mom died not long after the start of what was, I am sure, her happier marriage. She and Hum tried so, so hard – I could hear them if I pressed my shell-like ear to my little bo-beep wallpaper – to give me a brother or sister, but when mom was tragically run over by Franz Franks,[5] a local plutokraut,[6] in his chauffeured limo, all that came to an end with a bump.

I guess I grew up overnight. It is not easy to admit, but for a while I dreamed that re-widowered Hum was really interested in waiting till he could marry *me*. I insisted to him that he think of himself, but he did everything he could to keep me feeling that I was his special girl. How shocked he would have been if he'd known what went through my little head sometimes!

Sadly but inevitably, however, I began to feel like a butterfly[1] in a gilded bird-cage and I had to spread my wings. I hope I wasn't ungrateful, but the bard was right, wasn't he? Youth's a stuff.[2]

Mom's death pretty well destroyed Hum's equilibrium. He missed his Char-Char so much that he drove me all over America looking for a replica. Sweet old guy, he pretended that he was doing it to widen my horizons, which he truly did. I saw and did things with him that regular pre-teens don't get to do until much, much later in their lives. Eventually, burgeoning womanhood got the better of me. Where the hormones, there moaned I (Worn's joke)! So Hum and I mutually agreed together I had to make the break and quit Requiem High, Mass. He paid from his own fortune to have me privately educated, but books were never my bag. I was already addicted to fan-zines (as we *never* called them in those drear dead Icinghour[3] days). I dreamed twice-nightly of being an extra who had a star or two pinned on her door.

Amateur dramatics was a way in, I thought, and so did Dick Schiller. That was how I came to get pregnant for the first and – as it turned out, to my eternal regret – only time. I was sixteen years old and by no means equipped spiritually for motherhood. That is the reason I decided – rightly or wrongly, I agree – to give Dick his liberty. He had made it all too clear that, although he continued to love me, several times a day, he had married me out of duty. That was why, when I was grieving in the hospital, I sent him that telegram saying that I was dead, like the baby, which was completely true in the baby's case. I have these narrow hips, which are great for jeans and certain couturiers, notably *carissimo* Bartolomeo, but less so for motherhood. I never remotely thought that dear Dick would write one more memorable ten-line sonnet[4] and then

plunge into the nearest fjord. Of *course* I still blame myself, but
at the time I was sure that he had gone cold on me. I only
found out that Dick had been iced for good when I thought I
needed to divorce him before I could marry Harry Carry[1] for
the first time.

Would I have realised my dream of an acting career, if I had
not started waiting table at *The Enchaunted Shunters*[2] motel,
Moses, Mo. 23747[3] which was built in and around an old
railroad depot? The *de luxe* cabanas consisted of antique
pullman cars, but – as Chuck, one of the cleaner cleaners, told
me with a chuckle – you could sure pull women[4] in them too.
One day, in my red cap and apron, I happened, entirely by
chance (*or was it*, after all?), to get to deliver the specialty
Chuff-Chuff breakfast – consisting of juice-of-your-choice,
cereal ditto, *three* eggs over easy, coffee, $8.99, plus side order
of well-done bacon ($1.99) to guess who: the one and only
Clare Quilty,[5] playwright and showman extraordinaire. Woo
woo, we went, on our steam-puffin' electric trolley. Once
upon another time, C.Q. had come in person to Ramsdale to
see me perform in *The Strange Mushroom*, one of his now classic
plays. What that man didn't do for young people! Right there
and then in the Chatternougat Chow Chow[6] car – clang, clang,
clang went the bell![7] – C.Q. offered me a scholarship in his
secluded Film and Dramatic Arts Academy. Thanks to him, I
caught up on a lot of things I had been missing.

That led to the very last time I saw old Hum, although I
never guessed it would be. He came with his adorable new
wife, Reeta,[8] to see me receive the Open Rose[9] Bowl for my
graduation performance as Alice in *A Christmas Carroll*.[10] As I
had feared, without necessarily saying anything, C.Q.'s production was way, way over most people's heads, including Hum's,
it seems. He went what proved, alas, to be lastingly dipsy-

doodle over what he took, quite unjustifiably, to be the maestro's liberties with the March Hare.[1] When it was all supposedly over, he came back with a water-pistol filled with red ink and tried to correct Mr Q. with it. They took him away in a straight-jacket to somewhere where he was much, much happier. He wrote what he swore was a book about his life and loves in America but which was, I am sorry to say, so totally obscene and untruthful that Judge G. Rodias – *encore lui*,[2] as they say – ordered it available only to pathologists.★ It is a sad thing to have to say, but poor old Hum–Hum could not stand to see me become a woman with a woman's needs and drives. He wanted me to stay innocent, but what is innocence?

In spite of the unalphabetic disorder which Hum created in the synopsis-library at C.Q. College, I visited him at least one time during his prolonged incarceration in what he described, unjustifiably, as his 'death cell' (in fact, he had twenty-four-hour TV available and repro Van Go[4] on the walls until he threw them at the staff). He had pretty well lost it by the time we saw each other. I was already married to Boom-Boom, and had had meliorative surgery, and all he could find to say was, 'Where oh where is my little girl?' He missed mom that much.

I sometimes wonder whether all the attention which Hum lavished on me, before he lost his marbles, hasn't got something to do with my planned adoption of an Italian orphan cabin-boy, who was literally washed up on the beach below *Les Roches Roses*, after a yachting mishap from which he was the sole survivor. Umberto Umberto[5] – yes, isn't it *weird* how these

---

★ I have tried with might and main, and even a hint of *habeas corpus*, to obtain access to the one extant transcription of Dr Humbert Humbert's so-called 'confession', but without any avail. It is rumoured that a Japanese scholar has hacked into the archive, but Professor I. Ku[3] answers my e-mail only with suggestions which would take me far from my preferred field. – K.K.

coincidences can haunt your life? – is the light of my life and I hope that I shall be able to teach him something, if not all, of what H.H. taught me all those years ago. Umberto is certainly a willing pupil and I am going to give him all the love he needs.

NOTES

Compiled by Dr Appels N. Pears, jr.

p.147

1 Word used by VN, a surrogate female sexual organ.

2 Pun on 'Better Books', an English bookshop run into the ground by a, so to speak, Merkin.

3 Term used for vulva used by VN, passim.

4 Term used by, *inter alias*, Edna O'Brien, Irish writer, for the female sexual organ.

5 Variant on 'Haze', Lolita's surname in the original novel.

p.148

1 Film star to whom Charlotte Haze is compared in *Lolita*.

2 Pretentious film *auteur* inclined to prolixity.

3 K.T. is both a pun on Katie and the initials of the dramatic critic Kenneth Tynan. There is a hint here that Katie Kite has taken a flyer and is, in some sense, a reincarnation of K. Tynan, having undergone a sex-change perhaps which enables him/her to get under the skin of 'Lolita'.

4 L. B. Mayer, whose company did *not* produce *To Kill a Mockingbird* to which *Hummingbird* may be a (far-fetched?) proleptic allusion.

5 Reference to 'The Epic That Never Was', the film version of *I, Claudius* (Robert Graves), scrapped by (later Sir) Alexander Korda.

6 A pun on Warren Beatty, an actor.

7 More usually 'decathlete' but suggesting Gemujian's yachting affectations.

8 Did they have something to thank 'Lo' for as in 'Ta, Lo.'?

p.149

1 Pun on Quant, Mary, 1960s dress designer in 'swinging' London.

2 Pun (Italian) on Mad Max, title of and name of the hero of a series of zany films. Max Black, the philosopher, beat VN at chess.

3 Variant spelling of Klosters, as if it chimed with Gloucesters.

4 French. Fresh cream.

5 French. Please.

p.150

1 French. Red Rocks. Reference to site of Humbert Humbert's father's hotel and also place visited by Lolita and Hum on their cross-America jaunts. Cf. also T. S. Eliot (not admired by VN, who refers somewhere to 'Mr Eliot, a Jewish businessman'): 'Red Rock'. Would it be far-fetched to mention *Blight on Lock*, a work of Grim Gryn in which a young Chinese cook finds true love, but fucks it?

2 Reference to the film *Gigi*, directed by Vincente Minelli, which won six Oscars and in which a 'nymphet', played by Leslie Caron, raised to be a cocotte finds true love. Memorable for the song, 'Thank Heaven for Little Girls', sung (vilely) by Maurice Chevalier.

3 Ignorant spelling of Botticelli, Italian Renaissance painter. Waspish reference to T. S. Eliot's women's talk of Michelangelo?

4 French. Calm yourselves.

5 George Gordon, Lord Byron (1788–1824).

6 The quarterback seems to be fictional.

7 See class list in VN's *Lolita*.

p.151

1 Robillo is evidently one of Dolores' (many?) unlisted husbands. His Italian name is proleptic of Lo's last (to date) love.

2 Typical pious reference, in VN's style, to Nabokov sr.'s '*lieu de prédilection*', mentioned also in *Ada* by VN.

3 A fictional pop group with whom DH apparently performed a number of more or less obscene routines, in concerts on and off the stage.

4 See class list in VN's *Lolita*.

5 Penetratingly prurient punning reference to Annabel, Humbert Humbert's first love. A C-cup suggests large (pre-post-pubescent) breasts.

6 Cf. Maurice Girodias, publisher of *Lolita*. His behaviour after 1956, when *Lolita* was published, was the subject of protracted criticism, abuse and irony on the part of VN.

7 See class list in VN's *Lolita*.

8 See VN's *Pale Fire*.

9 See *supra*.

p.152

1 Is this the egregiously sane Dr Boyd who became the bio-hagiographer of VN? Certainly not. *This* Boyd was never in New Zealand.

2 Playful references are apparently intended to Anthony Quinn, Gregory Peck (a notoriously slow speaker), Warren Beatty (a famous lover), Diane Keaton, Meg Ryan, Sophie Marceau (a French actress), Robert Mitchum, perhaps Joan/Jackie Collins and, again maybe, Dawn Addams, who led an adventurous life and appeared in Fellini's *La Dolce Vita*. 'Dawn patrol' is also a nautical term.

p.153

1 A classmate of Dolores Haze in *Lolita*. The reason for her soubriquet is, it seems, pure malicious caprice, suggesting that she suffered from a common sexual infestation.

p.154

1 A reference to *Mystic Pizza*, perhaps. A variant MS has a reference to 'Miss Conti' as the director. This is a robust reference to Lucchino Visconti, the famous director and Milanese nobleman, whose sexual preferences were high, wide and handsome.

2 Vanessa Redgrave was a great actress. It is not clear who is being targeted by 'Shag Daley'. There was a Hollywood actor called Dan Daily. Another actor, Keir Dullea, may be the target. It is said that Noël Coward said of him, 'Keir Dullea and gone tomorrow.'

3 A transparent punning allusion to Vladimir Nabokov.

4 The poem by Sylvia Plath is rather laboriously brought in, though the point has a certain relevance.

5 French. (The) Professor.

6 The suggestion in the pun is that Charlotte Haze could not stop herself from yielding to desire rather than career opportunity.

7 French. In effect.

p.155

1 See *Lolita*.

2 French. Lit. The whole bazaar. As we might say, 'with the whole repertoire'.

3 A sardonic reference, perhaps, to T. S. Eliot's Princess Volupine, as well as, obviously, to a garrulous 'Royal', whose wardrobe received wide publicity. VN was considerably interested in the private lives of Royals and wrote a squib, of arcane perspicuity, on the subject of the 'tragic' love of Princess Margaret and Peter Townsend.

4 Christian saint whose lucubrations on the subject of time and of chastity (and its breach) are matched by VN in *Ada* and elsewhere.

5 Graham Greene, Catholic novelist and erotomaniac, lived at Antibes for much of the later part of his life. He was the lover of a large number of women and failed to receive the Nobel Prize only, so he seems to have thought, because he had incurred the enmity of a member of the Swedish academy. At one point he had been the lover of Anita Björk, an actress who starred in a version of Strindberg's *Fröken Julie*. There is no evidence that this has anything to do with the case.

p.156

1 The 'Gee Gee' theme is pursued here, not only in the initials given to the 'English philosopher' but also in the horse over which he vaults to his death. There is an English philosopher with the improbable first name of Galen. He is of no relevance.

2 See note 4.

3 Disparaging term for an Englishman. Merited in this case.

4 'Red neck' is a standard American term for an ignorant peasant.

5 Possibly an allusion to Francis Francis, a rich property owner in the Bahamas during the 1950s.

6 A reckless and, perhaps, unworthy allusion to the rich man's origins, not applicable to Mr Francis.

p.157

1 A reminder of VN's interest in butterflies, though they cannot, of course, be contained in bird-cages.

2 A jest at the deconstructionist use of truncated or mutilated quotation. 'Youth's a stuff' is, of course, the opening phrase of a longer, less crude, assertion. It won't endure, we are promised.

3 A pun on Eisenhower, general and President of the USA (1952–60).

4 A sonnet has fourteen lines, but freedom has its own prosody.

p.158

1 The film studio head whom Dolores Hayes is said to have married twice. Perhaps a sanitised version of Harry Cohn, legendary head of Columbia Studios.

2 Cf. 'The Enchanted Hunters' motel at which Humbert Humbert first becomes aware of the haunting presence of Clare Quilty.

3 VN was much given to this kind of reiterative onomastic play.

4 'Pulling women' is an English expression for sexual conquest, suggesting that Chuck may have been an expatriate.

5 See *Lolita*, in which Humbert Humbert ends by imagining (?) that he shoots the playwright and pervert many times. In this text, Dolores Hayes seems unaware of the playwright's death and believes that Humbert Humbert fantasised the whole episode, and much else.

6 The Chatanooga choo-choo (train) was immortalised in the popular song which Glenn Miller played.

7 A reference to *Meet Me in St Louis* (the name figures elsewhere here) and also to the vulgar notion of orgasm as a ringing of a woman's bells. There is also, of course, a possible reference to 'pull the other one, it's got bells on it'. Chimes within chimes.

8 The woman with whom for a while, on his account, Humbert Humbert replaces the lost Lo is, of course, called *Rita* in *Lolita*.

9 As VN would know, '*ouvrir la rose*' is a 'technical' term for sodomy.

10 A VN-style 'confusion' of the Dickens novel, *A Christmas Carol*, with the author of *Alice in Wonderland*, of which *Lolita* is a discordant version. Lewis Carroll, in his unassumed personality as the Revd L. Dodgson, was alleged to be a dedicated, if pure, paedophile.

p.159

1 Character in *Alice*, presumably impersonated by C. Quilty in a gross or libidinous manner.

2 French. Him again. But notice the punning reference to 'Louis', as described above.

3 There is no evidence, from Japanese Faculty Lists, that this professor exists. He seems to be a play on I.Q. The odd status of 'Q' suggests a possible reference to a reincarnated Clare Quilty.

4 Vincent Van Gogh, painter, is sometimes pronounced in this way by Americans. The assumption is that any form of pronunciation favoured by our author's assumed compatriots is
amusingly inept.

5 Umberto Umberto is a playful recurrence of Humbert
Humbert in youthful guise.

Firenze. Browneis University. 1995/6

The Siren's Song

1942. 'One cannot always like the unfortunate.' The second secretary from the British Embassy, Gareth Whitebrook, whom Iakobos has been deputed to see, makes this remark as if it established something in common between them. Neutral tone, neutral ground; nothing personal; on we go then, you and I. They are on a quayside on the Bosphorus; two men allotted the same short straw. Iakobos frowns, as if the English language, not the messenger who speaks it, were what puzzled him. 'Nothing more H.M.G. can do.' Having done what? Official sentence is passed; full stop. I. nods in disagreement.

Kurds in peakless white caps hurry away with bulging cargoes, like sacked secrets, on tilted trolleys. Others tote loads on their backs, with alleviating straps over their foreheads. Servitude is a Kurdish monopoly here. Every nation has its burdensome burden-carriers. *Mutatis mutandis*, don't you agree? Young Whitebrook's problem is the unfortunates above them on the *Broda*; these – they *would* be, frankly – Jews; pilgrims who can move neither forward nor back, at least until pushed. So, what's to do?

For Captain Rubik, an Albanian Epirot, they are a cargo of stinking fish; not his first. He has asked Iakobos to deal with the authorities because he is clever, and handsome, and because

Rubik is sure that he will fail (and a captain must avoid failing himself). Gareth Whitebrook implies that some higher power is dictating to the otherwise sympathetic British (their record on kindness to animals is, after all second to none). A consideration not of London's making forbids them granting the Jews visas to Palestine. 'Unfortunately'. Iakobos explains what Whitebrook knows: Ankara will not allow the Jews to set foot on land unless they have the means to leave Turkey. Without transit visas to Palestine, they are stymied.

'You'll simply have to sail somewhere else,' the Englishman says. 'Unfortunately. Isn't whence-you-came a possibility?'

I. is Greek, from Thessaloniki. He has commercial English (and some Ladino); his father was chief clerk to a ship's chandler, for some time, in Liverpool; I. worked more recently for a Jew chandler in Thessaloniki, hence the Ladino and an almost furtive concern for the passengers. I. amuses Whitebrook with the pupil's frown that corrugates his forehead at the simplicity of the message which comes to him in the King's English. I.'s dark eyes, curly black hair (not *oiled*, is it?), pouty lips are not what an Englishman always likes, but the two of them have in common this burdensome company leaning along the rails of the *Broda*; more heavy shadows than men. Glance at the pleading, accusing, hooded, unblinking, damnably hopeful faces! Isn't the hope what irritates one most?

'We've got engine trouble. Bad. Worn pistons. No power.'

'Ah well, this is a port. They must have people for that.' Work for other people has to be good news; almost an exit line. Get out of jail free. We're never far from childhood.

'And we're heavily overloaded. In England, you would not allow us to sail.'

'Not in England though, are we? Hence . . .' an English pause.

'And in very bad repair. Rust. Rotten plates.'

'No less out of my province, unfortunately.' Meaning: must you? Allowing: 'Look here, I must be getting back. Black-tie nonsense tonight. Unfortunately.'

'Black tie?' The young man is corrugated again.

One can still be nice: 'Dinner-jacket affair. Embassy do. Wish I could have been more helpful.' And, thank God, that's about it. Is that the time already? A dozen things to do!

Of his uniform, Captain Rubik wears only the anchored cap; from the neck down, as if he had already begun to abandon ship, the canvas trousers and the cotton vest (which ventilates sour armpits) rehearse survivor's anonymity. The kit of *sauve qui peut*. Without looking at I., Rubik tilts a bottle of *raki* towards two squat, clouded glasses and asks to hear what he knows already: whether I. achieved anything. I. tells him '*Tipote*'; nothing. Rubik says, 'The British are not human; they cannot be bought. If the Turks make us sail – *when* they make us sail – what then?'

His first mate is young; I. has been hired to be young, and guileless, but he needs no beard to know that the ship's certificate of seaworthiness has been bought; Rubik's is the voice that says nothing and at the same time tells him what he does not want to hear: once at sea again, the Jews and any officers or crew who stay to help them are doomed. When the ship goes, it will go – pouf! – like that. The facts shout; therefore, nothing needs to be said. Iakobos knows that his duty, and the Captain's, is to the passengers; that is why, in the circumstances, both men hate the Jews. Between the impossible and the immoral, man chooses freely. Rubik means to survive; and will. Iakobos can; and . . . ? This is a cargo ship; one does not die for one's cargo. 'If we are forced to sail, we are forced to think of ourselves,' the Captain says, as if such a thought were unusual with him.

'Why not tell the Turks that the ship is unseaworthy?'

'Never force people to hear things they know already.'

'We could sink her here. It wouldn't take much.'

Rubik looks at Iakobos as if his presence were now uninvited. 'Sabotage? I am the Captain. Think of the future. My owners tell me to sail, I sail.' Servility doubles as authority; callousness is dignity. Another glass? Sweet to refuse, when refusal carries no sanction.

The ship will sail and the ship will sink and the Captain instructs I.: Be ready with the lifeboat, the only seaworthy lifeboat, when the moment comes. Be glad that orders are orders: others must not get into it. Rubik is saving himself by saving I., and I. by saving himself. Discipline before morals. Unfortunately? Gareth Whitebrook's adverb has taken root in I.'s mind. Unfortunately, the ship is both unseaworthy and insured; and because she is not fit to sail, she will sail. Insurance is immortal; it cannot sink, has no location; it has pure being. It precedes (and defines) all acts of God.

The cargo is several hundred and some filthy stinking Jews who shit and piss and vomit and want food and water, water. In charge of them are four Zionists from the organisation which has chartered the ship; three dangerous men, and a woman (Irina), not underfed, not passive. They show their contempt for Rubik, and for the crew and – with different eyes – for the refugees they have to escort to Eretz Israel, *tant bien que mal* (Irina is Russo-French). Their suspicion angers and alarms the Captain. It also warrants premeditation; to survive, with honour, he cannot have witnesses to his survival. The Jews are dead or he is. He is Captain enough not to share his thoughts with I.; I. is cursed with his kindness.

I. is twenty-two years old, a sailor since he was fifteen. He is ambitious and without connections; there are no easy ladders for him. He will do what Rubik asks, and plans. As time passes, the inevitable fattens like a rat in the rancid, trickling innards of the *Broda*. There is strength, of a kind, in swallowing filth, in living in it, in learning to tolerate, digest, ignore it: degrading exaltation. It makes I. a man, or will, if all goes badly.

Rubik's confidence in I. flatters and disgusts the young man; the disgust lies in feeling flattered. Rubik's favours are reeking kisses which I. does not refuse; his whispered schemes are the siren's song which promises I. hateful salvation. Unfortunately.

Gareth Whitebrook has a double-ended black tie and it is a bastard to tie; his chin is high and his eyes are painfully lowered in order to see the knot. We all have our problems. Unfortunately.

The *Broda* cannot stay and she cannot go. The Turks fear what it is their convenient right to fear: typhus, cholera, dysentry. Providential bacillic trinity. The British have made their decision and hold to it as if it were not theirs; that is what British decisions are like (sorry about that). The owners insist that the ship must sail; to prove it, they can send no money for repairs. The Turks stand on the quay and look at the rust and do not see the problem. The Jews look down at the Turks, as if from below them.

A wide, flat tug sidles in; its cable cheeses the brothy water, tautens, sings. *Mehmet II* is sent to tow the powerless *Broda* into the Bosphorus, under the Anatolian breasts and pricking minarets of the mosques, past the little cathedral, low to the water; its cross is all there is to be seen of the city's Christian past. Two Lascars have jumped ship. I. remains; buoyed by the sombre levity that says, 'I am not only here; I am also ahead of myself; I see myself surviving.'

The Lebanese engineer has managed to make some mechanical noise come from below decks. A parody of power screws the *Broda*'s slow wake into sour green soup. The Zionists come to Rubik's cabin and say that if the ship re-enters the mouth of the Danube, they will kill him. In case he has any doubts. Their threats make cowardice wisdom.

When the ship is torpedoed, or hits wreckage, it splits soggily, soundlessly, like a paper bag full of water. A dud torpedo would explain it. The night is not rough; the indifferent sea shrugs and the *Broda* collapses. Soft coffin, it is swallowed in a single gulp. Already in the lifeboat, the Captain and the first mate are proved right; the Captain has saved Iakobos's life, and may be forgiven. The Jews are drowned. This is the Black Sea, not the Red. That is Ararat, where the stars are not.

1946. Piraeus. Iakobos has been in Egypt for almost four years. He is a medalled lieutenant in the Greek navy, a freshly risen sun in his glaring whites. He is a subsidised conqueror; part of what he has conquered – trust the British! – is his Greekness. He brings concocted freedom to his country. There are kinds of gratitude which enslave the grateful and embitter the benefactor. I. wishes he were less popular; it would make his compatriots less foreign to him. The unheroic hands that slap and caress him – '*Mprabo, mprabo!*' – also pick the pockets of his soul.

'Iakobos!' It is Rubik. Iakobos, laundered and creased like an

Englishman, frowns at his old (younger!) Captain with the fearful relief of a man recognised for what he is. Rubik too is disguised by valiant achievement; he has been the master of two tankers: the Persian Gulf to Suez, Suez to Sicily, Napoli, Genova, that has been his beat, with how many thousand tons of oil? He lost one ship in the Med, but saved his crew. Hero greets hero; liar, liar. Rubik is on his way to see old Tachmindji, the bastard. Coming? Iakobos declines, and goes along.

The long, file-filled upstairs offices are not changed. Look! The same old upright telephones, black daffodils. Here it is before the war; out there it is after. The dark ditch can be straddled at will. Tachmindji – has he suffered some kind of a stroke? – might have been happy never to see the two survivors again, but he is happier to welcome two hands which can haul him safely into the future. Iakobos has a good name with the British, Rubik has connections in the Gulf. Therefore: '*Kalos irthate!*' Welcoming Tachmindji has tears in his cold old eyes – where's that big silk handkerchief? – as nervous urgency rolls back the slatted top of his rosewood desk. He rocks the cork from a special bottle he kept for today, or tomorrow. On the narrow ledge above the desk is a silver-framed photograph. The old man (fifty-eight!) passes it to Iakobos: 'You remember Irine?' Peace with the face of a beautiful girl.

She is amused to be docile. She has a face like an Egyptian; the want of smile is a kind of humour. She is amused, and does not laugh; yielding, she does not give in. There is, Iakobos knows, and wishes he loved, something in her which he can never know and which can never love him. There is comfort in their incompleteness; it prompts desire which is manly, but cannot relax to affection. When they are married, and they soon are, Iakobos is armed by the submissiveness in both of them: Irine gives herself to a stranger; the stranger gives himself to her father. Their facsimile of passion is more passionate, more reckless (in secret), than passion itself. It almost makes them like each other; it almost generates love. They are Greeks; they understand what it is to be what they can never be. The past is no good to them. They dignify each other with the rigour of their falseness; if they could speak frankly, if they dared to love truly, they would teach each other contempt for their cowardices. Fraud rings truer than truth.

Irine's father becomes Minister of Marine for long enough to give certain favours; it is more important, he tells Iakobos, to distribute favours when you are powerful than to collect them. It is not only more blessed to give than to receive; in the long run, it is also more profitable, *pethimoo*. There is no better use for bread than to cast it on the waters. Jesus was a Jew, my boy; we are all alike, Jews, Greeks, Arabs, Turks, but very few of us are lucky. You need not believe in God, but never make the mistake of not thanking Him.

The Minister has a black labrador called Dick and another called Rover. He takes them, and Irine and Iakobos, to the island where he was born. It is a white bone wedged in the mouth of the sea. Solon spoke contemptuously of its poverty two-and-a-half millennia ago. The people call the Minister 'master'; they are still poor.

Iakobos buys surplus ships (some he scraps, some he scrapes). 1954. The old man *says* he wants only to build a retirement house on the heights above his birthplace. By volunteering to be older than he is, he secretes a little of his youth. He would like to make his island prosperous: a marina perhaps, where the English can come; not the Germans. Iakobos will take care of the business, and Irine. The Old Man (in his sixties!) plays at philosophy, but – for fun, for fun – likes to hear what deals Iakobos is doing, how he sees the future, what he hears. Iakobos is glad to tell him; it is in the telling that what he is doing takes on its meaning and plots its purpose. Fancy creates fact; the wet finger makes the wind, as the fishermen say on the island.

Thanks to the Old Man, something magic, powerful, almost noble, is fostered and grows in Iakobos. He is a visionary. Greed becomes superfluous; because he thinks clearly, because he reasons with superstitious accuracy and observant cunning, his head becomes clear, and as purely speculative as a saint's. Because he has no illusions about men or about himself, he can read the world as if its future were available to him in the facile text of a child's book. Contempt and respect cannot, need not, be distinguished; he sees Arabs and Jews, French and English, Americans and Persians as ciphers in a symbolic language which is void of prejudice: no one he meets or thinks about is required to bear the burden of being liked or trusted. Iakobos's attentions, public and private, have the diligence of a lover unembarrassed by emotions. He and Irine have a son, and another, and a daughter. Captain, later Commodore, Rubik commands a fleet of – according to the annual reports of an increasing number of companies, including one based in Liberia – twelve, eighteen, thirty-one, sixty-eight, ships. Then there are the planes.

1957. After Suez, Tachmindji and son-in-law are so rich that greed becomes an art, an exercise. Every disaster is someone's good luck, *pethimoo*. As if Iakobos didn't know, and had not already laid down keels in Japan for ships that would not, could not, use the canal! He has arranged their insurance too. All is for the best in the worst of all possible circumstances.

Iakobos's ruthlessness extends to his generosity. His kindness is as implacable as his acquisitiveness. It is as if, in both cases, the same piety is at work; fear and nerve, dread and hope, friendship and enmity. He prefers to do good by stealth; perhaps stealth excites him more than the good it does. He slides money towards good causes as if to corrupt them. The Old Man's island has a dredged harbour, a jetty for the ferry service; it has its marina, water supply, hospital, doctor. In due course, ruinous riches. These things, done by Iakobos, are credited to the Old Man.

1974. Iakobos's reticence is his fame; men have learned that to whisper of a misfortune in his presence is to be reminded that it is unlikely, very, that he can do anything about it. They are happy to be told this, since something will now be done. Iakobos makes no promises, and keeps them all.

Why? Rubik, the only man who might, never asks. The Commodore's irreplaceable silence jeers at the man who now governs a fortune which makes him a citizen of the world. Public orators have said as much in a dozen universities where he has been capped and gowned a doctor (having been benefactor). He has so many interests that he finds, at times (intriguingly in 1979, in London and Bombay), that he conspires against himself. His manifold balance sheets reveal that he sometimes registers successes in one of his companies by ruining another. He insures himself; he sinks himself; he is richer than he knows and still picks his own pockets.

To his fellow citizens, he is like Demetrios the Besieger, to whom the sceptical Athenians had no doubt that they should build an altar; more benefits stemmed from him than from the gods. All those he wounds go to his hospitals.

Iakobos is a benefactor who finds it salutary to remain a

bastard (a man must not allow his reputation to decline). He is grateful to his enemies for frustrating him; a prized poet tells him of Polykrates the tyrant, who threw a gold ring into the Samian Sea in order to avoid having everything he wanted, which – he had been warned – would excite the jealousy of the gods. When a fisherman recovered the ring in the belly of one of his catch and brought it back to the tyrant, Polykrates knew that his days were numbered. Iakobos throws gold where it cannot be known to be his.

1980. The Mediterranean is his pond; he sails his yacht, *Ithaka*, in it. He has many friends in the Gulf, he said, and he also gives money, in great secrecy, for the rebuilding of a synagogue in Thessaloniki. There remain very few Jews to go to it. How many speak Ladino now? When Irine says to him, 'You are a good man, *Iakobemoo*,' he replies, 'You too are among my accusers?'

'Am I a whore?' she says. 'After all you have done for me, how can I defend you?'

Next to them, all their lives, are the unused ghosts of the couple they might have been. As it is, their cruel sons are playboys; their distant daughter has been twice married at nineteen.

1986. Iakobos's official biography comes as a present from his Board. Once commissioned and furnished with all the facts, the biographer grows impatient with his own venality; impatience warrants impenitence. Treachery becomes a symptom of pride; he cleans his hands with dirt. As Gareth Whitebrook's late ambassador discovered, soon after the *Broda* went soundlessly to the bottom, if one cannot trust one's servants to betray one, whom can one trust? The biographer's name is Leo 'Ratters' Ratcliffe. He is blind.

'Ratters' is a blind man who sees. But sight, with him, is an inquisitive faculty: he asks many questions, takes many notes, and colours vivid prose with his informants' colours. He is authorised to 'see' the records of all the companies. Rubik, now younger and more eager than Iakobos (who has fattened on his rivals), is deputed to be his eyes. 'Ratters' scans the darkness which is his element and he sees Rubik and Iakobos like living print on the sable pages of his intuition. Rubik learns resentment late; his devotion to Iakobos curdles. Yellow with his own iniquity, he wishes it on the man who, having been for so long his master, he elects its originator. 'Ratters' reminds him of his captaincy, and the reminder notches new barbs in Rubik's hidden blade. Iakobos's favours have docked him of command of his own life. Having been given so much, he believes he must have been cheated of more; Tachmindji meant him to be the dauphin, who has become the major domo. 'Ratters' doubts all this, and fosters it by doubting.

Does Iakobos suffer from 'Ratters''s tactful inquisition? In the creaking saloon of the *Ithaka*, he submits – with a heavy sigh from the heavy man he is today – to the preliminary sizzle of the tape recorder. When the question is put – did he ever think he might have acted differently? – he looks at the dodging eyes of the blind man and makes, maybe, a franker face (crueller *and* gentler) than might be expected. It is as if, but only as if, he believed that 'Ratters' was *pretending* to be blind, just as he has pretended, no less successfully, to be invulnerable. 'Life,' he says (and the cultured voice resembles Lord White-brook's, his man in London), 'is like a game of simultaneous chess in which one sees a dozen and more games unfolding from the original position and in which one is allowed to play on only one board. Unfortunately.'

'Ratters''s eyes float here and there, twitching with greater mobility than sight could endure. He seems excited, unless he is embarrassed. 'The *Broda*,' he says. 'Tell me about that.'

'I was young,' Iakobos says, 'and I did what I was told.'

'For the last time?'

'I think not. I am after all, a very obedient person. I even answer your question! Cigar? My whole life, to be honest with you, has been a matter of question and answer. It has not, I sometimes think, greatly concerned *me* at all. And in this – I know I am not answering your question, but – in this, I am very much, despite appearances?, a Greek. We have many faults, many; but *egotism* is not one of them, in the sense – forgive me – that 'I' has no great meaning for me, or for us; I am part of something else and I have no notion that I *personally* have created anything, least of all the wealth which, believe me, is enjoyable only because it is not mine. We bring nothing into this world; we shall take nothing out; all that is commonplace with you, but let me add this: we also have nothing while we are here. Nothing truly ours. Odysseus said he was nobody; Odysseus was right, but how can nobody be right? I am accused of generosity, but I have no more feeling that I am generous than I do of being a tyrant, of which I am also accused.'

'The *Broda*,' 'Ratters' says.

'Philip told you what?'

'That you met on board.'

'They wanted us to die; you know who. We survived. I *think* we survived.'

'Forgive me; I must put in another tape.' The blind man's fingers see to it.

'You've done a lot of talking.'

'Listening,' the biographer says.

'I wanted to sink her,' Iakobos says, before the tape can work again. 'I wanted never to be what I have become. But it was not my decision. As for who I am now, I have no idea who he is.'

'I'm sorry,' 'Ratters' says, 'I think I missed that.'

October 16th. 0145 hours. Cruising off Samos. Rubik comes into the saloon where Iakobos is on the line to invaluable Whiters in New York. Half-sitting, half-lying on the long cushions, he raises his dark brows (does he dye them?) at Rubik, who will not be warned. The Commodore goes to the chiming drinks cupboard and helps himself, as if it were a liberty.

The biographer is sleeved in his long darkness. He sits on the rubbered companionway that comes up, and goes down, to his stateroom and he is, as he listens, in a great space, memory's cave, a boundless place, before and after life, in which the future can be remembered as well as the past. He hears the burble of reproach and reminiscence, of accusation and amusement, and he sees what he hears as black on black. Iakobos and Rubik are alone in the creaking saloon, Greek and Greek; the slur of their contest comes, untranslated music, to the listener. The great man (whose corpulence now lends credibility to his fortune) moves little and yet seems to agitate Rubik, as if, in his case, *pushing* on the strings could dance his puppet. His voice leans back on the cushions and denies Rubik the comfort of dismaying him. Should he be provoked? He prefers to be amused.

Should he rebut the charges? He confirms them: cowardice, of course; cruelty, no doubt; duplicity, what else? He denies only that he is good. He is beyond that. 'Ratters' sees the smile through the closed door and smiles too. When Rubik says 'Cheat', it is in the words of the poet who called the moon a cheat for cadging the sun's light.

The nation of the moon brings Iakobos to his feet. His bladder takes him out to see it. No mountain kills the sky. There are, the Greeks said, as many souls as there are stars, and no more. Our souls are not our own; the soul has me; I do not have it. Is Iakobos drunk when he lurches to the rail and, with a vulgarity not usual with him, unbuttons? Rubik has no prospect of the inheritance; he cannot – can he? – imagine, at his age, that the dauphinate might still be his. Yet, with a smudged movement, he blunders against the pissing potentate and, as if by mistake, nudges him through the rail and into the soft Ionian Sea. The engines throb; *Ithaka* is an island that does not stop.

Iakobos is himself now. He feels hands reaching up to him from below. He hears the siren's song in his ears. The water closes its shutters on him and in his helplessness he is, at last, at home.

Rubik watches and waits. The perfect crime has been an accident. He hears the saloon door stub against its stop, and turns and . . . 'Help!' The blind biographer has seen it all. Unfortunately.

Son of Enoch

'You must have been up at Cambridge with Methuselah Soames,' people say to me, even in the depths of the Périgord. They are often retired professional people with very nice intentions and, in not a few cases, dark blue Volvos. If I am in yielding mood, I own the soft impeachment: I may have been (all right, I *was*) at the same college as Methuselah, but he always moved in a different, smarter, more exalted, Apostolic world than I. True, for one bright season we trod the West End boards together in a wickedly impertinent undergraduate revue. But even then, he was the unmistakable comet; the rest of us were but a train of concomitant dross, sparkling with reflected glory.

Witless watchers, who saw no further than the ends of their own ambitions, were sure that Methuselah would soon be assumed as a fixed star in the artistic firmament. How could they fail to see that he had the makings of a constellation? No wise man, however, could say, or dared to predict, in what illustrious form he would choose ultimately to reveal himself. In the chaste 1950s, no throne seemed quite ample enough. Literary editor? Chief producer (Talks)? Curator of the National Gallery? Brains Truster? Professor, but of what, and – in those narrow days – where? The University of East Anglia, the National Theatre, and Channel 4 had yet to be invented, though we did already have the wheel.

Methuselah had so many gifts, such prehensile insights, such oscillating purposes, that his genius lay precisely in his lack of precison. 'The centre of certain circles,' I once heard him lecture a Nobel Prize-winner, 'lies in a variety of places on their circumference.' Parody and paradox marched in step for him. From time to time, they twinkled into skittish dance. An intellectual Fred'n'Ginger, Methuselah's solos could also be *pas de deux*.

He was reluctant to declare whether it was literature, the stage (ballet, opera, drama, *tutti assiemi*?), the epic mural, the lecture room, film (forget crass movies) or the imminent world of mass media that he would make entirely his own. His modesty was the result neither of doubt nor of indecision. Should, could one ask a chameleon to come out in his true colours? Methuselah's quotidian appearance declared his versatility. The jeans, top and bottom, owned allegiance to Bohemia; the bare feet remembered the plight of the *sans chaussures*; the raven curls indicated that the Great God Pan was *redivivus*; his stammer – Methuselah had so much of significance to say that words jostled, and sometimes jammed, in the only exit available to them – argued for freedom of speech in the tones of an erudition which he never for one moment concealed or abated. His eloquent hands made distinct Wittgensteinian boxes for the sentiments his lips delivered wholesale.

Methuselah's father, he let it be rumoured, had gone to the devil as a young man but had returned, as the result of who knows what negotiated resurrection, to practise, briefly, at the Bar to which it was his only son's pious promise to be called. It was possible that our most brilliant contemporary would jilt the Muses to sit literally in judgement over the rest of us.

By the time that we were both down from Cambridge and I was writing novels in a basement in Chelsea, our roads were already divergent; his high, mine low. Methuselah's precociousness was as smartly applauded as his father's, in his *fin-de-siècle* day, had been notoriously scorned. But if revenge was sweet, it was by no means to be his main course. Still in his early twenties, Methuselah devilled by day, for a plump QC in the chancy Chancery Division. By night, however, he often dined, candle-lit, with a scandal-lit princess who, the toadies croaked, solicited from him an insolence of style which would have led her to banish another, instantly, from her table. When he told her not to inter-ter-terrupt, she put her gloved hand to her mouth as if it were she who had been guilty of *lèse-majesté*. Who has not heard the story that when she proposed marriage, he told her that she was beneath him? Some even say that, at the time, it was literally true. Such is the state of our journalism that these things are both reported and believed.

Methuselah's brilliance flashed like a short circuit in the Inns of Court. Long before he had eaten enough stodgy dinners to be called (his brilliant diary denied him time to eat frequently in dusty company), he was the talk of the Bar. His master, Brinsley Banks, who had never been in the first rustle of silks, was suddenly winning more cases than he lost. As Methuselah's diligence informed Banks's arguments and the prodigy's marginal glosses embellished his oratory, B.B. began to speak of himself – his favourite topic – as a future Lord Chief.

The precocious Methuselah's renown in mid-century London was so great as to be stultifying. Already the rest of us knew that we could contend only for second place in the history of our generation. Even Noël Annan had to concede that there was a boyish intellect younger than he was. Is it shameful to admit that I wished that Methuselah would soon take his Finals and devote himself exclusively to The Law? It was comfortable, if cowardly, to imagine his genius modernising British justice rather than bestriding the narrow world of the arts where he would throw the rest of us into permanent shadow.

Meanwhile the merest rumour of his latest apophthegm – he was extremely apophthegmatic – provoked adulatory apprehension in the pubs, green-rooms and tiled places where the Arts were venerated and cabals conferred. Admiration and dread were indistinguishable: every devotee of every Muse waited to be outstripped, ridiculed, Methuselah'd. We were not yet at the *fin de siècle*, but the odour of *fin de régime* hung muskily over all our endeavours.

At five o'clock one afternoon, I was amazed, and flattered, when our liquorice-black telephone rang and I heard 'M-m-m-Methuselah here.'

He wondered if we could meet.

'Why not?' I said. 'We're far from parallel lines.' My facetiousness was a callow symptom of a sense of election at hearing from so bright and so distant a star.

'P-parallel lines,' he said, 'meet frequently, at Sh-sh-Schmidt's. Sh-sh-shall we do the same?'

His smallest trumps won tricks.

Schmidt's was a Viennese-style lunch place, in Charlotte Street, where young publishers fed angry young men at three-and-sixpence a head. It was tactful of Methuselah, I thought, to choose somewhere within my means. The purpose of our meeting was not, at first, evident; over his *Nachwurst*, he told me that he had had an invitation to go to Germany, where the Arts were properly appreciated, and funded. He had been asked to stage the *Ring* cycle, *as a musical*, in a Brechtian decor recalling Albert Speer, Leni Riefenstahl and the Bauhaus.

'Eclectic of you,' I said.

'Eclectic is what one chooses to make it,' he said. 'You've written a novel, am I right?'

'I've written two,' I said. It sounded like a confession of failure.

'I mean to write one,' he said. It sounded like a promise of triumph.

'What about?' I said. Damn him, I was already in a posture of deference.

'*About?* You're joking.'

'Am I? Monsieur Jourdain and I.'

'What is the only thing worth doing today?' Methuselah said.

'Ah!' I said.

'Precisely.'

'And you mean to do it?'

'Or not to do it,' Methuselah said. 'Or *not* to do it.'

'Two possibilities there,' I said. 'Not counting their synthesis.'

'You know your trouble?' he said. 'Hope.'

'Ah,' I said. 'Of course. In what sense?'

'You hope for . . . promotion. I don't.'

'You can't go much higher,' I said, 'can you? Without encountering respiratory difficulties.'

'*I* have no desire to please *anyone*,' he said. 'One either creates a masterpiece or . . . one does not belong to the Arts.'

'Cyril Connolly,' I said.

'Yesterday's man,' he said. 'Tr-tr-transcendence or n-n-nothing. What is a novel exactly? Can you tell me?'

'How about a mark on the condemned cell wall?'

His unamused snarl poured pity on me, pitilessly. 'A dead form,' he said. 'Which must be brought to life or left to rot. But how?'

'Do I have guesses?'

'By not *writing* it,' he said. 'By *not* writing it.'

'Ah,' I said. It was becoming a sort of verbal hiccup. I sipped some water. And then, in the light of his silence, I went and did it again. 'Ah.' Blast it.

'By having done what has not yet been done, and can never be.'

'You've evidently cracked it,' I said. 'It remains only not to do it.'

'The age of the primary text is past,' he said, leaping decades ahead of contemporary thought. 'I mean to be the first novelist of – no, *under* – the meta-text. Subjacence is all. I am going to be the author of . . . presumably you've guessed. An unwritten masterpiece. Not *unknown*, *c'est déjà fait, ça*! – you may even have done it yourself, because who can't? – but a masterpiece which cannot ever be criticised, cannot be outmoded, cannot lose its *élan* because it exists, in full, only in the creator's mind and there as a *variorum* edition of limitless layers. Immune from readers, it will never age, can never be copied, never *conceivably* disclose its *richesses recherchées*.'

'God!'

'In a word. Only in this way can the artist be emancipated from criticism and abide forever above, below, and all round those who seek to decrypt him. There will not be even a vestige of my work in the vulgar, linear mode. As an author, I shall be to literature what reality is to appearance, what white is to the spectrum, say.'

'What white is to the spectrum.'

'You're right. They will guess, and may even carp, as we do

at Creation, without being able to say how it was done or what its complexities are. I shall escape exegesis, though not – of course – envy.'

'Of course not,' I said. Look, I was already envious myself.

'I am going to be, to embody, my own creation; the man and the work are one. *Natura naturans*.'

'*Nicht war?*' I said. One did at Schmidt's.

'As your own harmless novels reveal . . .'

Ah, the stiletto of friendly candour, how it pierces!

'. . . there is no printed narrative that has not been bettered, no grubby trail of linear print that can *ever* be wholly free of the second-hand, as great art must. We live in a time of obese satieties, of systematic superfluities, in which every form has been thoroughly used, and abused. Besides, we have more m-m-masterpieces than diligence can scan or f-f-f-fingers count.'

'Leaving us where?' I said.

'Apogee and nadir,' he said. '*Ars est necare artem.*'

'Art is at its end, you mean?'

'Nothing has not been done,' he said. 'And that is what I mean to do.'

Before I could gasp, let alone suggest that we split the bill, he had slipped away silently on those famous bare feet. As I walked home, empty-pocketed, to our Chelsea basement, I wondered why I had been honoured with Methuselah's confidence; he could as well have declared himself to Noël or Peter or Isaiah or the other, famous, Freddie. All were his familiars. I came to the humiliating realisation that he had chosen me as *the* witness to his unique project because I had just enough wit to understand his genius and not enough nerve to emulate it.

If I imagined, with silly sentimentality, that Methuselah might, from time to time, or decade to decade, renew contact with me, I underrated his economy of style. His absence from my life *was* the contact he had with me. Damn him to hell, he knew it. As my hair greyed and began to fall, I was always more conscious of what Methuselah had *not* done than even of the overt achievements of our epoch which dwarfed me daily as prizes fell, like leaves in Vallombrosa, first on my contemporaries and then on my juniors. As I soldiered on in my own unlaurelled way, I was all the while aware of the *miglior fabbro* who was doing *nothing* and would never be forgotten for it.

Methuselah had taken his Bar finals, and with the greatest possible distinction, but he neither practised nor pleaded. It was said that he sometimes consented to play the part of Mycroft Holmes and, without stirring from his, or another's, bed would offer speculative advice which trumped the pundits. One scorching parenthesis turned the Master of the Rolls into toast for a whole smouldering weekend. Of course, Methuselah did other things – an opera, a motor-cycle manual, a philosophical pop-up book which, controversially, featured Lady Ottoline Morrell – but I knew that what he was *not* doing was what he was really doing. His novel, I imagined, was growing, thickening, coiling on itself, inside the head which bore its secret, ramified, impacted, unpublished volumes.

For some reason, I kept the secret of Methuselah's endeavours, less from a sense of honour than because I liked to think that it preserved a link between us. Cf. Lear and his fool!

Two-thirds of a lifetime went by and then, one day, earlier this year, the fax began to susurrate and a white tongue of curling paper came stammering into my hand. The complete text read: 'Come to the Reading Room, the British Museum, June 3rd, 1997, 3 p.m. to meet my father – Methuselah.'

What could be more typical than for summons and invitation to be one? I told myself that I should not go; and went. I confess that I am a London Library man myself; the BM Reading Room baffles and intimidates me. I was not sure whether it was where it had always been, wherever that was, or somewhere else, wherever that might be. I will not embarrass the reader with the tale of panicky traipses past mummy cases and filched grey marbles. I walked; I ran; I resigned; I panicked; finally my dishevelled appearance won my entrance to the domed edifice where Methuselah was waiting in fretful tolerance.

'You've missed him,' he said.

'It's only eight minutes past,' I said. 'You didn't stipulate punctuality.'

'He could only stay a minute.'

'He must be very old,' I said.

'Longevity is something one has to live with,' Methuselah said.

'Why did you want me to meet your father?' I said.

'I didn't,' Methuselah said, 'particularly. He liked something you did. I can't remember what exactly. He's slightly gaga these days.'

'We're none of us getting any younger,' I said. 'You're not getting any older either, by the look of you, but shouldn't you think of, well, putting down a marker?'

'Meaning what?'

'The novel,' I said. 'Isn't your head a rather fragile receptacle for it?'

'You have understood *nothing*,' he said.

'And it takes some doing,' I said. 'Your father wasn't really here, was he?'

'I'm going to bring something out,' he said. 'In the form of an *avant-propos*. On the stroke of the millennium. You've written how many novels now?'

'*Avant-propos* be damned,' I said. 'At least my books exist.'

'At *most*,' he said. 'Where, do you suppose, will you rate in the literary histories of a century from now?'

'There won't be any,' I said. 'There will only be video games.'

'Life *is* a video game,' he said. 'Come with me. I want to show you something.'

'Not the cities of the plain by any chance?'

'Your references are no longer taken, you know; what you think of as allusive wit is a frantic tug at a bell that no longer rings. That's why . . . Come with me.'

He led me out of the crepuscular light of the Reading Room through a door labelled ABSOLUTELY NO ENTRY. We went into a sheeted lobby, where who knows what furtive treasures awaited reclamation by aggrieved parties, and up a flight of narrow, bright steps. It was as if some furnace glowered down at us. I winced at its heat, but Methuselah skipped ahead in panic glee until we reached an upper gallery, gleamingly pristine, and came to a door labelled THE FUTURE. Methuselah had the key, God knows how, and in we went. The huge room contained neither stacks nor catalogues. There were no stalls for scholars but little booths, with screens.

I looked for buttons or knobs or unintelligible instructions, but there were none. Methuselah walked up to a screen and, with his usual consummate confidence, merely said, 'June 3rd 2097, gissit.'

There was a rustling noise and then the word 'Deal' appeared in front of us.

'Literature. Methuselah Soames. Gissit.'

The same brief rustling followed and there was one single title: *Nothing*, by Methuselah Soames, frstpub. 1.1.2000.'

'Sales before publication. Gissit.'

'Eight. Million.'

'Specimen page. Gissit.'

The screen went blank.

'You've stumped it,' I said.

'Random pages display for my friend. Gissit.'

The pages riffled past my eyes. All were blank.

'*Avant-propos*,' I said.

'Critical attention. Gissit.'

'Specify media.'

'Academic journals. Gissit.'

A flurry of titles filled the screen and filed past like the names of the dead on a bloody war memorial.

'Media coverage. Gissit.'

An equally endless scroll of solemn sources and awestruck authors jerked past my eyes.

'Do you want to know what became of you?' Methuselah said.

Of course I didn't. 'Of course I do,' I said.

He hyphenated my name with Gissit. There was a little burpy pause. If the computer could be vexed, this was its vexation.

'Works in print. Gissit.'

'Negative.'

'Mentions in lit. hist. Gissit.'

'One ref.,' the computer said. 'Listed at university with Methuselah Soames.'

'You devil,' I said, 'aren't you?'

'Nothing to it,' he said. And suddenly, I was alone again, in the lustreless present and could, of course, remember nothing of what I had seen and heard.

Life and Loves

'Listen to this, Susie. About a newly-wed husband and wife. I quote: "As he took her in his arms and promised to make her happy, and as she promised him the same, it occurred to one or other of them to wonder, 'Which of us will be the first to take a lover, and why, and when, and whom?'" What do you think?'

'Which one of them is it supposed to be says that?' Susie Harkness Landauer says.

'He doesn't tell us.'

'That's cheating.'

'The novel's about cheating. That's the whole point.'

'Do you think it's *true*? Do people think that?'

'Don't they?'

Jason Landauer is wearing a white polo, dark grey slacks, white socks, no shoes. He reclines on a black leather lounger in the window of the third-floor Riverside Drive and 75th street apartment which he shares with his wife Susie. People who know he is forty-one admit he could be in his mid-thirties.

'Did *you* wonder it when we got married?' Susie is twenty-nine. She is blonde and trim. She has full lips that some people wonder about, but which she has had no treatment to improve. Her relationship with her body is fine; she has two kids, but who would guess that? She tells people, they can't believe it, which is nice. How does she manage to do a job as well? She manages, because that is the way she wants, and likes, it.

Jason says, 'Didn't *you*? Ever?'

That tactfully highlighted hair might be a glamorous burden, the way Susie brushes it away as it falls across her brow. 'Certainly not,' she says. 'No.'

'Not *and* no! Two negatives used to make a positive, but today who's counting?'

'You're editing me, Jason. *And* child-briding me.'

He lowers one white-socked foot to the shaggy fawn rug and puts a hand on the sill by the double-glazed windows that mute the traffic. 'Bedtime.'

'You're not wondering it now, are you, possibly?'

'No,' Jason says, 'so that has to be you doing that.'

Something fierce, that they do not want to wait for, has been primed between them. Susie watches Jason go out of the room. Is she delaying his pleasure or her own? And is it just for fun?

JASON'S HIGH-ABOVE-THE-AVENUE-OF-THE-AMERICAS OFFICE. DAY.

JASON's feet are crossed on his desk, in a fresh pair of raw cotton socks (fawn this morning). The feet uncross themselves and are crossed again the other way. He is making his heard-it-before-dear face. He knows, from radio experience, that the telephone can transmit attitude as well as words.

> JASON
> (on telephone)
> Paula, Paula . . . No, it isn't; it's very
> simple: what's simple is this, Samuel
> Marcus Cohen, my illustrious-client-of-
> whom-you-may-have-heard, since
> you've been publishing him for two
> decades . . .

The door opens and LISA, JASON's smart, unpretty assistant,
shows in GIL TEACHER, the unknown young author of the
first novel which JASON quoted to SUSIE before the passionate,
almost ferocious preceding night. Some mornings, tieless
JASON gets to the office as early as seven, but not this one.

LISA wrote the brief, admiring report on GIL TEACHER's novel,
Sheet Music, which alerted JASON to its 'tart art'. She has made
brevity, and candour, her convincing style. JASON considers it
his secret good fortune that she surely looks too like Agnes
Moorhead to excite predators. Her hobby is tournament
bridge.

JASON
(Continuing on the telephone, but with more *performance* in his
cadences)
. . . wants a two hundred grand advance
for his new one or I have to go
traipsing around the dozens of publishers
who've been insulted by his, and my,
loyalty to you all these years.

JASON's eye-contact with GIL suggests both complicity and a
salting of – let's say – tolerance: GIL *is* intruding, but he
would not be unless JASON had okayed it. So . . .

JASON
(As before)
Paula, I did *not* put Sammy up to this. I
don't know about his new lady.
Correction: of *course* I know about his
new lady, but not her part in this. His
part in her is something else again.

GIL is shy but not awkward. He is tall and has light brown
curly hair and blue eyes. There is a spray of freckles each side
of his straight nose. He wears a blue blazer, light blue shirt,

dark trousers on long legs. He seems scholarly, or is it provincial?

JASON

>Paula, my acute angular beauty . . .
>angular is not derogatory, not in my
>book. And I did not say cute. I said *a-*
>cute . . . I have in my office a brilliant
>new young novelist up from Buffalo
>who needs his lunch . . . *So:* cutting to
>the chase, I already have an offer on my
>desk of $350,000 for Sammy's next full-
>length novel. Sight unseen. I won't tell
>you who from. Which I'm instructed to
>accept − yes, by the Laureate-to-be − if
>I don't hear from you by two-thirty.
>Look at it this way, you'll be saving a
>hundred and fifty gees *and* sticking to
>KRM. Oops!

He looks up as he listens to PAULA and almost fans one hand: what can you do? Then he smiles for GIL, at what PAULA is saying.

GIL's eyes switch to the volumes in JASON's shelves, the novels and reportage of famous clients, or of those in the diary.

JASON

(Still talking to PAULA, and proving himself to GIL, he grins)
>OK is OK with me and will be with
>Samuel Marcus. He never wanted to go
>anyplace else. Done.
>>(A new, as it were undressed voice:)
>How's your multi-talented live-in friend?
>>(With a true smile)
>That can happen, once the cellophane
>comes off.

(Now with a one-sided smile, and look at his limited-edition
watch)

And you, Paulie, three times a night.

(Puts down the telephone)

Welcome to literature, Mr Teacher.

GIL

So that's how it's done!

JASON

That's how *I'm* done.

GIL

You were having a good time.

JASON

So you're the shrewd student of human
nature who authored *Sheet Music*.

GIL

If that's who your twelve-thirty is, I
guess I must be.

JASON

I'm Jason Landauer, your new agent.

GIL

I never had an old one.

JASON

And I hope you never will.

(He puts the top of his hand under his unsagging chin)

It's a masterpiece, Gil.

GIL

In other words, you quite like it.

JASON

I'm never insincere with my clients, at
least not until they start making big
bucks, and insist on it. Now, shall we
flirt some more or would you like some
lunch?

GIL

Can't we flirt over lunch?

JASON

A synthesis man! I know we're going to
get along.

They go to the door. JASON looks back, as if someone else
might be there whom haste has forgotten but prudence should
not ignore.

JASON

(As his head turns towards GIL again)
Buffalo! Tell me about that.

GIL notices that he stops for a whispered word with LISA
before they head on out of the office.

They go to Danny's Downtown, a new old-fashioned New
York chop house in what used to be the garment district. On
the way in, they pass a black-framed clipping blown up from
the *Times*, for which Susie Harkness Landauer (her picture tops
the column) writes a regular restaurant piece. She three-and-a-
half-stars Danny's T-bone steaks and the big potatoes with
chives and sour cream and she recommends the brandy-flared
lobster tails, oh, and the great, great salads.

Gil says, 'Are you two related?'

'No,' Jason says, 'married. We're husband and wife, but not
necessarily in that order.'

Jason gives the impression that he could do without the big
welcome from Danny Estorick, but Gil is also being reminded
of how well placed Jason is in the world to which he can
introduce the young professor.

Danny has his usual booth ready for Jason. The heavy dark
brown table swivels to allow access for customers less slim than
Jason or Gil. In their butchers' aprons and peakless caps, the
waiters look like happy convicts.

'I read a lot a lot of manuscripts,' Jason says, 'and ninety-nine out of a hundred are manushits, believe me. But I'm here to tell you: you're good, very good even.'

'That's what I'm here to hear,' Gil Teacher says.

'That girl – Maria? Maria! – is she your wife?'

'Maria's a character in a novel I wrote. My wife is a real live woman. Two distinctly different things.'

'I'm here to tell you (and you're here to hear!) – she made me cry. She walked out; I cried. She came back in; same thing. Back-of-the-hand, I'm-not-*really*-crying style tears, but . . . That's not something I do too much today.'

'Can you find me a publisher?'

'I never make promises. Unless I can't keep them. Yes, I think so. I'm not guaranteeing how much they'll pay . . .'

'We want to come to New York.'

'No, you don't. You want to stay right where you are. The place where the words get on to the page and don't get spilled on Danny's sawdust. I usually have the small *filet mignon* and a salad. You need food, though, this is your opportunity.'

'Same for me,' Gil Teacher says, 'and some coleslaw maybe.'

'Comes with it,' the waiter says.

'So I'm a hick,' Gil says. 'Thing is, I don't want to go on teaching.'

'Go on teaching. How old are you?'

'I'm nearly twenty-seven.'

'You're twenty-six. How about Maria?'

'My wife's name is Ethel. She doesn't like it too well, but that's her name.'

'New York's full of girls used to be Ethels and they're Veronicas and Anne-Maries and whatever they feel like being today. It's a wonderful town. Keep away. How long've you been married?'

'Two years. We've been together three.'

'And you can write those things about marriage that quickly?'

'We're very happy together.' Gil Teacher looks steadily at Jason with those almost lashless blue eyes.

Jason wonders where Susie is at this precise moment. 'I don't figure on getting more than maybe five thousand bucks advance for *Sheet Music*. You want to go find someone who'll promise you ten? Minimum? He's sitting right over there.'

Jason indicates a slim man of about fifty, with restless eyes which seem constantly to be having trouble with focus: he frowns, he tilts his head, he rumples his brow. His name is Ernie Berlin. He is lunching with Byron Sadleir, the English movie critic and *Vanity Fair* columnist. Ernie is paying close attention to Sadleir, but is aware of Jason's attention. Byron is both voluble and a stammerer. He jerks out his punch-line and stabs out his eighth cigarette since they sat down, looks at the watch he wears on the inside of his left wrist.

'I believe in fidelity,' Gil is saying. 'I'll give you till the end of the week.'

Ernie Berlin is at their booth now. 'Hi, Jason. Don't get up.'

'Did you see signs? How are you, Ernest?'

'You know Byron Sadleir, don't you?'

'Doesn't everyone? How are you, Byron? It's been a long time.'

'Since you were fucking my wife, you mean?'

'What else would I mean? This is Professor Gil Teacher and you're going to wish you'd read his unsolicited manuscript before I did, Ernie.'

Ernie Berlin shakes hands and says, 'Mr Teacher.'

Byron Sadleir shakes hands and says, 'I hate t-t-talent.' His eyes remain on Jason. 'See anything of Cassie these days?'

'I'm a married man, Byron.'

'Hence the question. She's living in Boston, I'm promised, f-f-fellating some seventy-eight-year-old cellist. One must make a living, I suppose.'

Jason leans back and smiles at Ernie Berlin. 'So you've signed Maxie Rifle.'

'He's promised not to beat me up if his income stays above a certain figure.'

'You're still playing the part of the credulous virgin? Congratulations!'

Byron Sadleir has moved towards the door, huddling in his tall way to light a cigarette as if it were a fuse. His shoulder-blades rise through the long jacket of his pale grey Douggie Hayward suit. Ernie touches Jason on the shoulder and makes his what-can-you-do? face at Gil and then it's gotta-go time.

'So tell me,' Jason says, 'so I can not tell them: what's the next book going to be about?'

'Why not this pale Englishman with cow's shoulders and a milky complexion and a stiletto tongue who neither forgives nor forgets?'

'He'd already left Cassie when I was with her, briefly. Ten, eleven years ago. He never loved her.'

'Since when does jealousy depend on loving people?'

'Affection kills; hatred enlivens. Isn't that what Maria says at one point?'

'Keep it short and you get quoted, it seems.'

'Short and smart,' Jason says. 'You need to have the new book ready when the first one comes out, is why I asked. Do you have children?'

'Yes,' Gil says, 'we do. A daughter.'

'Maria,' they say it together, and smile together, as if the simultaneity proved that they shared a secret.

THE OCEAN OFF PLYMOUTH. CAPE COD.

A dinghy is in difficulty in a squall which has recently blown up. As the boat capsizes, the sole SAILOR is flung into the water. He grabs at the overturned boat and tries to lie across it.

Jason and Susie are spending the Memorial Day weekend with his brother, Noah, who has a waterfront property right along from the theme park where the first Puritan settlement has been recreated and where local history freaks impersonate the passengers on the *Mayflower* for the benefit of those in search of American roots.

Noah is shaggily bearded, bespectacled, with a high-domed forehead and a barrel chest (and gut). For Jason, he is an object of both veneration (the brains!) and alarm (is this what it means to be fifty?). He has been scanning the lone sailor through binoculars for some little time and he is already on his way to meet the emergency. He and Laverne spend all their time on the Cape and he knows, and revels in, its sudden dangers. The buoyant inflatable which is bobbing at the jetty is designed to ride out the bucking Atlantic waves.

'Come on, come on. Don't look, leap!'

'Don't land-lubber me, Ahab, OK? You like this shit. I don't.'

'Life-preserver in the locker. Get it on you.'

'How about you?' Jason shouts above the rasp of the engine.

'Mine's built in.' Noah pats his belly.

Susie sort of loves what she can read as her husband's brave fear as he goes along with Noah. She is in cut-offs and a plaid shirt of Jason's that shrank. Their children, Nicky and Caroline (five and seven), are wincing at the spray which keeps the brothers huddled in the accelerating boat as it thump-thump-thumps towards the lone sailor.

Laverne Leapman Landauer comes out on to the wide porch of the clapboard house. She is a large very black-haired woman, who likes to cook, and eat. She has a voice to summon multitudes.

'Lunch-time. What's this shit?'

'Noah says they'll be right back.' Susie indicates what Laverne already knows.

'Wouldn't you know that big *lobbus* would pull something like this? That guy had all morning to drown himself. He has to do it now.'

Caroline says, '*Lobbus?*'

Laverne comes down the worn part of the unmown lawn. 'Get back in here, Landauers, or make your own next time.'

'Someone's drowning, Aunt Laverne.'

'So call a chopper. The *goyim* love that work. They like to winch; let them winch. We got eating to do here.'

ON THE OCEAN.

NOAH is having a good time. He has manoeuvred alongside the capsized dinghy and is leaning out to help the lone sailor aboard his own boat.

> NOAH
> OK, Columbus, you discovered your
> limitations. I pull you; you don't pull
> me. Get it?

The man, whom we shall know as BLAKE AMBLER, flounders into the boat and spews water and tries to become sociably casual.

> BLAKE
> Damn. My watch.

NOAH

Don't worry: I have the time. And it's
lunch-time. You want to go back and
look for it?

BLAKE

It was a present, is all.

NOAH

You ever pay any attention to what the
coastguard says around here? They
broadcast warnings to dumb fucks like
you. You hadn't heard? Now you
heard.

BLAKE

Blake Ambler. I appreciate . . .

NOAH

You should. Noah Landauer. My
brother, Jason. Easy to remember: he's
the green one. Jace, can you take the
tiller here? I'm going to try and . . .

He is leaning out trying to get a rope on to the dinghy which
keeps *almost* righting itself in the busy sea.

JASON

Noah, do you have to be such a
fucking . . . *admiral*?

BLAKE

Don't worry about the boat.

JASON

Do you have insurance?

BLAKE

It doesn't matter.

JASON

You don't, soon as we hit shore, I can
sell you some.

NOAH

Why do you imagine we do this stuff?
Fun? He's in insurance. He needs the
work. It's the least you can do.

BLAKE

Well . . . of course.

The brothers laugh (but not in quite the same way) at BLAKE's
polite dismay.

Gertrude Meyer Landauer, the brothers' mother, is coming
round the side of the house. She is seventy-two years old, but
lean and firm-jawed. Her make-up indicates that she has not
resigned from life. She carries grand-maternal packages, but
that khaki trouser suit says Giorgio Armani. Laverne has folded
her arms on the fence around the deck, miming patient
impatience. Susie and the kids, aiming to be loyal to all their
obligations, are loitering towards the house.

'What happened?'

Susie says, 'The good Samaritans are back in business,' and
gets through kissing her mother-in-law.

'A fine time they choose to turn into Christians,' Laverne
says. 'Right when lunch is on the table.'

'The Samaritans weren't Christians, were they?'

'Breaking news!' Laverne says.

Nicky and Caroline are seeing what Gertrude has brought
them, which has to be candy.

Susie and Caroline head on into the house, but Nicky turns
back to be with the men when they come ashore. Blake
Ambler seems to be quite a different person by the time he has
a pair of borrowed pants and a shirt and is being introduced to
the family. His short fair hair is almost dry; he shucks his briny
parka and accepts a beer without a glass. He has Cary Grant's
cleft in his chin and the same jaw-line. Something tells Jason

that he probably made Skull and Bones, not so long ago.

'OK,' Noah says, 'this is my apparently amiable but basically furious wife, Laverne. This is my brother's slim ditto, Susie the *shiksa*, and this is my mother, Gertrude, who – as you can see – has a flaunting side, and a right to it. This is Nicky, this is Caroline. Did I say that was Jason? I did, and it is.'

'Blake Ambler,' Blake Ambler says.

'Shock. You need food. I laid a place. Yes, you do; yes, he does.'

'How about a doctor?' Jason says.

'Christ!' Laverne says. 'Something we don't have. A Jewish family with no doctor. Semi-Jewish. Let this be an inspiration to you, Nicholas, even if you're not entirely one of us.'

Blake is looking at Susie, and is smiling.

DINING ROOM/KITCHEN. NOAH AND LAVERNE'S HOUSE.

> **BLAKE**
> You are some cook, Mrs . . . Landauer.
>
> **JASON**
> (To SUSIE)
> Investment banker? I'd say so.
>
> **LAVERNE**
> (Over this, to BLAKE)
> Tell *her*. She's only Susan Harkness
> Landauer. The professional palate.
>
> **BLAKE**
> You're the cook, I thought I'd tell you.
>
> **LAVERNE**
> My name's not Annie, but any time you
> feel hungry, go out in your boat, start
> drowning and my husband'll have you
> sitting down to table in no time. His

hobby is fishing for *goyim*.

SUSIE flutters a pale brown eyebrow at JASON, whose expression says 'What can you do?'

JASON

How goes it, mother?

GERTRUDE

I sold a house and two apartments last week.

LAVERNE

Are you married, Mr Ambler?

BLAKE

Yes, I am.

LAVERNE

Good-looking young guy, what did you want to do that for? Is she rich? She's rich!

JASON

Laverne, we've established you're Jewish. Don't you risk ramming it home?

LAVERNE

You're ashamed of your people. You marry out, that's what happens. I'm not prejudiced. I'm realistic. Also, I'm interested.

(To BLAKE)

She wanted the rock, am I right? The ring, before she'd . . . That still happens. Are you Catholic?

BLAKE

No, I'm not.

LAVERNE

Noah, he was ugly. He was an ape. I took one look I knew I had him. Here was a man had to get married if he

wanted it regular. Which he did, and
does . . .

JASON

Laverne, what are we proving here?

LAVERNE

That you're ashamed to be what you
are.
(To BLAKE)
You, you coulda had anybody. She's
rich and she's a beauty, am I right?

BLAKE

How about I fell in love?

LAVERNE

This guy! There's something to fall in,
he falls into it.

GERTRUDE
(Takes her mobile out of her bag)
Do you want to call her?

LAVERNE

The guy's on the lam. She thinks he's
on the bright blue sea. He's a free man
for ten minutes. Let him enjoy himself.

NOAH

How's he going to work that around
here?

BLAKE

Are you a painter?

LAVERNE

He's Vincent van Landauer. A genius
with pigment. A pig with geniusment!
How about you? What do you do?

BLAKE

As a matter of fact I'm . . . I'm a marine
underwriter.

They try not to laugh, and then they do, because BLAKE does, and goes red too. SUSIE is the only one who doesn't laugh, and then CAROLINE imitates her: team of two.

SUSIE

Shall I make some coffee?

LAVERNE
(Getting up)
My kitchen, Soose. My coffee.

NOAH

Truth is, if it matters, I'm an investment analyst with Goldberg, Hyams.

LAVERNE
(Calls back)
Best in the lousy business. He could be a millionaire ten times over. Didn't know that when he married me, because otherwise would he have?

JASON

Laverne, did you ever embarrass yourself? Go back as far as you can remember.

LAVERNE

Fuck you, Jason, you ten-per-cent merchant.

SUSIE

Do you have a place around here?

BLAKE

Yes, we do. You're *the* Susie Harkness, the restaurant critic, I realise. Belatedly.

SUSIE

It's never too late, so they say.

BLAKE

But they're wrong, aren't they? And your husband is in insurance.

SUSIE

Insurance? He's a writer's agent.

BLAKE

Oh, OK. I get it. OK.

NICKY

Mommy, can we . . . like . . . ? Outside?

LAVERNE

(Calls)

You kids want some ice cream?

The two blonde heads shake. SUSIE looks at BLAKE and then at JASON and then she gets up.

SUSIE

Let's go.

JASON

They'll be OK.

SUSIE

Yes, they will.

She goes out, leaving JASON and BLAKE looking at each other.

LAVERNE

(Calls)

Noah, how many cookies you want?
Because come in here and get 'em or
you don't get 'em.

NOAH pushes himself up from the table and goes out. BLAKE looks at the watch he remembers he isn't wearing and tucks one side of his mouth under a cheek.

A little later, Jason feels he has to go out and help Susie be with the kids: quality-time time. They are throwing pebbles into the churning sea, revelling in immunity from its boiling surge and hiss-and-rattle retreat through the shingle.

Jason is saying, 'I know, I know. Do I not know? But a guy

gets saved from possible drowning, he has to pay his dues.'

'She thinks it's *cute*. She makes him fat deliberately. Noah. So nobody else will want him. The way she babies him, he can't even *move*.'

'He moved pretty fast when it came to . . .'

'Does he ever go see Asa?' Susie says. 'He's *his* father too, isn't he? How come he leaves it all to you?'

'Ask him.'

'It's your family.'

'Aren't you joining? Does he remind you of somebody, Blake? He does me.'

In the house, Blake is refusing the cookie jar which Laverne has offered him. She has been explaining that, thanks to his connections, Jason got Susie her job as a restaurant critic. 'Since when she's on TV panels; she writes for fancy magazines; she's going to model panty-liners any minute now, who knows? "With *our* little secret on *your* little secret, you too can make Jello with the monthlies!"'

They go out on to the porch with a tray of coffee in varicoloured mugs (designed by 'that woman in Wales, England') and Laverne calls to Susie and Jason to come and get it.

'I guess I should really make tracks here,' Blake says.

'Let her worry a little,' Laverne says. 'You'll only get more loving when you get back.'

Blake breathes out with a little amused sound, but raises his hand: 'Gotta go home, truly.'

'Alternatively, how about we tell them you drowned out there? And you can go anywhere in the world you want. Totally free, born again. Think about it!'

Susie says, 'Laverne, do you *try* and be embarrassing?'

'No, sweetie. Like farting, it comes naturally. Only don't imagine I won't remember you asked.'

'*Please* remember.'

'Could we not do this possibly?' Jason says. 'In public.'

'I promised to take my kids karting,' Blake says. 'I should call and have someone come get me.'

'Why don't I run you home?' Susie says. 'Quicker. Jason, do you have my keys? He does.'

COAST ROAD. CAPE COD. DAY.

SUSIE is driving BLAKE towards his house. He is paying attention to her by looking away from her with exaggerated concern not to miss the turning.

> BLAKE
> I don't usually come this way. OK, now
> hang a right and . . .

They come to the gates of a big property, with a big white house at the end of a fenced driveway: there are pillars and an unsaddled pony nodding in a paddock with a knocked-down practice fence in it. SUSIE has to stop while BLAKE goes round and punches in the code that opens the electric gates. He is elegant now.

THE BEACH AND FORESHORE. CAPE COD. DAY.

The sun has come out and the sea is less noisy. NICKY and CAROLINE are running towards some rocks. JASON, still keeping an eye on them, climbs a ramp of weed-bound earth and sand.

He goes through a bamboo brake and stumbles on

Two MEN, one quite plump and middle-aged, in a seersucker suit, the other younger, wearing shorts and a tank top and a

Knicks cap. They are hand-in-hand, looking in each other's eyes. When they glance at JASON, without reproach or apology, he sees that their eyes are hot with tears, of emotion not pain.

JASON raises two hands and backs away, with his chin high, looking out for the kids.

When Nicky and Caroline run back along the beach towards Noah and Laverne's house, they find Laverne, in a big black swimsuit, dabbling her feet in the ocean. To Jason's uneasy surprise, they seem very glad to see her and she gathers them to her big bosom and lifts them both up, for a moment. Jason walks on up to the house, where he finds his mother, naked on the low rooftop deck of Noah's office, which opens right off the main building.

Gertrude is face down, but unembarrassed enough to roll half over to greet Jason.

'Don't burn now, mother.'

'Where are the kids?'

'On the beach. Scaling Mount Laverne. Think they'll need oxygen?' He does not look directly at his mother, but leans against the place where the deck meets the side of the house. 'All the time I was a kid, I never saw you without your clothes on.'

'Your father wouldn'ta liked it. In addition to which, I had more to hide in those days.'

'Hence more to show.'

'Hence that.'

'Isn't there some way we can get him out of that place?'

'Of course there is. Make a million. Make two, to be safe. I am trying.'

'Is that what you're doing, mother? Last time I was there, I took him for a walk, you know, the way I do, and I bought him this cigar –'

'Havana? You always were the good son.'

'– and he dropped it. I felt so sorry for him I wanted to push him under a truck. We were at this ped-exing, you know, with the trucks drumming past, big rigs, and I wanted to push him right under one of those damned metal monsters.'

Gertrude sighs and tries to put some oil on her back, and then looks to Jason, who sighs and hits the spot she can't reach.

'You never loved him.'

'You know how old I was,' she says, 'when he married me? Twenty years old. What did I know? Why did he want me? My *character*? My *talent*?'

'You played good piano.'

'My ass! You want to know the truth when I was a young woman unfortunately? Women were men's toilets is the truth when I was a young woman.'

'So now you punish him,' Jason says. 'You didn't know any better, how was he supposed to? Is now so much better?'

'I could do with some *now*, I know that much.'

'So, you sold three places.'

'Eighteen grand commission. In one week.'

'You really discovered money, didn't you, once you took over the business?'

'I discovered it's the only thing people'll kiss your ass for when you're over seventy. I discovered that all right.' Jason nods and looks at the sounding ocean. 'I can't do it, Jason,' his mother says, 'look after him at home. I don't have the physical strength.'

'Muscle you can always hire.'

'He gets good care in that place.'

'Have you *been* there?'

'Better than he could get at home.'

They hear the bang of the screen door as Laverne comes out and can smile at what they soon hear: 'All right, cake's ready to be cut. Jason, Gertrude, everybody . . . NOAH! Take a quick look at the ocean. Anybody's drowning, it's positively your last chance to go save him.'

Jason leans over the rail and says, 'Susie home yet?'

'Haven't seen her, Jace. But then there's been work to do.'

'I wish she wouldn't say those things,' Jason says to his mother.

'That's Laverne.' Gertrude has raised herself and is putting on a batik robe. 'Are you happy, Jason?'

'I think we're very happy,' he says.

'Are *you* happy? Was my question.'

'I wonder where she is.'

OUTSIDE NOAH'S AND LAVERNE'S HOUSE. EVG.

Through the window: LAVERNE's chocolate cake is being eaten by everyone present, which does not include SUSIE. A little time has passed and with it the day has become evening.

Suddenly, there is a crash of breaking glass. A stone has been flung through one of the widows facing the ocean.

A moment later, NOAH flings open the screen door and runs out, followed by JASON.

                    NOAH
                   (Yells)
          Come back here, you bastard.

He runs on to the beach, with JASON, and stops. He stands there panting at the shadows and the darkness.

JASON

Who would do a thing like that?

NOAH

Some *nudnik*, can't stand for anyone to
have anything that's ... how about
nice? I catch 'im, I'll kill 'im. Do I
mean it? Will we ever find out? They'll
drive home happy, probably, now.
Party's over. People today.

It is as if the two brothers have something else they should,
or should not, talk about. It keeps them dawdling there on the
now silent shore; the pebbles no longer rattle together as they
did in the daylight. The breeze and the sea have calmed down.
Jason says that he hopes that Susie didn't run into any trouble.
Noah says, '*No*', as if unpleasant things never happened.

When Susie fails to arrive at suppertime, Noah drives Jason
to the Goschen Beach police station and, being local, goes in to
ask the desk guy if anything unusual has been reported. Jason
waits in the car and is somehow displeased when Noah comes
out and says that nothing has.

'Did you mention the guy throwing the rock?'

'We also have girls with throwing arms around here. They
play junior league now. How about we go round to the
Ambler place? Cop says it's not far.'

'Noah, listen, if it turns out ... like we missed her and she's
back at the house when we get there, let's just say we went for
a beer.'

'I could use a beer too. Are you two having some problems?'

'Not in the slightest. This isn't like her, one bit.'

'Maybe she went for a beer,' Noah says.

EXT. THE AMBLER SPREAD. NIGHT.

Dogs bark as NOAH drives up the crumbling drive to the front of the pillared residence. A light comes on as NOAH leans out of the car window, his elbow way down on the door. A window opens upstairs and a head and shirt-sleeved shoulders appear.

NOAH

Hi. Excuse me, but . . .

SERVANT

Kindly stay in the car and state your name and business. You are presently under electronic surveillance.

(As NOAH makes to get out)
Kindly stay in the car and state your name and business . . .

JASON

Makes you want to throw rocks, doesn't it?

NOAH
(Calls)
We're not on business. My name's Noah Landauer. This here is my brother, Jason, the well-known . . .

(Turns to JASON)
What do you do for a living, pal?
(Calls again)
We'd like to see Mr Ambler . . .

SERVANT

Are you expected?

NOAH

No, we're unexpected. Tell Mr Ambler we're the people saved his fuckin' life a little earlier in the day. And we haven't come for the reward, just my sister-in-law, who brought him home this afternoon. After that doesn't ring any bells, we'll take a powder.

The front door opens a few minutes later and Blake Ambler comes out in a silk dressing gown and, as they see when they get inside, monogrammed, hard-soled slippers. He leads them across the usual checkerboard hall through double doors into the book-lined den. Jason notices how fear and anger and dread are socialised into resentful deference by the grandeur of the house and Blake Ambler's hospitable rectitude.

'What can I offer you?'

Jason says, 'Nothing, really,' but Noah is already saying, 'Do you have a beer?'

'What we're here for is, we wondered, do you have any idea where Susie – my wife – who drove you home, where she might be?'

'She's not home? She left here, oh, it has to be soon after six.'

'Three hours ago! Was she OK, when she left?'

'She was OK all the time, far as I could see.'

'Blake?' A female voice calls from the hallway, but higher up. She has to be on the stairs. 'Are you OK?'

'Be right there. My wife. Nothing to worry about.'

Jason points two fingers at the older man. 'Just what you'd say if we had a gun on you.'

'That could very well be so.'

IN THE CAR. SOON AFTERWARDS. NIGHT.

The brothers are heading for the main gate out of the property.

NOAH
The guy was fucking his wife.

JASON
Or wanted us to think so. My guess is,

he was reading the *Wall Street Journal*.

NOAH

And fucking his wife. The rich always
have something to hide. But what?
They have choices. *That's* what.

JASON

I'm rich, Noah, so are you.

NOAH

We're comfortable. He's rich.

He drives carefully through the gates, which close behind the
Traveler.

JASON

Why is it you never go see Asa?

NOAH

I go, if I'm in the city.

JASON

You never are in the city. Did you not
like him? Is that why?

NOAH

Do you go because you did?

JASON

Do. He's still alive. I go because he's my
father. I hope Susie's OK.

Susie says, 'So where the hell have you been?'
'We went for a beer. What happened to you?'
'Not a thing.'
'You see the kids before they went to bed?'
'Your mother took care of it. Gave her a kick. Are you
checking on me?'
'You coulda maybe called is all.'
'But I didn't. Is all.'
'Have you eaten?'

'In this house, can you get away without?'

It is now nearly ten o'clock. There are people in the house, but they do not have an evening together. It is a relief when they talk about going to bed, as if it were the only thing *to* talk about.

'You kids get hungry in the night,' Laverne says, 'there's stuff in the refrigerator. And there's cake left over. And chicken.'

'We'll be fine.' Jason closes the door on her and turns to see his wife looking out at the moonlit shore.

'Jason, why did you marry me?'

'I figured it was the moment to get married. I looked around for a wife and there you were in bed with me. So . . . Where were you?'

'Three hours in my life you don't know what I was doing. I drove to Provincetown; I drove back. Do I face charges?'

'What did you think of the Ambler place?'

'Fancy. I liked it.'

'You drove from there . . .'

'To Provincetown. Why? I don't know. What do you want to do?'

'I have choices? I'm going to bed. I'm tired.'

'Had a hard day? Away from the office. Those *are* the hard ones, right?'

He is in bed before she turns towards him from the window. 'Am I not supposed to give you a thought in those kinds of circumstances? I better know.'

Susie says, 'How many women did you fuck before you had me?'

'I forget now. And it's a little late to call my accountant. Likewise my ancient history professor. What did you do in Provincetown?'

'Had some fresh squeezed orange juice and talked some French. Are you going to hold me overnight?'

'Talked some *French*? Who to?'

'The kid squeezed me my juice. He was in France in the summer. I married *you* because I thought you were the most extraordinary man I ever met.'

'I was kidding. Susie, come on, I was kidding.'

When he wakes in the night, he opens an eye for Susie, but she is not under the duvet next to him. He has slightly dreaded seeing her (*why?*) and he is more annoyed than worried when she is absent. He gets up, as if he cared, and goes down to the kitchen, but she is not there. He goes to the screen door and finds it unfastened.

Susie has her nightie lifted to her chin. She is standing up to the quiet waves which beat softly against her naked body. Jason watches her from the shadow of the big tree that has the swing hanging from it. He is excited, perhaps by her nakedness, perhaps because, so far as she is concerned, he is not there.

When Paula Steinberg comes through with an offer for Gil Teacher's novel, Jason smiles a smile he cannot quite analyse: he has angled for her to want it and at the same time he is honestly surprised and pleased. Paula is a smart, independent judge *and* he has influenced her. He takes off his shoes when she tells him she wants to make an offer and pulls out the top drawer of his desk, pushes back his chair, puts his clean cotton feet in the drawer. He is going to enjoy this.

'Gil is going to be a major writer. I know you know, so you also know why I'm saying this. He needs encouragement and he also needs money. Because money *is* encouragement in our pluralistic culture. How about seventy-five grand? You need a drink of water, take a drink of water. *Ten?* What did I do? That you need to insult me. Wait till you meet him. He's . . . modest and bright and if they could get the young Harrison Ford that is who they would get, when they come to . . . Fifty grand is not a lot of money to mention to a young guy who wants to bring his family to the city and . . . the kid has to eat, likewise his wife and his daughter.' When Paula goes to thirty thousand dollars against a twelve-and-a-half per cent royalty rate, Jason takes his feet out of the drawer, stretches out and puts them on the desk. 'Paula, you're beautiful and brilliant, but I like you, a lot. If I accept this offer – *if* – he does get Mikey as his editor, doesn't he, assuming you . . . ? Fine. I think I did say "fine". Yes, I did. You too. I *never* called you cutie. But I will, unless you're very careful.'

Jason stays very still for a minute or two after he puts the phone down. He treasures the good news he has for Gil Teacher and, almost instantly, wishes that it were better. What can the guy realistically do with thirty thousand dollars today? Paula is going to have forced him to be happier to Gil than he really feels. He smiles at the grievance which he needs in order to arm him for further business with Paula.

'Lisa, do we have that number of Gil Teacher? Paula's fallen for *Sheet Music*.'

'That's great news. I have it here. Do you want me to get him for you?'

'Do it, will you?'

When Jason has finished telling Gil the news and inviting him and his wife to dinner the following Tuesday, if they can do it, which they can, he looks up to see Lisa in the door of his office, with a face that is somehow smaller.

'Jason, can I see you a minute?'

'What's the problem? Money? You go down doubled and

redoubled over the weekend and they're coming to break your legs if you don't pay up? What?' When she shuts the door, he says, 'Oh my God, he's a married man and you only just found out. You love him, he doesn't love you. *What?*'

'I love him and he's asked me to marry him.'

'Jesus, Leesie, how do you look when it's *bad* news? What's the big problem?'

'He's a Brazilian international.'

'International *what?*'

'Bridge player, of course. We met at a congress in Atlantic City.'

'Is Brazilian the problem or is international the problem?'

'He wants me to go and live with him in Brasilia.'

'Which you obviously can't.'

'What do you mean? Why can't I?'

'Because how would you get to downtown Manhattan by eight thirty in the morning? Brasilia is eight thousand miles from the nearest subway station. Everyone knows that. This is pretty sudden, isn't it?'

'I've known Raimondo for five years.'

'You're sure you're not rushing into this. Brasilia . . . How old is this character?'

'Fifty-eight. He was married before and now . . .'

'Does he have kids?'

'Who are happily grown-up; married one of them, Luisa.'

'I always hoped that kid would find the right guy. And you, Lisa, too.'

'You know how happy I've been here.'

'Yes, I do. And I hope you'll be happy in Brasilia and, forgive me, but how soon is that likely to be?' He goes round the desk and puts his arms round her and kisses her forehead. 'Because how am I going to do without you?'

INT. DINING AREA. THE LANDAUERS' APARTMENT.
NIGHT.

> JASON
>
> The fucking *bitch*, can you *imagine*?
> Brasilia! With a face like hers, I thought
> I was safe for life. You can't trust
> *anybody* these days.

ETHEL and GIL TEACHER both laugh; SUSIE has heard it
before. ETHEL and GIL have come to that celebratory dinner.
He wears his blazer, but he has had his hair cut (it looks
darker).

ETHEL is at once slim and breasty with young motherhood.
She has dark eyes and a somehow *articulate* nose. Her long
black hair is gathered in a loose bun at the back and is
fastened there with a small red bow. She wears a floral cotton
dress and beaded shoes she bought in Santa Fe. She seems
both to have taken trouble over how she looks and to care
very little for what New York expects of her.

> JASON
>
> It's been that kind of a week, folks. I've
> been frantically auditioning girls with
> eye-shadow so thick they can hardly
> open them, who promise me they love
> lit-richer and have no clear knowledge
> of what order the alphabet comes in. A,
> B and see you round.

SUSIE has come back from the kitchen with a vegetable terrine
and a *coulis* of tomatoes.

> GIL
>
> This looks amazing, doesn't it, Eth?

> ETHEL
>
> A cookery critic who can *cook*? Is that
> permissible?

JASON has the feeling that ETHEL is using a tone more natural to GIL. It is as if he has loaned her the wit he is not using at the moment.

SUSIE

First eat!

JASON

You saw Mikey Carossa. How did you like him?

(To SUSIE)

Gil's new editor over at Paula's.

GIL

He was fine.

JASON

You didn't like him. You don't have to. He's the best though. He wrote one very good novel . . .

GIL

Early Call.

JASON

Which – you're right – might have had a catchier title.

GIL

It was good.

(To SUSIE)

This is totally delicious.

ETHEL

Gil feels that the guy wants to change the emphasis, don't you, Gil?

GIL looks at ETHEL with the flushed respect due to someone who has bravely broken an agreement to be tactful.

GIL

He seems to want to . . . I don't know . . . put more sex in the sex.

(To SUSIE)
I swore I wasn't going to talk about my
book while we were eating dinner.

SUSIE
I can always bring the coffee right away.

JASON
We have a deal. You don't have to
change a word you don't want to
change.

ETHEL
Did you read it yet?

SUSIE
What I have read I thought was . . .
OK, *chilling*, to be honest.

JASON
To be honest, you would have to say
that it was *nasty*, which is the word you
used to me.

He smiles at the guests, but SUSIE does not smile at him, nor
does he look at her.

ETHEL
Gil doesn't feel like he needs a co-
author at this point.

JASON
Which is what he should tell Mikey.
Alternatively ask the bastard how *his*
novel is coming along. After fifteen
years, he just might have that dedication
straight by now. You know what it is,
don't you? It's your up-state
address. It brings out the Wasp-baiter in
him.

GIL
Didn't I say it was time to come live in
the big city?

JASON

Is that something you want to do too,
Ethel?

SUSIE collects the plates and looks very *slim* as she does it: she
has somehow withdrawn her psychic weight from the table.

GIL

Ethel can get some good experience in
Manhattan.

JASON

A lot of people do, I'm told. Experience
of what?

GIL

A good law office. I thought I told you:
Ethel is a qualified counsellor, but she
needs practical —

JASON

You're a beautiful *lawyer*? This . . . this
. . . peasant!

As SUSIE comes back, in yellow-check oven gloves, watching
her step with the *gratin* of chicken in white wine sauce, the
telephone rings.

SUSIE

Somebody's second draft just isn't
working after all.

JASON

(As he goes to answer)
Or somebody's second wife. I'm so
sorry.

SUSIE

But he isn't really, is he? Like they say,
what's ten per cent of peace and quiet?

JASON

(Answers phone loudly enough for the message to reach SUSIE)
   Sammy! When was talking to you ever
   inconvenient? Susie just happened to be
   giving birth at that moment, but . . .
   what's on your mind?

SUSIE

(To GIL and ETHEL)
   I told him to put the machine on.
   Samuel Marcus thinks he *owns* Jason. He
   does own him.

JASON's voice is loudly hushed. Has it been enough to cause
the little cry from the next room which makes ETHEL get up
and put her napkin in her chair?

ETHEL

My turn to be sorry.

SUSIE

You don't have to be.

She has not hit the 'you' too hard, but the nuance is clear
enough for GIL to smile at the view through the window.

ETHEL goes to take care of her baby. SUSIE comes back with
string beans and sits down in front of the unbroached dish of
chicken. She swivels to look through to where JASON is
crouched by the telephone. He makes a helpless gesture and
gets up and carries the telephone out of her eye-line.

SUSIE turns and, since they are alone together, has to look at
GIL, who is already looking at her.

JASON

(Sighs and is *very* patient on the telephone)
   Paula is giving us . . . no, she's giving us
   everything you asked for. Could you
   possibly live with that without going

227

rancid with frustration? Yes, we do have
people here. No, I am not hurrying
you. A brilliant young novelist and his
ravishing wife, who are so much in love
you couldn't even get Samuel Marcus
Cohen between them.

JASON blows exasperation through his lips, as if someone
might be watching, and can hear.

SUSIE

... *anything* was better than Philly, so I
got on the train and ... look at me
now!

JASON

(Coming back to the table)
Famous authors! I'm such an admirer of
theirs!

He mimes spitting.

GIL

(Continuing to be quietly interested in SUSIE's story)
And how did you two meet?

The telephone is ringing again.

JASON

I don't believe this.

SUSIE

Oh, I believe it.

The scene which JASON's return to the table seemed to abort
is now reconstituted by his return to the telephone. Shy smiles
admit that both GIL and SUSIE know it.

SUSIE

I can answer your unasked question, if
you want, while we wait for the Master
of Ceremonies to get back. Which is,

isn't it, what did I do when I first got
to New York? Alternatively, I can say
'presumably you'll use all of this in a
novel some day?' Like *tomorrow*!

GIL

I can't promise. But I . . .

SUSIE

How about I was a dentist's
receptionist? Studying design nights, but
. . . And one day, handsome, dynamic
Jason Landauer lost this filling and
instantly became pleading and needing,
all in a dark brown voice. I found him
an early cancellation and he was so
grateful he immediately asked me to
marry him.

GIL

That's true romance!

SUSIE

It's true at least. Then the anaesthetic
wore off.

GIL looks at his unused fork and then at SUSIE. Then JASON
is back.

JASON

That was – guess!

SUSIE

Honey, what you should do is . . .

JASON

Switch . . . I know; and I did it already.

SUSIE

(Starts to serve food)
OK, we already had Samuel Marcus, so
. . . that was Aaron Glasser. Who
couldn't wait to tell you what?

JASON

He had the recall from Hubie Chase.
Humpty Dumpty is all back together
again. So the A-team is off to the Coast
once more and he wants to change the
last chapter, so far, of his memoirs.
Hubie, it seems, is now *not* Martin
Bormann. He's the guy who wants
Aaron out there for from ten to a
million weeks. For real money,
fortunately.

GIL is elongating himself from his chair in the direction in
which ETHEL disappeared, but the baby is now silent and she
comes back, buttoning her dress.

ETHEL

I'm sorry.

SUSIE reaches and touches her thigh: they're practically sisters.

JASON

(Looks at ETHEL, but goes on:)
Aaron has just one little problem.

SUSIE

(With a look at ETHEL, as if they had *both* guessed)
Who is going to water his cats? It's time
Aaron had a Filipino.

JASON

And who'll water the Filipino? So will I
please think of something instead of
having people to dinner?
(He raises and drops two helpless hands and then looks at GIL
and SUSIE)
Oh my God, I thought of something.
You kids want ten to umpteen weeks
apartment-sitting in an exclusive place
overlooking the East River belonging to

the first screenwriter they think of when
they can't get anybody else? Do you?

GIL

Is this serious?

JASON

Don't chew his pencils, or his Persian
carpets; feed his cats, admire – but do
not use – his best crystal. Do what you
will between his satin sheets, but don't
get fresh with his freezer. Personally, I
still advise you to have little or less to
do with this corrupt, dangerous and
delightful city, but in case you're
unpersuaded by sane advice, when can
you start?

ETHEL

We have a baby.

JASON

And he has cats. Is that the problem?

ETHEL

No, it's –

JASON

Then we don't have a problem. As long
as nobody finger-paints over the
Hockneys. Oh, and also normally he
insists on *droit de seigneur* over his
tenants, but as you're a married man, I
might broker that down to a big kiss.

ETHEL

He's gay.

JASON

Before gay was gay he was gay.

SUSIE

You'll like him.

GIL

Is that an order?

JASON

Susie'd go to California with him if he
gave her the chance.

SUSIE

How about some more chicken?

The Landauers have a black Korean woman who comes in
three mornings a week. All the same, Susie likes to tidy the
place after they have had company. Even though nothing is
broken and little is out of place, it is always as if some kind of
violence has been done to the apartment and has to be repaired
before anyone, even the help, arrives to see it. There is a kind
of nervous anger in Susie as she makes everything look the way
it did before. Jason's anger, which is equally controlled, is about
having to feel bad because nice people came to dinner.

'What I liked about them,' he says, as he carries out coffee
cups, 'is how they were such a couple. Notice that? She really
pulls for him.'

'And pushes,' Susie says, as they coincide momentarily in the
kitchen. 'How come it gets to be your problem always who
waters Aaron Glasser's fucking cats?'

'They don't fuck. The vet took care of that.'

'He's supposed to be David Kersh's client now, I thought.'

'He's my friend and he's David's client. He asked me if I
knew anybody. I thought of a way to make everybody happy.
How bad a guy does that make me in your book?'

'I had a book, you'd probably want me to be happy too.'

'Susie . . .' He stands and waits in the kitchen while she goes
back to the living room for whatever else needs picking up.
'Your happiness . . .'

'OK. Take the point again. I'm sorry. Do you think she's brighter than me?'

'Is what's seriously worrying you? Ethel's a kid.'

'I know she's younger than I am, is she also brighter is what I asked you?'

'You want a book contract? I can get you one any time you say. Susie Harkness's New York. Do it. They keep asking me when you're going to. We're going to Paula's party, we can talk to her about it.'

'Why have a good time when you could be doing business?'

'This is taking the point again? This is what you call taking the point again? Fuck you.'

'Did you say that to me?'

'Yes, I did. What do you want me to do? Deny it? I said it and I'm willing to act on it, at a moment's notice. Susie, I love you.'

INT. LOBBY. DELMONICO'S. NIGHT.

JASON comes in from the street and sees SUSIE waiting for him. They are on their way to PAULA's birthday party. JASON carries two packages in fancy wrapping.

> SUSIE
> Two presents for one person? Isn't that
> possibly overdoing it, even for a
> deductible dear old friend?

JASON moves his head down and sideways, his spare hand up: take it easy for a second.

SAMUEL MARCUS COHEN comes into the lobby, wearing a camel coat and a fur hat. He takes off the hat and establishes the vigour of his full head of white hair. He is not a tall man, but he has a tall reputation, and knows it. He is sixty-four.

SAMMY

Oh am I glad to see you.

He shakes hands with JASON, who does a little back patting, and then he takes a good look at SUSIE before kissing her.

SAMMY

Did I keep you?

SUSIE

Were we waiting for you? The secrets I
don't know about!

SAMMY

Oh Jesus. It's not her birthday again?

JASON

Fourth straight year you forgot why
you're here. Shall I tell people?

SAMMY

I've had a *day*: a lecture, two interviews,
one in some depth, a piece to write ...
What'm I gonna do? I could not show.

JASON makes a face at SUSIE and hands SAMUEL MARCUS COHEN one of the two packages he has been carrying.

JASON

Here. From you to Paula. With your
hand-picked love.

SAMMY

You saved my life. What is it?

JASON

Don't you mean what do you owe me?

IN PAULA'S APARTMENT.

There is the big room, with the decorator's favourite art in it,
and, through Bauhaus-inspired chromium-framed glass doors, a
long, narrow glassed-in terrace, with many plants in it,
overlooking Park Avenue. Nice.

PAULA

Jason! Susie!

JASON

(Hands over the package)

Happy birthday . . .

SUSIE

. . . to you!

PAULA

You shouldn't have.

JASON

Don't get too excited. It's something we
bought for my brother, but it wasn't his
size . . .

PAULA smiles and puts the package on the fake mosaic table
with other unopened ones. She is already leaning away to
greet BRAD EASY, the designer.

JASON has seen BYRON SADLEIR talking to a WOMAN in a
very little black dress who seems to feel the need constantly to
press the ball of her thumb against her forehead while she
agrees with him.

LORD FOREMAN, the bearded English movie producer, is
helping himself to a mini vol-au-vent and checks his fingers
before coming to meet the LANDAUERS.

JASON

Fred, you remember my wife.

FOREMAN

Do I not? How is the unmistakable
Susie Harkness?

(To JASON)

And who are you again exactly? I've
finally closed that deal to make the Max
Rifle trilogy for HBO.

JASON

I know. And I'm happy for you,
Frederick.

SUSIE smiles and eases herself away from the two MEN. JASON
notices her go and, at the same time, the arrival of GIL and
ETHEL, who is in another floral cotton dress and a headband
and looks as though she is not wearing stockings. GIL's hair
looks longer.

SAMUEL MARCUS COHEN has PAULA by the elbow.

SAMMY

Jason persuaded me to accept this new
deal of ours, Paula, and I hope it means
what it says.

PAULA

Two hundred grand? It does.

SAMMY

In terms of being taken seriously. Jason
Landauer sweet-talked me as usual, but
that was for his sake . . .

Does he know that SUSIE is right there? He may well.

SUSIE

If you're going to bad-mouth my
husband, Professor Cohen, at least have
the grace to wait till my back is
turned –

SAMMY

(The charmer now)
But, Susie, I much prefer your front.
(To PAULA)
I don't want any mistake. The new
book – I admit it, if this is an admission
– has affinities with *The Field of Blood*,
but it isn't as – all right – *crude* in its –

PAULA

Not as crude? Sounds like the deal's off,
Sammy.

She and SUSIE have a moment of amusement together that is
almost an embrace.

SAMMY

Jason told me it was all settled.

PAULA leans and kisses SAMMY, reassuringly, but her lips are
somehow shaped for SUSIE, and her eyes are still on her. Each
woman has a thrilling sense of what it would be to desire the
other. How does that feeling differ from desire itself?

SUSIE sees that JASON is talking to GIL and ETHEL. There is a
tenderness in his attention to both of them which reminds her
of how much she loved him when he talked to her in that
way, even though it is a way which she would now resent.

BYRON SADLEIR is standing beside SUSIE with a glass of spare
champagne. His face looks as if it has been chalked.

BYRON

Have some probably non-vintage
possibly non-champagne and get it off
your chest, whatever it is, because your
chest in no way needs it. I've been
scheming to m-m-meet you ever since
you recommended that bloody awful so-
called *b-b-bistro* on f-f-forty-eighth street.
Presumably there's something between
you and the *patron*. Is it money or c-c-
c-cunnilingus?
    (He holds out his pale hand)
Byron Sadleir, as you know. How do
you do? I realise it's *often*, but *how*?

SUSIE

Great script.

BYRON

I thought so. So, tell me something you clearly shouldn't. Is he good in bed? Or anywhere?

SUSIE

Who are we talking about?

BYRON

Ah! You have alternatives. I'm encouraged. Your husband.

SUSIE

Perhaps you should ask your wife.

BYRON

Sharp, but a trifle obsolete. He hasn't fucked my present one. He did tell you about Cassie though.

SUSIE

It leaked out. We've been married for seven years.

BYRON

Seven years! What did he do? Meet you off the school b–b–bus and offer to do your homework? I bet he did.

SUSIE

Have you ever been real?

BYRON

Once or twice. I hated it. Will you have lunch with me next week, if you really want to wait that long?

SUSIE

Certainly not.

Gil and Ethel are still talking to Jason, quite as if they were at a different, more friendly party. The Teachers have moved into Aaron Glasser's apartment and seem amazed by their good fortune.

'No problems?' Jason says. 'Because he calls me.'

'Oh he calls us,' Ethel says, 'to make sure Theodore is still talking to us. The cat.'

'Who Ethel swears is really a dog in drag.'

'Give it some therapy, and it just might bark at you.'

'So far,' Ethel says, 'it only wags its tail and comes when I whistle.'

'Who wouldn't?' Jason says it to flatter Gil. 'Do you get a lot of . . . callers?'

'Gorgeous came by,' Ethel says.

'Gorgeous?'

'This eighteen-feet-tall black guy,' Gil says. 'The kind has to bend double to make a basket.'

'You're blending in some information here, right? Aaron's Afro-American friend – one of his friends – is vertically advantaged. How goes it with the rewrites? Happy?'

'Ah, no. But it does go. Slowly.'

'Do only what you want to do. There are always other publishers. And parties. Not even Paula Steinberg is the only Paula Steinberg. So: fight your corner. Mikey Carossa can be that little bit strutty. But he's . . . good, isn't he?' Jason looks over at where Susie is still talking to Byron Sadleir. 'Does she need rescuing, would you say?'

'We'll be fine,' Gil says.

'You are fine,' Jason says. 'How am I, would you say?'

ANOTHER PART OF THE FOREST: THE PARTY CONTINUES.

BYRON

You weren't born Catholic by any
chance, were you?

SUSIE

They started two blocks over. I'm a
split-level Presbyterian.

BYRON

Only there's a certain brand of Catholic
girl who m-m-marries Jews, if you've
noticed. They can't do without sex, but
they associate it with something slightly
unpleasant, hence . . . I thought perhaps
you might be of their p-p-persuasion.

SUSIE

I was always told you were witty, I
now have evidence that that was a typo.

BYRON

Which must be why you are seriously
proposing to have this outrageous affair
with me.

SUSIE

You know something, Byron? You are
truly slightly dated.

BYRON

Well, these are excellent times to be
behind. Which happens to be my
favourite position anyway. What's yours?

SUSIE

And to think that I used to admire
those no-holds-barred pieces of yours.

BYRON

Ah disillusionment! As the beach-boys
say in California: when we're young, we
lie on the sand and gaze at the stars, and
when we get older we lie on the stars
and gaze at the sand.

The level of the conversations seems to change all at once, in all corners of the big room. Faces are looking in from the terrace too. Fred Foreman is sitting low in a chair, pressing his face with a silk handkerchief. He looks at it as if he feared blood; there is only sweat there, but his face is bloodless just the same. He makes a slow wriggling gesture and his velvet jacket slips off his shoulder. He seems to be trying to get away from it, as if it were an importunate intruder.

By the time Paula reaches him, he wears the ghastly smile of someone asking for help by pretending nobly that he doesn't need it.

'Fred, what's the matter?' Paula looks round and is happy to see Jason, in an only slightly irritated way. 'Jason, I think Fred's not feeling so well. Can you call a doctor?'

'It's the heat,' Fred says, as if it were a long statement. He still tries to extract himself from his velvet jacket. His armpits are dark with sweat and one of his cuff-links has come off. Black hairs can be seen through his wet shirt.

'Don't you have a doctor here? With all this money to eat and drink?'

'Jason, don't get clever, get busy. Imagine it mattered to you to find a doctor.'

'So sorry,' Fred Foreman says, 'about this . . .'

'They should maybe loosen his tie,' Susie says. Concern puts her arm through Byron Sadleir's.

'How about his title? They should loosen that too. It never was too good a fit.'

'Why are you so terrible, Byron?'

He looks down and sees her hand. 'You're playing the wholehearted friend. That's very touching. Indeed.'

Samuel Marcus Cohen has adopted the medical style as he supervises Foreman's removal to Paula's bedroom. Sammy's

novels are noted for their mastery of physiological detail. Fred
Foreman is restless enough to claim that he is all right now.

'You will be, Fred,' Paula says. 'I saw you sitting there, but I
didn't react right away because I assumed it was the usual
reason: you had an erection and . . .'

She gets the smile she was angling for and, as Fred Foreman
presses a hand to his chest, she has time to sigh, slightly, at what
this has done to her party. By the time she gets back into the
main room to tell everybody that Fred is going to be fine, the
guests are already moving towards the door, as if the liner on
which they were travelling had listed very slightly and
everyone was thinking of how to abandon ship without
creating a rush. Jason has called Paula's doctor (who will be
sorry that he was not asked to the party) and the concerned few
are waiting for him. Byron Sadleir shows no wish to deprive
himself of free luxury before it is necessary. Susie is taking pains
to look like someone who is only waiting for her husband.

'So tell me,' Byron says, 'do you think that Greta Garbo ever
farted in the bath-tub?'

'Not while she was being Greta Garbo, did she?'

'The unspoken pleasures, let's talk about those as the solemn
music plays.'

Samuel Marcus Cohen himself opens the door when the
doctor is said to be on his way up.

'What greater warrant of the seriousness of Fred Foreman's
condition,' Byron says, 'than that S-s-sammy himself should
step down from his p-p-pedestal to play the b-b-b-butler?'

Dr Lacey is dressed like a banker and carries a flat, business
briefcase, as befits someone who deals, as it were, in futures.

'I do admire a man,' Byron says, 'who finishes his fuck
before he consents to do something as trivial as saving an
arriviste's life.'

'At least Fred's an arriviste who actually arrived.'

'Oh,' Byron says, 'and when do you expect to get here yourself?'

Having examined Fred Foreman, the doctor says that they have to get him to the hospital. The sick man responds as if to a threat. He says that he wants to go back to the Carlyle. When the doctor insists (not least to Paula), Foreman gestures to Jason to come closer to him and, as arrangements are made on the phone in the other room, he asks a favour.

IN A CAB. NIGHT.

> JASON
> (Breaking a silence)
> He has no right to hate me. Byron. He
> hates me, doesn't he? But he has no
> right.

> SUSIE
> He doesn't hate you. At least not
> because of . . .

> JASON
> Cassie. Who had every right to hate
> *him*, if you want to know.

> SUSIE
> And do I?

> JASON
> I don't know what *you*'re so snappy
> about.

> SUSIE
> But I'm supposed to know why you
> are.

> JASON
> This has to be it.

The cab has stopped outside the St Regis Hotel.

SUSIE

I thought he was staying at the Carlyle.

JASON

You and his wife. And you were both
right.

INT. BAR. MANHATTAN. NIGHT.

It is down the street from the St Regis. Dark, and gleaming,
with lights that confer anonymity.

JASON and SUSIE look along the bar. A young WOMAN is
sitting with a white wine spritzer reading a paperback. Waiting
is not a problem for her. She has her long, dark-stockinged
legs snaked around each other.

JASON

Has to be her. The best-looking woman
in the place.

SUSIE

Lucky I'm not here to hear that. Go
ahead, if you're sure she's the one.

JASON goes forward and SUSIE enjoys the careful confidence
which being watched gives him. He even coughs before he
speaks to the WOMAN.

JASON

Good evening. Are you conceivably
waiting for someone? Because . . .

WOMAN

You could say I was spoken for.

JASON

Fred asked me to stop by. He's . . . not
well. He's in the hospital as a matter of
fact.

WOMAN

Oh, I'm really sorry.

JASON

That's right. I'm a friend. Jason
Landauer.

WOMAN

Do I possibly know you?

JASON shakes his head, looks back towards SUSIE in a way
that draws her to the WOMAN's attention.

JASON

We were at the same party, and ... like
that. And he evidently ... can't see you
tonight. Is there anything ... that needs
to happen?

He means does she want money. Her look tells him not.

WOMAN

He needs to get better, tell him.

JASON

You'll be OK?

WOMAN

(That's a joke, right?)
I'll be fine.

JASON walks back to SUSIE, as if they had both done their
duty.

SUSIE

Which of us will be the first, isn't that
the question?

JASON

To do what?

SUSIE

Is the right answer.

It is a fine evening and there are plenty of cabs, but they seem to prefer to walk, in silence. When they reach Columbus Circle, Jason makes a questioning face: want to take a cab? Susie shrugs and they walk on. One of them, it appears, is not doing what he or she wants, but neither is sure which.

The noises they make in the apartment and the brief assurances from the sitter that the kids have been fine, and even Jason's nicely expressed gratitude, do not break the specific silence between Susie and her husband. Who is punishing whom, and for what? Those kinds of unasked questions seem to silt a bar between them.

By the time they are undressing for bed, it is almost a game of dare: who will dare to speak first, or not dare not to?

Susie says, 'Did you pay her off?'

Her tone refuses to be part of a game at all. She speaks with aggressive banality, as if there had been no silence to break.

'You were there. Fred has an account. They see each other quite regularly when he's through town.'

'They have a lot of guts, those women, I think.'

'Guts and bruises both.'

'Suppose I was out of town and you just happened to see her someplace. Would you be tempted?'

'I don't like to buy my women.'

'You do like to sell them though.'

'Meaning I sell you?'

'To the magazines, didn't you? You were very . . . helpful to me.'

'Can that never be forgiven? Because what's the matter with you these days?'

'Should I say nothing? I should.'

'What?'

'I think I caught something the day Noah fished that guy out of the ocean I shouldn't.'

'Noah and I fished that guy . . . So what did you catch?'

'It made me think. I don't know what exactly.'

'What it made you or what it was?'

'That's right. So. It'll pass.'

'Susie, tell me something. Please. Because it could be important and I can't tell you why, because I don't know, but did you throw that stone?'

'Excuse me.'

'I beg you, as my wife and the mother of my children, tell me the truth.'

'I don't even know what you're talking about.'

'While you were . . . wherever you were, that night . . . supposedly.'

'Provincetown.' She happens not to have put her nightdress on, but her nakedness is very proper now.

'Someone threw a stone through Noah's living-room window.'

'That's how it got broken. Since when can I throw a stone straight and hard enough to do that kind of damage? You know I have no throwing arm whatsoever.'

'That's from before when you started working out.'

'I work out because I'm a professional eater. "Supposedly" is nice coming from my husband and the father of my children.'

'I wouldn't blame you if it was true. Blame is not . . .'

'You're saying Provincetown was an *alibi*, is what you're imagining?'

She reaches under her pillow for her nightdress. He reaches there first and takes it and holds it away from her.

'I'm imagining you had every right to be something . . . I don't know you to be. That isn't . . .'

'Any of your business, and now you want it to be. I went to Provincetown. I had some juice —'

247

'And you talked French.'

'He talked; I listened. Pretty well.'

He comes round the bed and holds her shoulders until the expression in her eyes changes. Her smile doesn't match the look she is giving him, but it offers some kind of a promise, and then he is kissing her and knows what she wants him to do, though she will never say so. He turns her round because he loves the fall of her breasts away from her chest, though maybe what she likes is something else: the kiss of his hips against her butt.

He is already in her when she looks over her shoulder, which always excites him, and in an already slightly breathless voice she asks him, 'How much do you figure she gets? Per screw? As a matter of interest?'

There they are, strangers, fucking in the half-open mirror on the door of the walk-in closet.

JASON'S OFFICE. DAY.

JASON is checking the overnight faxes and opening the mail. He hates faxes and loves the mail. Even though he is alone, there is something public about his expression: he is making it known, if only to himself, that – despite the cheques and the promises he is finding – he is not happy about something.

The door of the office opens and we see what is the matter. His new employee is called MARTINA; she is young and pretty, in a Slavic way, and she is ready to smile, or sulk, depending on how things go.

MARTINA
(As if this closed the subject)

I'm sorry.

JASON
(Because it doesn't close it)

Subway have a flat again? Yet another
bomb scare I'll never get to hear about
from any other source?

MARTINA

I missed my connection. I coulda called
in sick. My mother *is* sick. What do
you want me to do?

JASON

How about get to the office at the time
we said? *I* do.

MARTINA

One of those mornings, right?

JASON

Very nearly one of those afternoons.

MARTINA

So this isn't going to work.

JASON

This isn't going to work, or *you* isn't
going to work?

MARTINA lifts her skirt and pulls down her panties and doesn't
mind a damn what he sees before she turns round and shows
him her ass, which is a lot hippier than he expected.

JASON

I appreciate the offer, but I'm going to
have to ... think ... about ... it.

He has spaced out the last words because there in the
doorway is GIL TEACHER.

GIL

Excuse me.

MARTINA steps out of her panties, straightens up and walks
out of the office.

GIL

Bad moment?

JASON

One of the better ones of the day so
far. If you're looking for a job as my
personal assistant, you may have noticed
that there's an opening.

GIL

And quite a pretty one too.

JASON

Next thing is, I'm accused of harassment
and my wife is standing by me. That's
when all else fails. What's happening,
Gil? Don't tell me Aaron's cat started
barking.

GIL

I'm on my way to murder Mikey
Carossa. I wanted your permission.

JASON

Where's my rubber stamp? Only I
thought everything was . . .

GIL

I got this new set of notes from him.
This morning. Do you want to see
them?

JASON

Did you?

GIL

Why is single-spacing so damn
threatening?

JASON

Go talk to the man, one on one, and
. . . *then* kill him. You want me to call
him first?

GIL

No, no.

JASON
Anything else bothering you?

Chez André is a bistro favoured by the movie crowd and recommended for its shrimp and red pepper soup *à la Michel Guérard*. There are pictures of French actors and directors (yes, Louis Malle is still there) and the red-check tablecloths and napkins that art directors used to associate with unspoiled country restaurants. The *patron* is called Jackie (André Martinez was the chef, but he has his own place now). Susie finds Byron already at the quiet table Jackie has kept for her, quite as if they had something to hide, or could have the smallest hope of hiding it *Chez André*. Byron is drinking a glass of champagne and is reading the *New York Review of Books*, which he has folded in a deliberately bulky way, as if he might soon lose patience with it altogether.

'I'm so sorry,' Susie says.

'Please don't get up,' Byron says, still sitting there.

'I was at the magazine and could I get a cab?'

'You should have kept me waiting a little longer. It's good for my morals.'

'That's the first I ever heard of them,' Susie says.

'The apt quotation is the mark of the good little girl, to whom nothing will happen. Is that what you want?'

'I guess eating with a legend gives people the shakes.' Susie is taking off her alpaca jacket. 'I used to get off on those savage profiles you did of famous people, when I was in college. I always dreamed maybe I too could be a public executioner.' She frowns at him looking at her as she puts the jacket over the back of her chair. 'What is it?'

'The nicest moment in the world is when a beautiful woman first begins to . . . how about *disrobe*?'

'I love to disappoint a man. This is as far as it goes.'

ABOUT THE SAME TIME IN JASON'S OFFICE.

JASON has PAULA STEINBERG on the line, and GIL TEACHER
watching him. GIL is sitting on a steel and leather couch by
the window, knees almost to the hands holding his chin.

> JASON
> (For GIL, to PAULA)
> On the contrary . . . on the contrary,
> because . . . let me say this now, please
> . . . I know pretty well exactly where
> we are on this thing. I don't say I like
> the neighbourhood too well, but . . .

JASON listens and gives the silence some punctuation by raising
his eyebrows, conducting what GIL cannot hear, opening and
shutting his mouth without saying anything.

> JASON
> (At last)
> I have another suggestion. No, this
> comes from me. Let's send the original
> manuscript, which — let me embarrass
> you — you described as a masterpiece, to
> some other sensitive publishing person,
> off the record —
> (He listens again, but supplies no punctuation this time)
> You want your money back?

> GIL
>
> Jason, please —

> JASON
> (A silencing hand to GIL)
> No, I personally will send it back to
> you, because this is a book I believe in,
> and a writer . . . No, Paula, I'll tell *you*
> what. You're not a decision-maker. You

have many qualities; you are not a
decision-maker.

He hangs up.

> GIL
> Jesus Christ, Jason.

> JASON
> Gil, I did not come rushing into your
> office; you came rushing into mine.
> You wanted something done; I did
> something. Now let's have a beer and
> not be here when she calls back.

> GIL
> I don't want you giving me your
> money.

> JASON
> And I don't want to do it, so that's not
> going to spoil the party.

JASON opens an icebox with the covers of best-sellers (which
he does *not* represent) pasted on the door.

> JASON
> Ethel working yet?

> GIL
> Three days a week, for Standish Nichol
> and Riley.

> JASON
> (Holds out a beer)
> I told you not to come to this stupid
> city. You came; you saw; now how
> about you hang in until you conquer?

The telephone rings and he puts a hand on GIL's forearm as
they listen to it.

When the ringing stops, JASON's hand stays there for another
second or two.

★

Susie is enjoying the squash flower stuffed with 'caviar of eggplant' that comes with her *rouget*. Byron pushes his unfinished plate of lamb sweetbreads away and watches her work.

'So what are you hoping for? A distasteful incident or what?'

'I'll take what.'

'Are you unhappy with Jason Landauer?'

'Why add Landauer like that?'

'To make you think. Why are we having lunch?'

'Because I used to be such a fan of yours?'

'This food is not very special, you know. Are you going to write something cruel about it?'

'Mine's quite special. You want to say something, that's a tongue you have right there in your mouth.'

'Ideally, I'd like it to be somewhere else entirely.'

'Oh boy.'

'I'm sending it back.'

'This is what you mean to do to me, is it?'

'One must fight to maintain standards, my dear, come the four corners of the earth in arms. Waiter!'

'Be right there, *monsieur*.'

'*Monsieur* comes sweetly in a Brooklyn accent.' Byron holds up the empty bottle to the returning waiter. 'We could do with another one of these, couldn't we?'

'I don't promise to drink a lot of it.'

'Don't worry. I promise to.' He takes her hand, as if he were re-establishing some broken continuity. 'I want to tell you a secret.'

'You have one left?'

'Don't flirt with me, darling. I'm not worth it.'

'And that's the secret?'

INT. THE LANDAUERS' APARTMENT. EVG.

JASON has come home in time to play with NICKY and
CAROLINE. He is down on the floor building them one of his
special, very tall card-houses.

> JASON
>
> How many storeys is that, Nix?

> NICKY
>
> Sixteen.

> CAROLINE
>
> Seventy.

> JASON
>
> Seven*teen*, I make it. We'll have to
> make a hole in the ceiling pretty soon,
> it's getting so high.

> NICKY
>
> Who are you kidding?

CAROLINE and NICKY freeze as they hear the sound of a key
in the front door. Then NICKY is on his feet and running.

> NICKY
>
> Mommy, mommy, come see –

The front door slams shut. The breeze from it is *just* enough
to make the whole elaborate structure of the card-house tilt,
very very slowly. NICKY and the street-clothed SUSIE are just
about in the living-room doorway in time to see all the cards
flat on the floor.

> JASON
>
> So all of a sudden we're playing
> Pelmanism!

> CAROLINE
>
> You've just ruined everything, Susie
> Harkness.

SUSIE

Oh, sweetie, I'm so sorry.

JASON

Some things are made to fall down.

SUSIE

Have you guys eaten?

NICKY

We were waiting for you.

SUSIE

And here I am. Go wash hands, I'll be
right there.

NICKY and CAROLINE look at JASON. Then they sigh at each
other and go out of the room.

SUSIE

How was your day?

JASON

Short. Eight till five-thirty. My new
assistant is now my old one. Gil Teacher
is no longer Paula's pet. You didn't
drive to Provincetown again, did you?

SUSIE

I had lunch with Byron Sadleir.

JASON

Talk French at all?

CAROLINE
(Back in the doorway)
So now we have clean hands.

SUSIE

Listen, at this point, Byron is like a
piece of Sixties history.

JASON

He's like a piece of Sixties *shit*.

CAROLINE

So now what? Because . . .

The telephone starts to ring. SUSIE indicates for JASON to deal with it and then she goes and presses CAROLINE, with the flat of one hand behind her blonde head, towards the kitchen.

Jason's usual people do not have a car available and he has trouble finding a cab that is willing to go to Brooklyn. The driver of the one he does get, finally, has no idea how to find the street where Gertrude lives. Jason does not know where his anger has come from, but it seems to make him incomprehensible to the driver who is soon blaming him for his own incompetence.

'The streets have changed,' Jason says.

'And I'm supposed to know?' The driver raises his voice over the Haitian radio station he is listening to.

Finally they turn into the street and see the police cars and the ambulance. Jason pays the guy off and runs to his mother's house.

Gertrude is sitting in the ransacked living room. She is rocking herself on a low chair. Stuff has been dumped all over the place. She looks up and rumples her brow at Jason.

'I had company,' she says.

'How many?' Jason crouches in front of his mother and his hand is on her narrow knee. 'And who were they?'

'Two punks. They didn't introduce themselves.'

Jason looks up and sees one of the paramedics, who is about ready to go. He has been to a lot worse incidents than this one.

'Does she need to go to the hospital?'

'Ask her,' Gertrude says, 'because she isn't going. She's OK.'

'She needs watching,' the paramedic says. 'But . . .'

'Thanks for being here,' Jason says.

The paramedic makes the usual face and he's on his way.

'What did they take?'

'What is there? The crown jewels were in the bank. Why wasn't I?'

'How did they get in?'

'They rang the bell.'

'And you opened the door?'

'That's what doors used to be for.'

The police sergeant stands there, bulging with professional gear. 'OK, Mrs Landauer, that's about it for us. We'll have someone bring some pictures up here for you to look at later, in case you recognise somebody, but . . .'

'You don't advise me to?'

'I never said that. Did I say that? You identify them, we'll go after them. I'd never say that.'

'Thanks for being here, sergeant.'

'Take care of your mother.'

Jason starts to pick things up. They have even thrown pictures off the walls. Hatred and fear make him furtively angry with his mother. 'You need to get some new locks.'

'Locks!' She is looking at herself in the mirror from her bag. 'Right now, I'd settle for *looks*.'

There is a tap on the window. A black man is leaning across from the steps up to the front door.

Jason says, 'Yeah?'

'Gertrude home?'

'Who are you?'

'Curtis Lamming. Who are you? You're the son!'

'I'm a son.'

'Curtis, that you? Come on in.'

'She was mugged here this afternoon.'

Curtis goes into the living room and crouches down by

Gertrude in pretty well the same attitude as Jason when he first got there.

'I tried to call you.'

'I heard you had. Goddamit, I had my mobile switched off. I came soon as I could.'

'You want a cuppa coffee?' Gertrude is on her feet.

'Like when don't I?'

'I'll go make it,' Jason says.

'So what happened here? What did they do to you? I know: I should see the other guy, but I'm seeing you, Gert, and I don't like it as much as I did.'

Why does 'Gert' make Jason feel so sick that he has to wash his face in the kitchen basin when he overhears it? He makes the coffee and is not sure whether he is dawdling in there or hurrying to get back into the living room. Unworthy thoughts crowd into his head like spectators jostling after an accident.

'So: your mother tells me you're in the agency business.'

'This is black. Did you want it black?'

'I like it black,' Curtis Lamming says.

'Curtis works with me. He also writes.'

'I'd like to see something,' Jason says.

'You kept quiet about him, Gertrude.'

It is a relief to hear Lamming use Gertrude's full name. 'So what sort of thing do you write?' Jason says.

'I write a lot about my dad.'

'OK. What kind of a man was he?'

'I don't know. Never met 'im.'

'OK.'

'I dream of being a mean sonofabitch, but I can never quite make it unless I'm being him.'

Gertrude has her legs back now. She is tidying the room, fitting drawers back into the bureau, picking up ornaments.

Curtis Lamming watches her as he might watch a child, with concern, but with no active participation.

'How about your wife, Jason? Don't make me let you neglect your wife.'

'I'll call her. I'll stay here with you tonight.'

'Jason, go home now, OK, will you please?'

'I'll be here,' Curtis says. 'They come back for the couch and stuff, I'll take care of them. Tell me something: how do you rate Jorge Luis Borges today?'

'How do I rate Borges? Like Mexican silver. Nicely worked, but doesn't finally weigh too much. Not a question I get asked a lot. Is there still a cab-stand down on the corner of Third?'

'Or you can get the bus. Back into Manhattan? You can get the bus. Next time you're coming over, tell Gertrude, and I'll dump some material on you. Mexican silver. Right!'

EXT. GERTRUDE'S HOUSE AND STREET.
BROOKLYN. NIGHT.

How can JASON both hurry away from the sight of CURTIS LAMMING with GERTRUDE and, at the same time, somehow be reluctant to leave them together?

He walks down to the corner, apprehensive, yet with aggressive motions of his jaw, as if he were looking for trouble. He is almost disappointed to see a cab waiting on the old stand.

IN THE CAB:

The driver has no problem taking him to Riverside Drive. He wants to talk about baseball, which JASON has not followed again since the big strike.

JASON tries many positions to be comfortable. How can it be

that he doesn't fit too well in a taxicab? His mother is all right; she is not alone; he has not had to stay the night. What's the problem?

INT. THE LIVING ROOM. THE LANDAUERS' APARTMENT. NIGHT.

SUSIE is wearing her glasses as she works her notes into a piece for the magazine.

JASON is sitting on the lounger with a manuscript on his knees, but he is not reading.

                    JASON
        He's fucking my mother.
                    SUSIE
        Good for her.
                    JASON
        You're kidding.
                    SUSIE
        It's not good for her. It is too good for
        her. I should look so good at her age.
                    JASON
        She's almost certainly giving him
        money.
                    SUSIE
        You give me money.
                    JASON
        Dad was right probably.
                    SUSIE
        Well, I think it's spunky.
                    JASON
        Spunky.
                    SUSIE
        A woman over seventy years old who
        refuses to . . . you know. Go quietly.

JASON

You didn't see him.

SUSIE

What's threatening you so much? You
want her to be alone? You want to
move back in with her? Is he tall and
good-looking?

JASON

He's tall. She probably paid by the yard.

SUSIE

Fred Foreman has an account with a
call-girl and that's cool, you think.
Remind me what the difference is.

JASON

I will when she gets herself killed.

He frowns. From the kitchen comes the sudden then steady
beep of the smoke alarm.

JASON

Have you got something on the stove,
babe, possibly?

SUSIE

Jesus Christ. Jesus Christ.

IN THE KITCHEN:

Flames have had time to leap from the black saucepan on the
stove to the paper-towel roll and they are flaring towards the
ceiling.

JASON

Stay back. Get the kids and get them
out of the apartment. Then call Stefan,
get him to call the fire department . . .

SUSIE

Jason . . .

JASON is filling a saucepan and throwing water at the flames.

> JASON
> Do as I fucking well tell you. NOW!

He pushes her out of the kitchen and shuts the door.

> SUSIE
> *Jason* . . .

> JASON
> You goddam fucking bitch.

He seems almost sorry when there are no more flames and, except for the smoke which makes him cough, quietly, there is nothing left to be masterful about. He stays in there with the door shut and opens the window and leans out, breathing the freedom of the night.

The kitchen door opens and the JANITOR is there with an extinguisher.

> JASON
> All taken care of, Stefan.

> JANITOR
> You sure?

JASON indicates to look for himself.

> JANITOR
> I called the fire department already.

> JASON
> What'll I do? Start another fire?

> JANITOR
> OK. I'll tell them . . .

NICKY and CAROLINE are looking into the kitchen from the door.

> JASON
> Go back to bed, you guys. Everything's
> fine.

The telephone is ringing. JASON shakes his head, picks up.

> JASON
>
> Yeah.

INT. THE LIVING ROOM. SAME. NIGHT.

JASON standing in the window looking out at the traffic whitening Riverside Drive with its lights. He senses SUSIE has come back into the room.

> JASON
>
> Guess who that was on the phone.

> SUSIE
>
> No.

> JASON
>
> Samuel Marcus.

> SUSIE
>
> And?

> JASON
>
> Why didn't you tell me he came over here tonight?

> SUSIE
>
> He came over here tonight. What did he want?

> JASON
>
> He left some books he bought at Rizzoli. Some he couldn't bum from the publishers, I guess. They should be in the closet. You cooked for him.

> SUSIE
>
> What are you suddenly? A special prosecutor? You come in and tell me about this black dude who's fucking your mother and I'm *indicted* for not

confessing to an hour with Samuel
Marcus Cohen?

JASON

What did he want?

SUSIE

You. Me. Anything he could impress his
powerful personality on.

JASON

Funny night.

SUSIE

Too true. Goddam fucking bitch is
where we're at now, is it? Well, let me
tell you something.

How might someone guess, from her posture, and theirs, that Laverne is being an elephant for Nicky and Caroline, *because* there is a problem between their parents? Is it her heavy patience as she lurches along the edge of the grass above the foreshore? The sea is quite placid and the slow tide gargles in the shingle.

Noah and Jason are over by the telescope with which Noah scans the ocean for opportunities for aggressive philanthropy. It is as if they were in a different room in the garden, where the kids cannot see or hear or guess from their father's attitude that anything is wrong. Susie's absence fills the scene.

'Kick her the fuck out the house,' Noah says.

'She says she's in love.'

'So? Kick here the fuck out the house.'

'What's that going to do for anybody?'

'She crossed the line. Love or no love. You have to be strong. You're not strong, you're weak.'

'So maybe I'm weak. What about the kids? She's confused. Suppose this is a time to be gentle.'

'It's not.'

'How would you know? Strong. Strong is not going to see Asa, right? That's what strong is for you. Doing what suits you best, is that strong?'

'You know what he needs to do? Eat is what he needs to do.'

'I thought you were with the kids, Laverne. What's happening here?'

'They ran over to Mrs Blofeld's. She has that bouncy castle they like. They're fine. Not like you, Jason. Maybe she wants you to tan her hide, ever occur to you?'

Noah says, '*Laverne*, will you please?'

'Who does she think she is? You have to do something.'

'I have this friend, people say that, he immediately does nothing. Which is often the smart thing.'

'What do your friends say?'

'I'm not telling them.'

'Think they don't know?' Laverne says. 'Because what's she doing, your pretty little *shiksa*, while you mope around being understanding? My book, you know what you should do? What that character shoulda done – what was his name? Blake Ambler! – which is grab your opportunity with both hands. Start over.'

'Opportunity? With two children? Are they really OK?'

'I gave them something to eat. They're fine. She wants out? She's out! You look terrible. Live a little.'

'She's my wife.'

'Come on, Jace,' Noah says, 'be honest with yourself.'

'I be honest with *my*self? How about you?'

'This is what you come to my house to say to me?'

'Your safe little house, where you play safe, where you're the king of the castle, where . . .'

'Enough.'

'Enough is right.'

'You guys finally,' Laverne says.

'Because Gertrude gets roughed up, some punks rough her up, do you go see her? Do you send her a single stick of flowers? What do you do? *Ever?*'

'You still have a tongue, don't you, little brother?'

'It's been up a lot of asses, but it still has other uses.'

'You despise yourself; you despise other people. Why?'

'Could just be they're despicable.'

'Everybody has to be your father.'

'Everybody except my father. Know when this started for me? Fucking Blake Ambler. I wish you'd left him to drown.'

'No, you don't. Imagine we had. You don't.'

'So why're you leaving me?'

Laverne is already almost back at the house. She turns and calls to them. 'We have some cold cuts. Do you want baked sweet potatoes? The micro, they take ten minutes.'

'Go home,' Noah says. 'Break some china. Jesus. You had to marry a trophy wife . . .'

'Noah, stop this, is my advice, right now.'

'HEY, THE TWO DEAF BROTHERS!'

'So what happened with Blake Ambler, that this is all my fault?'

'Nothing probably. Nothing, she says.'

Noah puts an arm around Jason and leads him towards the house. It is more like an arrest than a fraternal embrace. Noah is bulky like the cop who came to Gertrude's house. As they go up the steps on to the porch, Jason shrugs himself free.

'So be angry with me.' Noah says.

Laverne is in the kitchen door. 'How about I do some *gefilte* fish, which I have ready, potato salad, diced carrot, I chop a few scallions in there, plus I have some hard-boiled eggs.'

'I couldn't eat a goddam thing, Laverne, and you know it. A joke's a joke, OK? I'm going to have to head on back into the city.'

'Gertrude doesn't want me over there,' Noah says.

'You're a fucking mind-reader, Noah. You know what everybody wants, which always fortunately turns out to be nothing whatsoever from you. Think about that.'

'She'll come back,' Laverne says. 'She'll get even and then she'll come back. Don't worry about the kids. We love 'em.'

'Even for what?'

'Have you been faithful to her all the time?'

'I wanted a wife. I wanted a marriage. I'll be back Saturday morning. Have I been faithful? What kind of question is that?'

'And what kind of answer is that?'

'Trophy wife. What kind of a way is that to talk about your sister-in-law?'

'Why pretend?'

'Pretend?' Jason says. 'Pretend what? You know what worries me most: the kids. Something happening to them. And her being . . . all right: *pleased*. Like it would prove that I was . . . This Mrs Blofeld? She's that way, right? You don't like her, Susie; you never did, did you?'

'You don't want the truth,' Noah says, 'don't ask for it.'

'The truth!' Jason says. 'Know what the truth is? The truth is what people tell you when they want to hurt you without telling a lie, is what the truth is.'

AARON GLASSER'S LIVING ROOM. NIGHT.

The Manhattan skyline glitters outside the big windows.
JASON has called to make sure, he says, that GIL is not

reacting badly to the situation with *Sheet Music*. He is sitting on the couch, under the big Hockney, with Theodore, the Siamese cat, glaring at him and slowly moving its tail.

GIL

How's Susie?

JASON

You've heard.

GIL

Heard.

JASON

She . . . we're not together right now.

ETHEL

What happened?

JASON

I wasn't going to say anything, but I did. As much as I want to. She's seeing somebody else.

GIL

You sure you don't want something to drink?

ETHEL

Or eat.

JASON

I'm all fuelled up here. All I need is a good recipe for what I'm supposed to do.

GIL

Beautiful mistresses are supposed to help. My book of basic plots informs me.

JASON

Right. What I need is a deeply understanding woman who can accept that I'm all out of emotional energy, but I do need some straight sex, and we can take it from there.

GIL

What happened to that girl in your
office?

JASON

In my office, nothing happened to her.
Martina. She's long gone. So . . .
(He manages at least to *touch* the cat, then he gets up)
Time I was too. Stay happy, you guys.
It's a neat trick if you can swing it.

GIL and ETHEL look at each other, while JASON forgets the
cat and uncricks his neck.

'Something you forgot,' Jason says. He is holding out the
Rizzoli bag.

'You want to come in? I'm all by myself.'

Samuel Marcus Cohen has what he likes to call a *garçonnière*
in a serviced building right across from the Algonquin Hotel.
He is often out of New York, teaching a semester at UC at
Santa Barbara and a regular stint in Jerusalem, but his books and
mementos (and awards) and cigar-smoke have given the place a
distinct flavour. He is wearing brown corduroy pants, a
collarless cotton shirt with a cotton baseball jacket over it and
Timberlands, with no socks.

Jason says, 'So, you'll be finding another agent.'

'Never occurred to me.'

'You think I sold you short to Paula, don't you?'

'Nothing to do with it.'

'So how do you figure it from here on in?'

'This is not a nice thing to happen. I fully recognise that. No
one's happy.'

'Come on.'

'About that. Do you want something to drink?'

'What are you going to do? Pretend to be grown up?'

'What else can grown-ups do?'

'You're the one man, Sammy, I had undiluted respect for. Ever since I was your student. The one person I always defended.'

'Against . . . ?'

'Listen, people say things.'

'I'm listening. Say what?'

'You're tight with a dollar, for Christ's sake. You know that.'

'Who says that?'

'The whole fucking chorus of Hebrew slaves says it. Jesus, Sammy, when did you last buy anybody a cup of coffee? Not to mention a birthday present. You're budget-conscious, Samuel.'

'Put Paula's present on my tab.'

'It's on your fucking tab. I came here to say that you're a dirty bastard, Samuel.'

'Is that going to help?'

'You're a dirty bastard, Samuel.'

'Why am I?'

'You're fucking my wife, for Christ's sake. Don't tell me you hadn't heard that either.'

'Can we try to be adult here?'

'Fucking was never adult. Never. Fucking is a low-down dirty business and you know it. Be sensitively and life-enhancingly sensual in your books, but don't try that shit with me.'

'I never meant it to happen.'

'You put that line in a book, Sammy, and I don't care *who* you are, it's out like a bad tooth. Have you met my children,

Sammy? I mean, I know you never gave them a *present*, not so much as a candy bar —'

'You mentioned teeth . . .'

'Shut up when I'm ranting, OK? How many times have you been in our house? And how many times have you asked *us* to anything? Who's counting? What's to count?'

'You're understandably angry and upset. You're also in a double bind.'

'Spare me the clichés. Use them in your next overwritten satire on success and all the other things you hold so dear.'

'Does it occur to you, Jason, that you are pretty well *enjoying* this?'

'What are you going to do? *Charge* me?'

'I'm a little disappointed in you, Jason.'

'Are you, professor? Well, I'm . . . what am I? You probably have a word for it; I don't.'

'Because I thought we might handle this without — but I see that that's impossible.'

'Oh you do? On a clear day you can probably see right to the end of your nose. Wait a minute: I'll think of something closer.'

'That's self-hating and unworthy.'

'Well, that's exactly what I am.'

'What are the real issues here?'

'The real issues! You screwed my wife. You're still doing it.'

'I've now had many long talks with Susan. She needs air.'

'She gets that with your dick in her mouth?'

'Don't demean yourself, Jason. I used to like you.'

'But my present behaviour is leading to a revision of my case? I ought to wring your neck. I should add to this city's frightening tally of brutal and undetected killings.'

'I always suspected that you are a violent person, Jason, afraid of your own violence. Hence the excess of deference and *disponibilité*.'

'Don't talk fucking French to me.'

'Your marriage wasn't working,' Samuel Marcus says. 'You knew it. Susan certainly knew it.'

'It only remains to tell the kids.'

'It's perfectly understandable that you would use your children, whom you do not always cherish, as a screen . . .'

'How often do you see your children by your eight previous marriages, liaisons and signing sessions? I mean, I know about the junkie and the hooker, but are there others? Who says I don't cherish them? Is that what Susie says? Because what is she doing right now?'

'I don't consider that my business. Susan feels –'

'Fuck *Susan*. OK, you did that already. In my own apartment you did that.'

'It's in your joint names, she tells me.'

'You've checked my fucking *lease* already? You are a fucking *ghoul*, Samuel Marcus. You are a treacherous, shameless old fuck.'

'I'm not your father, Jason. This anger is misplaced.'

'Susan – why am *I* calling her Susan now? – told you that my *father* did something to her?'

'I never said that.'

'Are you sure you don't want to say it? It might be useful to have some allegations of that kind available against a helpless old man who would never behave like you behave. My father!'

'One thing is definitely beginning to emerge, you know, Jason, from this.'

'Well, keep it in your pants until Susan gets back. You complacent asshole, really.'

'I may have to seek different representation.'

'Does that bring me up short? I can't wait to blow you out of my ass. Don't wince like that. You write those things, why is it so painful to hear? You write those things all the time. "Glorying in the vernacular", isn't that what you called it in that interview on A and E?'

'They never paid me – do you know that? – at least that I heard.'

'I embezzled ten bucks now?'

'Your problem, Jason, as I see it, is that you feel obliged to keep up this pretence of innocence.'

'Innocence. Do I? Of what am I guilty?'

'Everybody knows about you and Paula.'

'Paula. They do, huh? Do they also know about the earth being flat and God having a long white beard? What the fuck are you talking about? Who told you this? Or does it represent the full total of your fictional output on a day when you've *understandably* had other things on your mind, and places?'

'Somebody told Susan.'

'Did he or she? The plot thickens. Or sickens. It sickens. Because although I make a *show* of finding Paul Steinberg irresistible, I resist all along the line, and always have. *Who* told her, Samuel? You, to get her into pants? You, to get into her pants.'

'You will never understand what there is between me and Susan if you insist on thinking of it only in those terms. Never.'

'Byron Sadleir told her. I just might put a contract out on both you two pricks. He probably fucked her too. Literary Figures Linked in Twin Slaying. There's a chuckle in everything if you dig deep enough. How do I get to punch you in the nose now, Sammy? I seem to be all spent here.'

They hear the front door open and heels on the walnut block floor in the hall. Susie comes in, looking good. Then she sees Jason. She puts down packages and magazines and tries to have no particular expression on her face.

Jason says, 'Nobody gets kissed, right?'

'Jason and I have been having a talk.'

'I hear you already took inventory on the apartment.'

'Sammy, we have just thirty-five minutes to curtain time.'

'Susie . . .'

'Jason, is this the moment really?'

'The moment? When will the moment be? I wouldn't want to miss it. Did you speak to Nicky and Caroline?'

'I called in earlier. They seem fine. It's only that we have these tickets.'

'House seats, no doubt. I have to talk to you, Susie. Alone. Privately. There are things . . .'

'I know.'

'There damn well are.' Jason's face is red and swollen and – it's the last thing he wants to have happen – he is swallowing tears. 'The kitchen . . . is . . . being taken care of, but . . . I . . . we . . . need to choose . . . Wednesday noon the guy is coming . . .'

'I'll stop by.'

JASON'S BEDROOM. NIGHT.

He is reading a manuscript and making notes in his usual red Le Pen. He knows that he is pretending to be what he really is, but what else can he do?

The telephone purls and, again, he pretends to be reluctant to answer it. He answers it.

> GIRL'S VOICE
>
> Mr Landauer?
>
> JASON
>
> Yes. Who is this?

GIRL'S VOICE

Yes, I'm calling in response to your
advertisement.

JASON

Advertisement. Oh, about needing an
assistant . . . How did you get this
number?

GIRL'S VOICE

No. This is your Thousand and One
Nights Straight Sex and No Shit
Service. Which I understand you were
wanting.

JASON

Who the hell is this?

GIRL'S VOICE

You wouldn't want me to come to
your house, of course. So how about
we meet at your office in – not much
traffic at this hour – say twenty minutes?

JASON

I can't do this.

GIRL'S VOICE

You can't do what you want to do?
Why is that? Sure you can. You can do
things to me you didn't do with her.
I'd . . . appreciate it.

JASON

You're putting me on, right?

GIRL'S VOICE

Like a glove. Tight as tight. I'm not
going to be wasting my time, am I? I'd
hate that.

JASON

Is this – ?

GIRL S VOICE
I don't mean to be . . . boastful, but this
is basically the Girl of your Dreams.
Now or never. Twenty minutes. I'll
wait five. And that's it.

'I've never tried to get into the building this late. I just hope these keys . . . We don't want . . . Oh, OK, it seems to work.'

'I love these places at night.'

'So long as we don't set anything off. Think the elevators are working? I don't know anything about these things.'

'I don't mind stairs.'

'I never figured you'd show.'

'I wasn't sure you would.'

'I'm not sure I did. I mean, this doesn't seem like me at all. Or you. OK, they work.'

'Can I press the button?'

'Eighteen. Press it.'

Jason watches her, as if she were a child. There is no problem getting into the office, though it seems a different place with no telephone ringing, no voices from David Kersh's offices.

'We're better in here probably. My partner deals with movie people. He's better furnished than I am. Big liars have to be. Now what's all this about, seriously?'

She takes off her hair-band and shakes the dark hair loose, as if the feeling of it over her face and mouth is the primer she needs. 'It's about you want to fuck somebody and I want it to be me.'

'Ethel . . .'

'Let's not do names. Let's do things.'

'I'm sorry.'

'Nothing to be sorry about. I'm someone you don't know. You thought you did, or thought you should, but I'm a total stranger who wants to do what you want me to do. What's going to stop us? A fuck without strings. Don't call me Pinocchio and I won't you.'

She unbuttons the front of what should be that same dress she was wearing when she came to dinner and had to go feed Maria. She steps out of it and right away she is unhooking her bra and showing him breasts that are faintly blue-veined and milky-white. One long black hair glistens on the left nipple.

'Does he know you're doing this?'

'Why talk? You don't want to talk. Or do you want to talk?'

'You're very beautiful.'

She takes off her shoes, now, and pulls down her panties. Yes, she has a thick black muff and it shows a glimpse of pink between her legs as she stands there, feet apart, hands on hips. She turns and shows him the back view. She has a slim back and tight white buttocks, not one bit like Martina.

'This is me. Where are you?'

'OK, but whatever you say, or don't, this could have . . . it has to have . . . consequences.'

'It is a consequence. Of what you said. And what you wanted. And what I did, and do. Are you chickening out here? I'll forgive you, but will you forgive yourself?'

'Either way, will I?'

'I heard you were quite a stud at one time.'

'I thought you two were so happy. I really like . . . him.'

'Gil and I are not a single item. Or is it you'd sooner he was here and not me?'

Jason takes off his clothes awkwardly, as if for a physical. He wishes quite seriously that he did not have to go through with this, at least until she sits down, cross-legged, on the deep carpet and looks very closely at what she is doing until she looks up at him, with lots of white in her eyes, and he grabs down at her and kisses and kisses and kisses her and then he can hardly wait till she is crouching on the floor, looking back at him, and he has to have her the first time, fast.

'I'm sorry, if – I needed that, like that.'

'I'm here for that. We have all night. Don't we?'

'I guess we do. I just . . . my kids are with my brother. If anything happened, they needed me . . .'

'What could you do? Do you want me to go to work on you right away, or what?'

'Am I supposed to understand why you're doing this? Does that play any part in your pleasure, or does my *not* understanding . . . ?'

'Probably.'

'Ethel, something happened. I can tell. What?'

'Do you like a girl to . . . while you fuck her? I can bite the nail off so it won't hurt. Unless you want it to hurt. Oh look, he has a rule, your partner, that bends! You want to do things to me with it? Or . . . if you want me to.'

'He dared you and you did it, is that what happened? Did you do this before? Is he happy you're doing this?'

'By the way,' Ethel says. 'Your friend came home.'

'*Aaron* did?'

'He finished his script. The studio loved it. They paid him all the money and he came home. They were high and he . . . was higher. He read Gil's novel in like twenty minutes and then they started working on it together while I was at the office. You heard about my office? I was there, they were . . . in the apartment. Pretty soon they were working on each other.'

'How did you find out?'

'The usual way. Gil is very honest. He spilt the beans. Spilt beans are his favourite recipe. Fatherhood is not his bag, he had to tell me. And I had to listen, with Aaron in the other room feeding the cat.'

'He loves Maria.'

'He did, but she's been sick a lot, croup. It keeps him awake; it keeps me *busy*, but it also keeps him awake, and you know what writers are: they do need that clear head in the morning. Are you ready to start again? Oh look, it's moving of its own accord! Or can you make that happen consciously? Do they all go clockwise like that?'

'Clockwise. I guess so. Do you want a drink or anything?'

'I'm all lubricated here without. I guess there were indications, which I have to say I never saw. Like when that guy came by, Gorgeous, the photographer friend of Aaron's. Gil talked to him for a long, long time. He's an information gatherer, but he was also, in retrospect, fascinated.'

'So Gil told you about him and . . .'

'Yes, he did. Very . . . *gently*, I have to say. Like I never realised before how little he thought of me, you know? Now he *was* thinking about me, I realised everything, including that I married a guy who, basically, wasn't one.'

'Did all this happen *before* I came by the other night?'

'It *had* happened, but I didn't know that. I knew that . . . something was different, because everything *seemed* just the same. It all started out, everyone was very civilised and . . . practical and unexcited. Aaron especially. Aaron was frankly a delight and didn't want anything to change, necessarily.'

'Why do people always produce that shit at times like that?'

'That's right. No, don't be shy. I like it there. You know what I'd like to do, with this? Guess. You can.'

'I don't think I can do that, Ethel.'

'You don't have to hurt me. And we can still go on talking,

if you want to. Don't do it *hard*. Medium rare, please. Nothing more. You read *The Story of O.*, didn't you? Think of me as O.'

'Ethel, you are bad. So, what do they think you're doing at this minute?'

'I don't suppose they care. Because . . . something happened.'

'Something happened. Which was what?'

'OK. I threw Aaron's lousy Siamese out of the window.'

'You did what?'

'I threw his cat out of the window.'

'You threw Theodore out of the window? *Where?*'

'Where? Where I was; where it was. The penthouse. I couldn't take it anywhere and do it exactly.'

'You couldn't have done a thing like that.'

'Of course I couldn't. I equally couldn't have called you up, not little Ethel of Ethel and Gil limited, and asked you to come and fuck me up the ass. Yes, I could. Yes, I did. Murder makes you hot to trot, isn't that what they say?'

'*Then* what happened?'

'This *is* then, Jason. This did. So: two major clients gone in a single week, is that possibly what's going through your mind?'

THE LANDAUERS' KITCHEN. WEDNESDAY NOON.

There is no sign of scorching. SUSIE has approved the new curtains. The units that were damaged (and a couple that were not, but didn't match the new ones) have been replaced. There is going to be a new cooker. The kitchen is better than ever.

SUSIE
It looks great finally.

JASON

So do you, I have to say.

SUSIE

You don't.

JASON

I appreciate that.

SUSIE is wearing a pink pants suit with little black button boots and has a Hermès scarf over her newly done hair. She uses her hands more when she speaks to JASON than she did when they were living together.

SUSIE

You're not sleeping. That's bad.

JASON

Don't worry about it. But I do have to talk to you.

SUSIE

I figured you might.

JASON

You don't have a lunch?

SUSIE

I'm going to have to stop doing it. I'm getting reproachful messages from my liver, like . . . *must we*?

They go into the bedroom because Susie says she needs a pair of shoes that go better with what she is wearing than the new boots. She is glad to be doing something while Jason tells her what it is he needs, or wants, to tell her.

'Left field,' she says.

'Left field is right. It means nothing. Meant nothing. To either of us. That's the deal.'

'And you rightly wasted no time in closing it. Or telling me.'

'You have a right to know. I wouldn't want you to feel guilty for nothing.'

'I don't feel guilty, for anything. There was no call for you to be so thoughtful. So what was it like with a woman you don't have to have breakfast with? She *was* your breakfast, right?'

'Interesting. How are things with you?'

'Sammy is a genius.'

'So he says. So I always believed. How does that register in the sack?'

'I don't intend to talk about it.'

'At least it isn't Byron Sadleir.'

'I like Byron. A lot.'

'Is he next? I think I need to change my shirt. Is that permissible? Or is next simultaneous now? What do I know?'

'Jason, if you hate me, say you hate me. Say what you really feel. Also what you really want to have happen.'

'Do I know either thing? There's what you want and there's what you'll settle for.'

'That one. That's a great shirt. Put that one on.'

'Susie, you may be having a great time. *Susan*, you may be having a great time too. But I'm not, and I didn't tell you about Ethel to give the impression that I am . . .'

'But you still could be.'

'Whatever I'm doing, you are fucking my most illustrious client — ex-client in all probability — and in the process wrecking my business, my home life, and also my children.'

'*Our* children. Who are fine, because I talked to them.'

'That makes them fine? Come on.'

'Meanwhile, it doesn't mean a thing that you are screwing Ethel Teacher —'

'Oh! Guess who I saw yesterday.'

'There's more? There is more.'

'Cassie Queiroz, who used to be Cassie Sadleir. Isn't that astonishing?'

'Probably. Why?'

'Did I see her? It's astonishing because I did see her. After all these years. In the same week that . . . all this happened. He's still alive and, what's more, he's giving a recital at Carnegie Hall, which is why they're in town.'

'Was she glad to see you?'

'She didn't see me. I saw her and it was . . . strange. Because I didn't feel anything *now*, because she's quite aged, though still . . . but I did sort of feel what I felt *then*. Flashback to an emotion I no longer felt. So what, right? I remembered how I just couldn't believe my luck when I felt the tip of her tongue between my lips.'

'That's how I felt.'

'Yeah?'

'With you.'

'And him.'

'Sammy is sixty-two years old. I'm thirty, you may remember. I'm not the only one who's lucky. I also know what Sammy is like. He's told me, very frankly.'

'Very frankly, he's told anybody who will listen. Fifteen million sold. How soon will it be, did you ever stop to wonder, before you – and I – appear in print?'

A PENTHOUSE WINDOW IS BEING OPENED.

'I had to do it, Jason.'

'And you did it. So what do you have to do now?'

'You never really wanted to marry me, did you, that much?'

'How much is that much? I loved you. I asked you to marry me. You didn't want to marry *me* that much.'

A MAN STANDING IN AN OPEN WINDOW HAS A
BABY OVER HIS SHOULDER.

'I wanted you. I don't know too much about marriage. Does
anyone any more?'

'What you wanted was what happened last night, only all the
time. With different girls.'

'I had plenty of that. Before I met you. Is that what got to
you? I couldn't do anything about that.'

'I can take the kids up to my folks Saturday. I know you
never like to have them the whole weekend.'

'Don't bother. They're staying up at Cape Cod. With Noah
and Laverne. It's all fixed. And sorry, but you're wrong: I am
too going up there to be with them.'

'To keep them away from me, right? That's cheap, Jason.'

'How was I supposed to know what you'd be doing? For all
I know you could be addressing the Knesset with Samuel
Marcus. You're welcome to come. I wanted them to have a
nice weekend is all.'

THE MAN IN THE OPEN WINDOW IS SHOUTING
BACK AT SOMEONE IN THE ROOM WHO IS
YELLING AND CLOSING ON HIM FROM BEHIND.

'The first time you seriously think about them is when you
can use them to do something to me.'

THE MAN IS LEANING OUT OF THE WINDOW. A
MAN BEHIND HIM CANNOT REACH THE BABY.

'Get your clothes off, Susie. I want you like hell.'

'I have to go now. I'll see you Saturday, I guess. You want
to fuck *him* is what you want.'

SOMETHING IS FALLING FROM A WINDOW.

'You're not around, what's Samuel Marcus going to say?'

A BABY IS TURNING IN THE AIR LIKE AN EASY
SWIMMER IN WATER. ITS WRAPPER UNWRAPS
AND FLIES ACROSS THE FACE OF THE BUILDING.

'Whatever it is, it won't be to me. Samuel Marcus is on a
two-day weekend seminar at Columbia, on media melding.'

'Bullshit into art. Of course he is. And so you've got time on
your hands to be a good mother.'

'Thanks for being shitty. It makes things easier for me.'

'What's this all about, Sooze?'

'Me wanting to be somebody, isn't it? On my own.'

'Which is why you had to rush and be Sammy Cohen's meal
ticket. Literally.'

THE BABY FALLS. THE BABY FALLS. THE BABY
FALLS.

THE BABY HITS THE CANOPY OF THE BUILDING
AND BOUNCES.

IT RICOCHETS OFF THE CANOPY AND INTO THE
TRAFFIC.

'Let me be the goddam bitch from hell, Jason, why can't
you, for just a little while?'

The telephone has been ringing. Jason has left Susie to finish
her question, but now he picks up. Sorry, but it might be
important.

EXT. APARTMENT BLOCK. THE EAST RIVER. DAY.

A black DIPLOMAT, in a silk suit and yellow tie, with
diamond slide, is standing beside his black Mercedes with
diplomatic plates, talking to a COP. There is an ambulance
parked in the street and plastic tape marking off the area.

> DIPLOMAT
> Elle est tombée carrément du ciel.
> C'était un coup de tonnerre,
> littéralement, a l'intérieur de ma
> voiture –

> COP
> Someone is going to have to translate.

JASON is getting out of a taxi and walks slowly towards the
building. He is in shock and in no hurry to get where he has
hurried to get to.

JASON gets to the ambulance and sees the sheeted bundle
being put into it. It hardly weighs enough to count as a body.

Is that ETHEL standing on the far side of the street, among the
usual morbid and curious CROWD? It is ETHEL.

JASON thinks that he should not go to her. He also thinks that
he should. But he does not. He is there and he is not there.
It is not his tragedy. Why did GIL call him?

There is GIL. He is coming out under the canopy from the
apartment house with a sheaf of manuscript pages in his hand.

JASON watches GIL as GIL watches AARON GLASSER, in
burgundy-coloured brush denim pants and a fawn cotton,
collarless shirt (they are *everywhere*), come out of the building
in plastic handcuffs.

He is led by the elbow by a COP who puts the usual careful

hand on AARON's head as he gets into the car.

JASON manages to be standing next to GIL without having come up to him, so avoiding the need to shake hands, or not.

> JASON
> How did it happen?

He might be talking to someone not directly involved.

> GIL
> She murdered Theodore. He murdered
> Maria.

JASON looks over, and it seems *miles*, to where ETHEL stands in her floral dress with the buttons down the front.

> JASON
> You let him do this? You let him?

GIL looks at him and JASON sees how many freckles he has on his face and how pale his blue eyes are and how sweet his lips and how white his teeth. As if GIL were truly smiling.

> GIL
> He loved it and she threw it out of the
> window.

He *is* smiling. He is smiling, if that's a smile, and he is letting the breeze, which is considerable suddenly it seems, snatch the pages from him and fly them, like the baby's wrapper, along the street.

The ambulance backs up and moves away, without urgency.

Jason hails a cab and tells the driver where to take him. He is glad when the guy says it's quite a way. He huddles in the back like a man who has been knifed. He cannot say exactly where the pain is, because he does not know what pain exactly he is in. He is not even sure that it is his pain. No, it is not his pain, and that is what he feels, without feeling it. The horror, the horror, is what he *thinks*, but that will not quite define it, because he was taught Conrad by Samuel Marcus Cohen and what he feels is a composite of too many things for a common quotation to cover it.

His father is not in the big room where the old Jews play pinochle and Scrabble, some of them, and the women play Canasta when they're not watching soaps. Asa has had a slight stroke, they tell him: nothing to worry about (as if he had been nothing to worry about before). They have him in a bed, racked almost to a sitting position. His mouth is a little bit twisted, perhaps, but he does not seem different. God help me, Jason thinks, I don't truly know what I hoped, because how long can this go on?

'You bring a joke for me today, Jasy? Usually you do.'

'Not today, I don't seem to have. Today has not been so funny as some days are.'

'Jason . . .' Asa beckons his son's ear to his lips. 'I don't want to be in this place.' The old man leans back, with his mouth open and his eyes bright, to see how that one goes down. 'Do you understand me?'

'I know you don't, dad.'

'I want to go home. Take me . . . please.'

'Dad . . .'

'To 1,1,7,1. I want to see my house again.'

'Dad, we don't own that house any more. 1,1,7,1; we haven't owned it in years and years.'

'Is where I want you to take me. Please.'

Jason feels young and strong asking them to get him a wheelchair and never mind what the doctor says. He will take responsibility for whatever happens to his father, just like he pays the bills whenever he needs anything not covered by the overall financial arrangements, so do this for me now, please, will you?

He walks Asa like a baby in a stroller, through the Brooklyn streets where he was once a father younger than Jason is now. By the time they come to 1171 Statler, Jason knows what made him run to Manhattan and become whoever it is who doesn't live in the narrow, greying house with the tyreless truck parked in front and the rusting swing-seat with the burst cushions on the porch. The neighbours are shouting at each other in Spanish.

'Eleven seventy-one, Colonel.'

'I want . . . to go . . .'

'Me too.'

'. . . inside,' Asa says. 'I left something . . .'

'Dad, you sold this house like eighteen years ago. We can't go inside.'

A woman comes out of the house with an expression that says that she was expecting to see someone entirely different.

'What's the matter?' she says.

'He used to live here.'

'Yeah? Wanna buy it back? It's yours.'

'I want to go . . . inside . . .'

'Can we possibly, for a moment?'

'Help yourself.'

There is a bicycle in the hall and a folded bed with a crushed mattress in its jaws. Jason cannot push the wheelchair through the available space, even though it has a special device for racking the wheels closer together. He leaves the chair on the porch and picks his father up in his arms and takes him in that way. All the time he is in the house he is going to be afraid that someone is stealing the wheelchair.

'It's a slum,' Asa says, 'my house . . . it's a . . . slum. You smell that smell? That smell was never in this house.'

'Dad . . .' Jason is afraid the lady will be upset, but she is just making sure they don't take anything or hoping, maybe, for a dollar or two.

'Jasy . . .'

'Yeah.'

'Shall I tell you a joke for a change?'

'You have a joke? Tell me.'

'She isn't your mother.'

'He senile?' the woman says.

'I didn't mean to say that,' Asa says. 'I meant to say the other thing.'

'That's the joke?'

'The joke . . . ? The joke . . .'

'Does he wet himself? Mine wets himself.'

'That's the house, dad.'

'The joke is . . . I'm not your father.'

'Do I get it?'

'Think about it.'

'*Oh*, it's a think–about–it joke. OK.'

'You're why . . .'

'Thank you very much,' Jason says.

He gets out of there quickly and he doesn't give her any money because his hands are full of his father and by the time he could give her money, he is down the steps with the wheelchair (which is thankfully still there) and why bother?

'. . . she doesn't come see me. Why . . . no one does. Only you.'

'OK, dad.'

'Is the joke.'

There is a problem with the rental car when Jason gets to

Boston and it is already past two o'clock when he gets to Goschen Village. He just knows that Susie will have gotten there early and she has: Laverne says she packed them a picnic, because that's what *she* seemed to want, to be alone with Nicky and Caroline.

'How have they been?'

'Great,' Noah says. 'I beat shit out of them; we understood each other perfectly.'

'Jason, you need to eat.'

'I brought you something,' Jason says. 'Small thank you.'

Noah unwraps a small Abercrombie and Fitch compass. 'Top quality. You should have, you should have!'

He hugs Jason and Jason uses the moment to look like there's something else. 'The old man,' he says, 'he's going downhill.'

'His age, who goes up? You know who came back? The phantom rock-thrower. Did it again. FBI think it's extraterrestrials, but they won't admit it.'

'You don't want to hear this, but he is. I took him back to eleven-seventy-one.'

'No kidding.'

'There was a little kidding as a matter of fact. He told me this joke.'

'Did he so? What was that? How was the place?'

'It was a slum. When is a joke not a joke? That's the question. And the answer is, when Asa tells it. Like, he told me he wasn't my father.'

'He told you that?'

'You knew.'

'Did I?'

'Want me to throw a rock through your living-room window for you? I'm forty-one years old, Noah. If you knew, tell me.'

'I didn't.'

'What did you?'

'I guessed is all, that something wasn't possibly entirely kosher.'

'Turns out it was me. Is that why you . . . don't like to see him?'

'I don't think so. I never liked him too much. And he *is* my father.'

'So you knew. You knew. Where has she taken them? Susie, the kids?'

'Down the beach.'

'In a car? Did she take them in a car?'

'Relax, Jason. They're fine; she's fine. Very possibly it's all bull.'

'What's that?'

'He likes to fantasise. Get back to Gertrude. How is she, by the way?'

'Your phone not working? Because ask her.'

'Jason, just because we looked after your kids for four days doesn't mean you have to . . .'

'I'm sorry. The minute he said it, Noah, I knew. Like I'd always know. Little things came back to me. Her voice one time on the telephone, talking to *him*, I guess. Who was he? You don't know, do you?'

'Don't get your hopes up: you're still Jewish.'

'Jason, come in here and eat this stuff, will you?'

'She fucks you with food,' Noah says, 'is what she does finally.'

'Did you know anybody coulda been him? Some uncle who wasn't an uncle . . . ?

'Who knows? Some sonofabitch maybe has you down for a

million in his will. Live in hopes, fella. It's more than I do.'

Laverne has the television on while she cooks, and it is still on while Jason eats his chopped liver. Laverne has just put a plate of corned beef and sauerkraut and mashed potatoes in front of him when the news flash comes on that the man in custody for the death of little Maria Teacher has killed himself in his cell.

THE BEACH. CAPE COD. DAY.

The pace at which SUSIE and JASON are walking along the beach shows that AARON GLASSER's death has been conveniently sad for them. It has allowed them to change their mood, at least for the moment, and dawdle at the water's edge reflecting on what really matters and can never remotely be expected.

> SUSIE
> Poor Aaron. He was so much fun. To
> do a thing like that.
>
> JASON
> Come on, Susie, after what he *did*.
>
> SUSIE
> I guess. Where does this leave you and
> Ethel, do you suppose?
>
> JASON
> Ethel and I were never anyplace to start
> with. You know that.
>
> SUSIE
> Think she and Gil . . . ?
>
> JASON
> (Shakes his head)
> It's been some week. Because guess
> what.

SUSIE

There's *more*?

JASON

My father isn't my father. I went to see
that old bastard when no one else
would and he springs this on me.

SUSIE

Look at it this way maybe: you could
possibly have better genes than you
know. Who is, do you know, your
father?

JASON

Listen, it could still be him. Except ...
Gertrude never loved him. And – I
don't like to think about it too much –
but she has to have been a pretty sexy
woman.

He looks with a sequence of several expressions at SUSIE.

SUSIE

Still is. Is what you don't like to think
about.

JASON

You're ... I love you, Susie.

SUSIE

You want me to say everything is all
right.

JASON

Do I deny that if I'm smart? I'm not
too smart.

SUSIE

You're pretty smart.

JASON

I feel sick every minute I'm not with
you. I want to tear your clothes off and

I want to wring your neck. How do
you read that?

SUSIE

I wish you'd be halfway honest with
me, Jason, sometimes.

JASON

About what? My bowel movements?
You certainly gave me the runs all
week. I was taken short talking serious
money with the President of Random
House. Is that honest or what?

SUSIE

I don't want you to be unhappy.

JASON

No? It's a kind of victory, isn't it? But
then so's making people happy. Maybe
there isn't too much difference. There is
though.

SUSIE

Cassie Sadleir.

JASON

Did I tell you? I did.

SUSIE

Marcus and I went to the concert.

JASON

Fuck you.

SUSIE

He was wonderful. Queiroz. But I'm
talking about when you and she . . .

JASON

That was before you. Way before.

SUSIE

(Shakes her head)
There is no time in these things, Jason,

and you're smart enough to know that,
whatever you say.

JASON

I went through hell with Cassie. She
tied me in knots, and she tied the knots
in knots.

SUSIE

My point.

JASON

Which is?

SUSIE

Don't worry about the kids. Don't
pretend to worry about them. They're
happy we're together. She fought you to
a standstill. You needed something
easier. I was it. You admitted it one
time.

JASON

I have no memory of that.

SUSIE

She never came; you never conquered.

JASON

Oh that!

SUSIE

And you only had to be inside me ...
sometimes not even that.

JASON

Do you go down on him as a matter of
interest?

SUSIE

What can you possibly be hoping to
achieve with a question like that? Sure.

JASON

Suicide? That's what happens when two
people really respect each other's

intelligence and discover how
unexpectedly much they have in
common.

SUSIE

You're either a raging hypocrite or a
Puritan suddenly.

JASON

How about I had a *pilgrim* father?

SUSIE

It all began with the two of us talking.

JASON

Doesn't everything?

SUSIE

He made me feel like there was
something about me that was worth
more than magazine work.

JASON

I told you that.

SUSIE

Something unusual and . . .

JASON

You're not going to say 'special', are
you?

SUSIE

You see? You see?

JASON

He said the exact same thing to Dot
Gould and also to Naomi Pratt, if you
can believe that. She could.

SUSIE

I'm Naomi Pratt to you. And you talk
about love.

JASON

Shit, Susie, he told me *I* could be an

important novelist. After one short story
I did for him to avoid reading the
Leatherstocking trilogy. If I have to bite
on a bullet, let it be a soft one.

He starts walking towards the row of black stakes which seem
to diminish as they nail down the surface of the ocean.

JASON

I don't think he wanted me in the sack.
He flatters other people because it's the
best way he has of flattering himself.
And an even better way, I'm sorry to
bring this up again, is taking younger
men's wives.

SUSIE

To you, in other words, I'm totally
incidental. So why did you want me?

JASON

Remember Veronica Flugelman? He
dumped his second wife for her. Third;
third. And why? Because Jake
Flugelman, now a forgotten man, won
the National Book Award with a
volume of stories that even Sammy had
to say were 'important', however
important that may be. Sammy dreads
death.

SUSIE

He loves life.

JASON

Meaning young girls.

SUSIE

Young people. Think of all the teaching
he does. Jesus!

JASON

Remember when he played tennis with
us and his son Daniel when he was in
rehab? He had to partner you – the
usual writing on the wall, only I didn't
read it – and he called everything out
the kid hit that wasn't a net cord. No
wonder Danny's in Thailand someplace.

SUSIE

Successful fathers are never easy to live
with.

JASON

Nicky is not going to have a problem
then. On the few occasions he sees me.

SUSIE

They're going to see you a *lot*. No
matter what.

JASON's nose goes right to one side, which makes her smile,
just.

JASON

Do you want to marry him?

SUSIE

I don't ever want to get married again.

JASON

'*Sibylla, Sibylla, ti theleis?*'

SUSIE

Hoping I don't recognise the quote?
Because I certainly don't want to die.
He makes me feel – I'm sorry –
important, Jason.

JASON

Susan.

SUSIE

Yes, he does.

JASON

And what do your children make you
feel?

SUSIE

Our children are never going to be
short of love.

JASON

Whatever happens, you said.

SUSIE

Yes, I did.

JASON

Let's hope you're right. But you know
what they love most, which just shows
how early folly can strike? Us. The two
of us together.

SUSIE

Jason, today –

JASON

I know. To allow them to put their
faith in an obsolete social arrangement
like monogamy can only be the prelude
to a lifetime of contempt for everything
we have hypocritically pretended to
stand for. Think I haven't read that shit
for myself? *Read* it? I've sold it for over
half-a-million dollars. Several times. I'm
selling the agency, by the way.

SUSIE

No, you're not.

JASON

While the going is bad. David is buying
me out. I have this vocation suddenly to
be a restaurant critic. Now you're going
to be Marcel Proust, there has to be a
vacancy, doesn't there?

SUSIE

You won't necessarily get it. Everyone's
entitled to be happy, Jason. Every now
and again, we're allowed to do what we
really need to do.

JASON

Are you though? Are we? And what
else did we ever do, our generation?
We're like kids who've been given the
run of the place to do what we want,
only we don't know too well what
exactly that is. So you know what I
think we do, subconsciously maybe? We
listen for the sound of that tail-finned
gas-guzzler with the old folks in it
coming home to tell us to cut it out
and get upstairs to bed. And all the time
the mess gets worse and worse and now
we're beginning to be seriously afraid
that they're never going to show and
the house is ours to take care of and the
old folk can't hack it any more and
now what are we going to do? Do
what you want to do? Sure. You want
something more? I hope Sammy can
give it to you. Almost sincerely I do.
It'll be more than Big Daddy ever gave
anybody before, but who knows?

SUSIE

It doesn't bother me, him being tight. I
kinda get off on it. I feel independent
even when I'm with him. Less of a
possession. You, you took such trouble
making me smell good, I sorta
wondered maybe you didn't like the
original flavour too well.

JASON breathes out through his nose and picks up a small rock and heaves it at the sea as if he hopes it will break something. Which would not help one bit.

                    JASON
          OK.

To his surprise, the danger of tears, and anger, has passed. He can look her full in the face and not feel a tiny twitch of apprehension that he will look anything but the way he means to look.

                    JASON
          Some week. Monday, I had a family; I
          had a wife; I had a father; I had a
          business. Saturday and nothing is like I
          was sure it always would be, and you
          know something?

SUSIE raises her eyebrows: well?

                    JASON
          I still think of that little mole you have
          just where the fur starts and I still wish
          I at least still had that to myself.

                    SUSIE
          I'll save it for you.

They are walking towards NOAH and LAVERNE's house now. They can see NICKY and CAROLINE playing with her kids on MRS BLOFELD's inflatable castle that her dog has not quite gotten used to yet; the children are whistling to it and slapping their thighs but it continues to hesitate.

                    JASON
          You want me to be honest? I don't
          think you're the greatest woman ever
          lived. I married you because it was
          going to be an easy ride? Not quite. I
          wanted you to think you were a pretty

lucky girl? That's true. I wanted you to
be happy and I wanted me to be. I was.
I thought you were. You and me both.
That was my . . . my big lie, I guess.
And I was proud of it. Our marriage
was the only long fiction I ever got
round to.

SUSIE

And I don't want to be somebody's
fiction.

JASON

Then don't be. But I do have a
question. When did Samuel Marcus
Cohen ever write any non-fiction worth
a fish's fart?

They are going away from us and now they diverge. JASON
turns up the beach towards MRS BLOFELD's and SUSIE walks
on, alone.

When Jason hears that Susie has gone to Israel with Samuel
Marcus Cohen, he is slightly ashamed to wonder how she will
stand being in Jerusalem for a whole semester. He has not sold
the business. How else is he going to pay for the kids' school,
and the much more experienced lady than they had before
who takes care of them? He has a new secretary, Francine, a
Creole woman who has taught him to do things on the
computer that he can hardly believe he can do. He likes to
think that he hates the office, but it is for him what the theatre
was to Stanislavsky: a second home.

He spends more time with the kids, and gets to like it. He
likes himself for liking it. His agency has not suffered losing Gil
Teacher to Ernie Berlin. It hurt a little bit when *Sheet Music*
came out and did very well. Paula said she had always, always

believed in it. The movie is going to be wonderful. The potentially bad publicity about Gil's private life did the book no harm whatsoever, which proves that there is no bad publicity. As Samuel Marcus is alleged to have said, *Les Fleurs du Mal* always smell sweeter than most.

Jason hears that Susie is coming back to New York early; meaning alone. She finds him one December morning snowballing with the kids in Central Park and he throws one which, with lucky accuracy, knocks her hat right off. They all start snowballing together, without a word spoken. 'Just like in the movie,' she says when they are catching their breath finally.

INT. HOSPITAL ROOM. DAY.

BYRON SADLEIR is under an oxygen tent. He is dying of emphysema. SUSIE is sitting with him. He gestures to her to put her ear down to him, because he does not have enough breath for full volume. She listens to him and she makes a face like she does sometimes to one of the children when they ask for something they truly should not have.
BYRON touches the transparent plastic of the tent, so that her hand feels the touch of the fingers that cannot close over hers. SUSIE sighs, without regret or reproach, and goes and closes the little lid which fits over the judas window in the big blond door. She slides the bolt across and then she smiles at BYRON SADLEIR and uses the back of one heel to slide the shoe off the other foot, and vice versa. Then she takes off her alpaca jacket and starts to unbutton her blouse. She takes her time, as if she were giving it to BYRON, who watches as she does what he asked her to do.

After a time, however long it was, or short it later seemed, she came back to him and they lived together again, wiser and maybe better than before. Now that they needed to have no more illusions, they trusted each other totally, almost. Susie had a wonderful letter from Samuel Marcus Cohen, who also wrote to Jason, wondering — in a postscript — whether Jason was going to want commission on the movie deal for the novel, even though he no longer represented him. He assumed not. He was wrong. Susie was entirely on Jason's side, and her support had nothing to do with the news that Samuel Marcus and Paula Steinberg were going to get married.

INT. LAW OFFICE. MANHATTAN.

A WOMAN who twists her wedding ring round and round her finger is explaining to ETHEL, who wears a dark suit and has cropped hair, why she wants a divorce and what the grounds are. ETHEL wears no lipstick, but austerity gives her a certain new nakedness which works well with her businesslike style.

Susie and Jason have found new, secret urgency in their desire for each other. Neither cares to discuss why, or what exactly it is, or means. They do not see as many people as they used to. They often sit in the apartment enjoying whatever it is that makes them feel so separately together. Only occasionally does either of them yield to the sweet luxury of wondering who the next lover will be, for him or for her. It keeps them happy though. The kids are great.